The Curse of the Dark Horseman

A Novel

Kristina Stangl

In dedication to my parents, Robert & Dilek, thank you for always being by my side and supporting me.

To Melissa, thank you for being the best sister.

To my own paternal grandmother, Maureen, who serves as the namesake to the characters in this novel.

CONTENTS

Also by Kristina Stangl

The Enchanted Forest Saga:

The Curse of the Dark Horseman

The Sleeping Knight

The Emerald Prince

Silverheart:

Cupid's Serenade

Sex, Lies & Politics:

The Ambassador's Wife

Wake Up, Darling

My Life is a Soap Opera

Kill Me, Kiss Me

www.kristinastangl.com

CHAPTER 1

Lady Kassandra Stanton stood firm and still, as she concentrated on the portrait that hung before her. Ever since her childhood, it was a picture that she often admired but yet, knew very little about. Whenever she stood inside the grand salon, located within her family's private estate at Wiltshire Hall, Kassie always sought for a quiet and somber moment to peacefully gaze at the portrait. It was there inside that very room, which was currently owned by her legal guardian and grandmother, Maureen, where the portrait hung. Tucked away in the furthest corner, behind the piano and nearest to the window overlooking the blooming garden attached to her family's grand home, was the precise location as to where Kassie's most beloved and cherished portrait was proudly displayed.

The portrait was that of a dashing young and handsome gentleman on horseback. His hair was as black as night, while his face was as white and as transparent as that of a mere ghost. His eyes were emerald green, just like the hanging ivy vines and sprouting oak tree leaves, which grew in great abundance throughout their remote and sleepy English country village located in Northern England. Additionally, his clothes appeared rather old fashioned and seemed to be at least a hundred years older than the current fashion worn by other similar gentlemen of equal age and social stature as he. Furthermore, seated above his black stallion horse, the 'Dark Horseman'— as Kassie preferred to reference him as — stood right there in the center of the portrait, surrounded by the dark and evergreen forest behind him, along with a blackened and shadowy road in the background and lastly, accompanied by the night sky illuminating right above him.

With the moon shining down upon him as his only source of light, Kassie squinted her eyes and noticed that for the very first time, right there behind the Dark Horseman, situated upon a small hill, appeared to be that of a vast estate. However, due to the dimly painted paint strokes and darkly shadows, it was rather difficult to detect. But there, upon closer inspection, Kassie certainly did see something. Moving her observation away from the estate, Kassie reverted her attention back to the horseman. For some odd reason, she was always pulled to him… like a strange and unexplainable gravitational force that constantly drew her back in and directly towards his path. Whether or not she was interested to look elsewhere in the painting, one way or another, Kassie consistently found herself staring straight at his face— particular at his eyes. For if truth be told, there was something vexing about his eyes that always caught her attention. It was as if, by some odd occurrence, that he was somehow watching her. Impossible, right?

Of course, Kassie, naturally knew better. After all, she was a modern and educated lady, living at the turn of the twentieth century. It was the year 1900. But somehow, by some odd and rare notion, Kassie always felt within her heart that in another lifetime, she knew the Dark Horseman. Really knew him. Personally. More than just as the man, who remained forever frozen in-time on horseback in a simple portrait painted by an unknown artist.

But what was even more strange and peculiar, was that ever since she was a young girl, the Dark Horseman was always in her dreams. Following her. Haunting her. Helping her. Although Kassie seldom hardly ever recalled any of her other dreams; however, whenever it came to the matter concerning the Dark Horseman, she always remembered her dreams about him most vividly well after she awoke, come the next morning.

What were those dreams, pray tell? Well, it was rather difficult to say. Although Kassie vaguely recalled in such little details as to how their original paths crossed; but either way, in each dream, she always found herself on horseback and wandering through the dark and gloomy woods late into the night… lost… alone and… scared. Fearful of the darkness and the mysterious creatures that lurked inside of the woods during the midnight hour, Kassie closed her eyes tightly shut, as she quietly hoped and prayed for a miracle. And then, just before she lost all hope, her prayers were miraculously answered. Furthermore, before Kassie had enough time to even bat an eyelash, the Dark Horseman was off, galloping away from a far-off distance, on his way to rescue her. As soon as he scooped her up within his strong and sturdy arms and then whisked her away with him, Kassie would suddenly awake and return back to her current realm.

Who he was and if he was based on an actual historical figure was something that Kassie always wondered about. Was he rooted upon fiction or was he real? Was he intended to be a good character, or was he designed to be evil? Kassie never really knew the truth to be sure. But either way, whatever the original artist's intentions were, it really didn't matter. For Kassie, the Dark Horseman was good and kind to her. He was her hero, after all. But more than anything, had he been a real man, then Kassie was absolutely certain and convinced that her mysterious horseman would have been her equal match. An ideal husband. That, if he were actually here, standing right before her in real life, then she would have much rather have preferred marrying him than her current fiancé, Walter, in an instant. Walter, a man whom she was engaged to marry, was a union born out of necessity and sadly, not of love. Tragically, this was a harsh reality that many ladies of her time, with similar social and economic backgrounds, had to face: an unwanted engagement due to the pressures of their respective families. But apart from all of this, Kassie remained convinced that had her Dark Horseman been a real man, then her life would have taken a much different course. Furthermore, Kassie also knew within her heart that had her fantasy been an actual reality, then he would have madly loved her and she, in return, would have madly loved him, too.

"Are you still obsessing over that painting?" asked Maureen to her granddaughter, Kassie.

"I thought that I was still alone in the room," Kassie bashfully admitted.

"Ever since you were a young girl, I could never pull you away from that painting," sighed Maureen, as she walked over to join Kassie's side.

"Is he real?" asked Kassie, suddenly and bluntly.

"My dear child," began Maureen, "Whatever do you mean? He's a painting. Of course, he isn't real. He's no more than paint."

"I mean, is he based upon a real person? A historical figure?" Kassie clarified.

"Well, that's more like it," laughed Maureen.

"Well? Is he?" asked Kassie, once more.

"I'm not entirely certain," admitted Maureen. "But personally, I think he might have been."

"Really?" asked Kassie, surprised by her grandmother's admission.

"I've never told you about the legend of the Dark Horseman of Galloway Manor before, now, have I?" asked Maureen, with a raised brow.

"The legend of the Dark Horseman of Galloway Manor…" Kassie excitingly repeated, in amazement.

"From your reaction, I take it that I haven't," said Maureen, as she sarcastically laughed on.

"I suppose," Maureen continued, "That the time has finally come for me to come clean and tell you more about him."

"Wait, so you knew of him?" quickly asked Kassie, in return.

Walking towards her sofa nearby, Maureen decided to take a seat and enjoy a fresh cup of tea; which at this very moment, was conveniently being served right on time for their daily scheduled afternoon tea service.

"Let us discuss more about this matter over some tea," Maureen suggested, as she already began to pour Kassie a cup, without her even agreeing to it.

"One or two lumps of sugar?" asked Maureen, as she placed the teapot back down onto the table.

"None," replied Kassie, with a bold smirk.

"Ah, yes," Maureen laughed on. "That's right. You prefer milk, just like your dear late mother."

"Actually," Kassie interrupted. "It was my late *father's* favorite."

"Yes, I stand corrected. Wise girl," replied Maureen, as she sadly recalled her own son's and daughter-in-law's unfortunate passing.

"Anyways," Maureen continued, "Why don't you come and join me, so that I can share my tale with you."

"Very well," replied Kassie, as she walked over and took a seat nearby her grandmother.

Once Kassie joined her side, Maureen added a dash of milk to her tea and then, she handed her the teacup, along with a small almond biscuit to serve as a side snack. As Kassie took her first sip of her tea, Maureen stared on at the painting, as she prepared to reveal the legend behind the mysterious rider.

"Once upon a time, or so, as they say," she began, "There was a young gentleman, named Lord Henry Galloway of Galloway Manor."

"Wait, so the horseman was based on a real-life person?" Kassie inquired, most curiously.

"Yes, he was," replied Maureen, as she took another sip of her tea.

"Did you know him? In real-life?" asked Kassie, once more.

"Unfortunately, no, as he was around well before my own time," admitted Maureen.

"How long ago?" asked Kassie.

"About a hundred years or so," replied Maureen. "Anyways, it's best that I continue on with the story."

Almost immediately, Kassie nodded her head in agreement. Although Kassie wasn't often considered to be an avid listener; however, this time around, she was all ears. Ah, yes, Kassie was most eager to hear the story of this most intriguing tale.

"A hundred years ago, Galloway Manor was the most lavish, exquisite and famous estate in our entire village; if not, in all of England, for that matter. Naturally, as a result, the Galloway family was one of the wealthiest, respected, famous and most powerful families around. In fact, they owned most of, if not, all the land inside this very village. Amazingly enough, practically everyone living here was once employed by them."

"Really? If so, then why haven't I ever heard of their surname before? Up until now, I've never encountered anyone related to their family. Not once. Let alone, an estate called Galloway Manor," remarked Kassie.

"Well," began Maureen, "A lot can happen over the span of a hundred years."

"What about our family?" Kassie inquired.

"My child, bear a little more patience with me, for I am getting to that," answered Maureen.

"As I was saying," Maureen continued, "A hundred years ago, the Galloways owned everything. The father was an earl, known as the Earl of Galloway, and he had a son named Henry. Lord Galloway was a kind and generous man, who was once married to a distant relative of my mine, named Sarah. Shortly, after Henry's birth, Sarah tragically died from complications associated with childbirth. Naturally, Lord Galloway was devastated by this painful loss, for he loved Sarah unconditionally, with all his heart. But as unfortunate as this untimely tragedy truly was, Lord Galloway was, at the same time, also blessed with the birth of their only son Henry, who was now the sole heir to his vast ancestral estate, title and fortune. And so, in time, Henry grew up to become a dashingly handsome, educated and well-mannered gentleman. However, for as handsome and as wealthy as Henry was, he was also, just like his father before him, kind and generous to everyone, regardless of their lack of titles or lower social and economic statuses."

"He sounds too good to be true," Kassie reflected.

"Perhaps," added Maureen. "But, like all tales, Henry's upbringing was also filled with several challenges along the way."

"Really? How so?" Kassie inquired, as she remained glued to her grandmother's every passing word.

"Like you, Henry also grew up as an orphan," Maureen revealed. "But before his father's passing, the earl married another woman by the name of Vera. Not much is known about her apart from the fact that she was a foreign-born woman, who was also rumored to have been descended from an ancient Russian family with some traces of Gypsy blood in her, too. But from what we do know, during Lord Galloway's many travels to the far east, one day he returned back to our village with a new bride. Through his second marriage to Vera, Lord Galloway sired another son, named Phillip, who was the half-brother to Henry. Naturally, Henry, as the first-born son, remained as the sole heir to his father's title, estate and fortune. However, this did not deter nor minimize, Vera's bitterness and resentful envy of him."

"How unfortunate that must have been," remarked Kassie.

"Yes, how unfortunate that must have been, indeed," agreed Maureen. "Needless to say, unfortunately, Lord Galloway succumbed to an untimely death; a horseback riding accident that left him paralyzed. Sadly, due to his severe injuries, he shortly soon afterwards, fell into a deep coma and never awoke. Many say, that had Vera not been around, then there was a hopeful chance that Lord Galloway might have recovered. But again, these are only speculations."

"Did people honestly believe that there was some sort of foul play?" asked Kassie, most concerned.

"Yes," answered Maureen. "Sadly, that's precisely what the villagers thought. Personally, that's what I believed happened, too. Regardless, upon Lord Galloway's passing, his title, estate and fortune were immediately transferred over to Henry, as his inheritance. However, at the time, Lord Henry was still a young man, who was busy away living abroad and not quite yet ready to manage the daily affairs of Galloway Manor. As a result, his stepmother, Vera, served as the head mistress of the manor, in his absence. Unfortunately, her rule was so cruel and authoritarian, that most of the servants quickly fled the estate soon afterwards. For the ones who reluctantly stayed behind, they were subjected to harsh working and living conditions. Sadly, Vera's cruel nature and heartless administration of the manor went on for several years— up until the arrival of Lord Henry, upon his thirtieth birthday. By this time, Henry was a grown man, who was already well established and ready to take over the rigorous affairs and responsibilities of his late father. However, this didn't sit too well with Vera, who wasn't yet ready to give up her power so easily over to her stepson. A man, who wasn't of her blood, and whom, she regarded, as far less suitable and ideal than her own son, Phillip. Ah, yes, Vera favored Phillip over Henry, and she was most determined to steal Henry's inheritance away and transfer it over to Phillip."

"How dreadfully terrible!" exclaimed Kassie.

"Yes, it was," replied Maureen. "To make matters far worse, Lord Henry was to be engaged. Now, if Henry had married and produced another heir of his very own, then Phillip would have most certainly, stood in no direct chance of ever inheriting Galloway Manor. Therefore, something needed to be done. And so, a curse was enacted."

"A curse?" asked Kassie, in amazement.

"Yes, a curse," confirmed Maureen. "A curse beyond time, space and measure. As for the specific details surrounding the curse, I'm not entirely certain. But from what I do know, Vera was directly responsible for what happened to Lord Henry."

"What happened to him?" asked Kassie.

"On the eve of his wedding, Lord Henry was out riding on horseback through the woods. It was late at night, around the midnight hour. Just like every other night before, dating back from his own childhood, Henry rode his majestic stallion down the open path. However, unlike before, this time around, he failed to return back home."

"What do you mean? Did Henry go missing?" asked Kassie, most intrigued.

"Well," began Maureen, "I suppose this is where the curse begins."

"How so?" asked Kassie, as she took a bite of her almond biscuit.

"As you can safely presume, there was no wedding the following morning; for Henry had long gone missing. Although all of the servants and local villagers searched high and low for Henry, no one could find him," Maureen revealed.

"Did he and his horse run away?" Kassie inquired.

"It's possible, but where could he have gone? Even now, the nearest town isn't for miles on end. Plus, there were no footsteps, nor any horse tracks along the way. One way or another, it seemed like Lord Henry, along with his black stallion, Midnight, simply vanished," said Maureen, as she threw her hands up into the air.

"If Lord Henry vanished, then what became of his family? Why have I never heard of them or their manor, until now?" asked Kassie, while desperately trying to better understand this intriguing tale.

"I'm getting to there, my dear," replied Maureen. "After Henry's disappearance, rumors began to circulate that his fiancé, Julia, and his half-brother, Phillip, were secretly lovers. With Henry out of the picture, Julia and Phillip were free to marry. And so, the couple soon ran off together and eloped to Scotland to marry. Nevertheless, they were never heard of ever again. As for Vera, well… with both Henry and Phillip gone, she remained as the new sole heir and owner of Galloway Manor. But, as my own grandmother use to say, 'evil means will always meet a violent end;' and this holds many truths, especially with regards to Vera. But before I get to Vera, let me first return back to Henry."

"But I thought that Henry was already dead," Kassie interrupted.

"Presumed dead," Maureen corrected.

"Really? How fascinating," Kassie remarked, as she took another sip of her warm tea.

"That night… that fateful night… in which Henry blindly rode out into the forest with his black stallion…was the very night that ultimately came to seal his fate. Although Henry rode a hundred times over before in that same dark and gloomy forest; however, this time around, this was the night, in which Vera finally cornered him… and enacted her curse," Maureen revealed.

"Wait," cried Kassie, in astonishment. "Was Vera a witch?"

"Yes, that she was," replied Maureen, calmly. "She was indeed, a witch. And, a most envious and sinister one at that."

"How utterly dreadful," Kassie remarked. "What happened to Henry, when he encountered her?"

"Well," Maureen continued, "Just like his father before him, Vera also intended to have Henry killed and then blame his untimely death as an unfortunate 'accident' due to horseback. However, I should also mention, that Vera was a practitioner of black magic; meaning that her powers stemmed from all of the negative energies and dark forces of the earth. In order for Vera to have enacted her powers on that fateful night, she needed to call upon all that was evil, in order to do her bidding. And so, it was there in the middle of the forest, where Vera came face-to-face with Henry. Alas, as she revealed to him her true ugly and witchy form, she also summoned all of the dark powers and energies from the forest to come attack and kill him."

"Fascinating," observed Kassie.

"Yes, it was," agreed Maureen. "Once she committed this evil deed, Vera quickly vanished straight into thin air; all the while, leaving poor Henry and his horse alone to meet their dreadful doom. Meanwhile, as the thick ivy vines, trees and prickly plant thorns sprang up into the air to strangle and squeeze him to death, Lord Henry managed to say a little prayer. Even with the pesky vines suffocating and pressing down against his very throat, Henry still miraculously managed to say his prayer aloud, before his mouth was eventually sealed shut by the protruding leaves that had quickly engulfed him. But Kassie, my dear, please do remember that where there is darkness, there is also light… and where there is evil, there is also good, just waiting right around the corner. Shall I continue on, my child?"

"Yes, please do," Kassie pleaded.

"Very well, as I was saying," Maureen continued, "As the forest continued to consume and devour Henry and his horse, a magical light suddenly appeared. But before Henry could fully comprehend as to what was about to happen next, the forest abruptly ceased attacking him and in no time, all of the vines, plants and trees quickly released their tight hold of him. After Henry was freed from his attackers, he quickly glanced towards the light. To his amazement, he noticed a beautiful woman standing right in front of him. And ironically, this lady also just so happened to resemble his own late mother."

"Wait, was this woman his mother, Sarah?" asked Kassie, in surprise.

"Yes, it was Sarah," Maureen confirmed. "Just like the angel that she was in life, so she was well after her death. Hearing the cries of her son from heaven, Sarah returned back to earth to come to her son's rescue. Although Sarah had freed him from his attackers, she unfortunately couldn't stop the evil and powerful curse that Vera had already enacted. By saving Henry and preventing the forest from consuming him in death, a debt was now owed back to the forest, in exchange: his own mortality. Sadly, with his life having been spared, Henry was now doomed to remain as a creature of the forest; never again permitted to leave its grounds, for all eternity. Was this a fate worse than death? It's hard to say. Needless to say, after his mother revealed this sad but bitter truth to him, Sarah also pleaded with Henry to remain hidden within the forest. In addition, she also forewarned him to never seek revenge on Vera; for if he did, then the consequences of his actions would not only be irreversible, but they would also prove to be regretful. However, Henry, being the determined young man that he was, simply couldn't stand by this injustice and do nothing. And so, after waiting and hiding for one long month inside the forest, Henry eventually returned back to Galloway Manor. Since the estate stood within the same land and forest as his curse, Henry was able to ride home and enter back into his house late into the night. With Vera busy away enjoying her last supper while seated as the new head of the table, Henry abruptly entered the room and without waiting not a second longer, he plunged his dagger straight through her heart, killing her instantly."

"I see, so Henry got his revenge in the end, didn't he?" asked Kassie.

"Yes, he did; but sadly, it also came at a heavy price," Maureen revealed.

"What was the price?" asked Kassie.

"Having acted upon his rash impulses and selfish desire for revenge, Henry most unfortunately and permanently sealed his own fate. By slaying the one woman, who knew the precise remedy to his curse, Henry was now doomed to forever remain bounded to it. Tragically, now, even as I speak, neither sleep nor death, can ever befall upon him. He lives and rides on his horse forever more, as a prisoner of the forest and of Galloway Manor. Time knows no boundaries to him, yet distance does. After that night, most of the servants fled and no one else has seen him or Galloway Manor, ever since. It was as if, both Henry and the manor simply vanished into thin air. That, or, they were all hidden away deep within the forest, where no human eyes can ever lay their sights upon them, ever again."

"If that's the case, then how did this portrait here, come into being?" asked Kassie, with a raised brow.

"Well, long after Vera's death, Galloway Manor, along with its inhabitants were all slowly but surely forgotten. A blemish in history. A forgotten family name and estate. However, the memory of Henry continues to live on, through the legend of the Dark Horseman. In fact, some of our own villagers profess to have actually seen the Dark Horseman occasionally riding out in the forest, so late into the night. Even to this very day, some still claim to have encountered him, face-to-face. For some travelers, they regard him as a saint, coming to help aid them along their night journey through the woods; while for others, he's the very devil, himself, sent to summon them to their violent dooms. But whether he's a saint or the devil, I suppose that's really up to the individual. As for myself, I personally think he's an agent of good. A somewhat gothic and legendary Robin Hood, of sorts."

"I see; so, Lord Henry and his black stallion, Midnight, are the same Dark Horseman and horse from your picture. Furthermore, he's not only a legend, but he's also based on a real person. But still, that doesn't explain as to how you came to acquire this portrait of him?" asked Kassie, who was determined to press on for more concrete answers.

"As I said before," Maureen continued, "His mother, Sarah, was a distant relative of mine. Besides, this portrait was painted well before he became the legendary Dark Horseman."

"Henry seems like an interesting character," Kassie reflected. "I wish that, perhaps, in another lifetime, I could have met him."

"Be careful what you wish for Kassie," Maureen warned. "The curse of the Dark Horseman might be a myth, but magic still runs true in our part of the world. Why, our own village is so incredibly superstitious, that we don't even have any black cats living inside of here! Imagine that!"

"It's because we have more dogs around, used for hunting, that's why," Kassie insisted.

"Perhaps, but the mind is also a powerful force. What you believe, you often see. And what you hope, often comes to be," said Maureen.

"If that's truly the case, then why must I marry Walter?" asked Kassie, with the tone of her voice sounding purely melancholy in nature.

"But don't you care for him?" asked Maureen calmly, in return.

"Walter is kind and decent, but I don't love him. He's just a friend and nothing more," replied Kassie, boldly and as a matter of fact.

"Eventually, in due time, you can grow to love him," Maureen reassured her. "Kassie, I'm not going to live forever and without a mother and a father, I also need to make sure that you're properly taken care of well after I'm gone."

"But I've gone to university. I can take care of myself," Kassie reminded her.

"I have no doubt. However, as a woman, your chances are still limited in your career choice. Plus, our family's estate and fortune will ultimately come to pass over to your male cousin and not you, if we don't take action. Besides, Walter is a family friend and a decent fellow. He will treat you with respect, which is more than most husbands do," advised Maureen.

"But I don't love him," Kassie cried.

"Love is such a rarity, my dear. Not everyone experiences the same romantic love, as we read in stories. Sometimes, it's far better to live a safe life, than to risk otherwise," Maureen reflected.

"Are you really still insisting that I marry Walter, come tomorrow?" asked Kassie, with desperation in her eyes.

"My dear, you already know my answer. Now, please come to accept it," said Maureen, firmly.

"But…" began Kassie; however, sadly, she couldn't find the words to finish her own thought.

However, her grandmother already knew what was secretly hidden away, within her own heart.

"Kassie," began Maureen, "Men like Henry are legends. They exist only in our romanticized tales. But men like Walter, they're real. My dear girl, please don't waste any more time chasing after your dreams and fairy tale like aspirations, in the hopes of achieving a happy ending. Such endings are not designed for everyone. Kassie, my dear, it's best that you come to accept your reality now, rather than later."

And with that, Maureen got up from the sofa, kissed her granddaughter goodbye and exited out of the salon to retire for the rest of the afternoon. With Maureen gone, Kassie stayed behind and continued to stare and admire the portrait. Just an hour ago, she knew nothing about the Dark Horseman. But now, she practically knew his entire life story. What would it be like to meet a man, who spent the past one hundred years living in a curse? A curse, in which no one knew how to break it? Or that, he was once, a real man? Was he lonesome, or was he content on living his life in solitude? Did he even miss the outside world? Kassie was more curious than ever. Had he not haunted her dreams these past few nights, then Kassie would have reluctantly accepted her fate to marry Walter. But now, as soon as she closed her eyes, she saw only the Dark Horseman, aka Lord Henry Galloway, instead.

CHAPTER 2

While seated above her white English Thoroughbred horse, Faith, and wearing her newly sewn white and silk bridal gown, Kassie was expected to depart from her childhood home, ride down the hill from her family's estate and enter into the local church to meet her fate on horseback. In exactly an hour, Kassie was going to come face-to-face with her new groom; and with that, her entire destiny was about to be sealed, once and for all. But shouldn't she have been happier? Joyfully thrilled? Blissfully at ease? Ecstatically excited? Why, most brides were, after all.

But sadly, unlike most brides, this marriage wasn't of Kassie's choosing. No, not at all. Kassie had other dreams and ambitions. Why, she never intended to be a wife; let alone to a man like Walter. In fact, that's why she went to university, in the first place. While most young women her age preferred to stay at home and marry; Kassie, in contrast, was determined to get away and attend university. Luckily, for Kassie, her family, came from wealth, so she was awarded with the financial opportunity to further her education. Although she was orphaned at a young age, her father was a nobleman. As a knight formally appointed by the King of England himself, who went by the name of Sir Robert Stanton, Kassie was known formally as Lady Kassandra Stanton of Wiltshire Hall.

While her father was the first generation in their long family's tree to have formally acquired a title of nobility and rank; Wiltshire Hall, on the other hand, had been their ancestral seat and residence for at least the greater part of the past one hundred years or so. Dating back from her own great-grandfather, their family achieved their wealth through the sales of their own manufactured gun powder, which were previously used in the English wars fought abroad. Over time, beginning with her great-grandfather and down to her own father, each generation acquired more wealth, than the previous one. Shortly, before her parents' tragic deaths due to a severe case of malaria that they unfortunately contracted during their last trip to India, Kassie's father had previously inherited both Wiltshire Hall and their family's business from his own late father, right before his travels abroad. In his absence, Robert appointed his mother, Maureen, to serve as the administrator and caretaker of the estate and the business. However, after her parents' untimely passing, Maureen subsequently sold their family's business to a private firm located outside of London. Afterwards, she kept the bulk of the proceeds to fund the upkeep of Wiltshire Hall, with the remainder set aside in a private bank and reserved solely for Kassie's care. Since, at the time, the family had no other direct male relatives, Kassie was expected to inherit Wiltshire Hall and its remaining fortune, with Maureen having been formally appointed as her legal guardian, until she became of age.

Over the years, Kassie grew up happily and privileged, with the expectation that she, as a financially independent heiress and lady, was going to pursue a life of her own choosing. Therefore, when Kassie grew into the ripe age of eighteen, rather than debuting into society as another new debutante, she opted to attend university, instead. As unorthodox as that decision was, it was there at Oxford University, where Kassie studied about philosophy, history, languages, science, math and everything else in-between. Furthermore, when she wasn't studying, Kassie was either busy away venturing the outdoors or practicing her equestrian skills at the horse track. Although she studied several subjects, her favorite by far was writing. Through writing, she was able to express herself in ways that she couldn't otherwise do in real life. By the power of the mind and with the stroke of the pen, Kassie had the rare and keen ability to create new worlds, while documenting her own internal feelings onto paper; that otherwise, couldn't be so openly expressed in front of polite society, especially by a young lady of her stature. Unfortunately, such passionate and willful emotions were automatically deemed as 'unlady' like, when uttered so publicly aloud and in-person.

Eventually, after graduation, Kassie originally planned on returning back home to Wiltshire Hall to carry on with her writing, in the hopes of completing her first novel, while also managing Wiltshire Hall on the side. However, upon her arrival, Kassie was devastated to learn that during her absence, an unknown male relative had suddenly emerged with new claims to her inheritance. As a fifth cousin twice removed from her father's male line, Sir Douglas Marley, now had legitimate rights to legally acquire her late father's grand estate and fortune. Furthermore, Douglas was not only expected to inherit Wiltshire Hall, but it was also rumored that he actually planned on moving into the estate as well, upon his next upcoming visit.

Devastated by this unexpected turn of events, Kassie was almost ready to give up on Wiltshire Hall altogether and to seek employment as a governess back in London. However, her grandmother, Maureen, devised another alternative plan. Given that Douglas was already married with children of his own, the prospect of ever matching Kassie to him in marriage was simply out of the question. Furthermore, Douglas was a notorious gambler. As a result, it was well known back in London that he had previously acquired several thousands of pounds in debt and owed a lot of money to his creditors. With that being said, rather than freely surrendering Wiltshire Hall over to him, Maureen suggested that Kassie marry Walter instead, as an alternative.

Ironically, Mr. Walter Thornton also came from a wealthy family, in his own right. For many generations, his family were wealthy feudal owners, who owned most of the farmlands in their country village. However, with all of the wealth and land that his family possessed, they had no formal estate or title to show for it. Unlike Kassie's family, Walter's family did not maintain the same equal amount of high expenses that the Stanton family had, with regards to the operational upkeep of Wiltshire Hall. Currently, as it stood, even with Douglas outside of the picture, given the high cost of maintaining Wiltshire Hall, their family's funds were starting to dwindle down, with no further income coming in. Therefore, by marrying Kassie to Walter, Maureen was convinced that not only could he purchase Wiltshire Hall upfront from Douglas paid in-full and thereby, settling his financial debts to his various creditors back in London; but that, they could also use their combined joint Thornton and remaining Stanton wealth to continue to fund the estate's operational expenses into the future.

Thus, Maureen was wholeheartedly convinced that this deal was simply too good to be true and as a result, Douglas would have to be a complete fool to turn it down. Thus, he'd have no other choice but to relinquish all of his inheritance rights over to Walter and thus, ensure that the estate would continue to remain within the grasp of the Stanton family. This way, not only would Kassie and Maureen continue to live peacefully and comfortably within Wiltshire Hall; but that, the estate would eventually come to pass to Kassie's direct descendants in the future.

A perfect plan, right? Well, not so much for Kassie. While Maureen was delighted and thrilled at the prospect of remaining at Wiltshire Hall, the real truth was that Kassie had secretly wanted her ancestral home to pass down to Douglas, instead. Had Douglas inherited Wiltshire Hall rather than herself, then Kassie would have gained the newfound freedom to live her life on her own terms. While being a governess might not have been such an ideal and glamorous sort of life; but at least, this way, by working as a governess in London, she'd have her freedom. Freedom to earn her own living. Freedom to write. However, by now agreeing to marry Walter, there was no longer a guarantee that he'd even allow her to continue on with her writing. In fact, Kassie believed wholeheartedly that Walter wanted her to do nothing else, other than being his dear sweet, loving and devoted wife— a role that Kassie already despised and greatly detested.

But what was so wrong with Walter? Well... nothing really… apart from the fact, that he wasn't the sort of man that Kassie had ever envisioned herself marrying, in the first place. For starters, he was rich and handsome. Standing just over six feet, with blonde hair, brown eyes and a fair complexion, Walter was more than a decent looking fellow. In fact, he was considered as rather handsome, too. Some might even say, that he was quite the catch; for all of the other ladies in their village often fought hard to capture his wandering attention. But unfortunately for them all, Walter only had eyes for Kassie.

Ever since they were children, Walter had always loved Kassie. From the time they first played together in the sandbox, Walter was determined to grow up and marry her, one day. Surprisingly enough, Maureen, being the keen elder that she was, secretly knew this truth all too well. Therefore, with the threat of possibly losing Wiltshire Hall over to

Douglas, Maureen was determined to marry Kassie off to Walter, in order to secure the estate and fortune back into their family's direct possession, once and for all. Naturally, Walter accepted Maureen's proposal and as a result, Kassie, due to the ongoing pressures from her family, had no other choice but to comply. For if she didn't, then not only was she going to lose her childhood home of Wiltshire Hall over to Douglas and his family; but, as a consequence, she was also going to lose the love and respect of her dearest grandmother, who was the only living relative that she still had left in this world and by whom, she regarded as a most beloved parent. And so, against her own better judgment and wishes, Kassie reluctantly agreed to their proposal. However, at the same time, Kassie still held out hope for a miracle, while she secretly prayed for a way to escape her unfortunate fate.

But why couldn't Kassie just love Walter? Wouldn't that have been easier? Simpler? Make everything else in her life, so much smoother? Especially, for her? After all, she knew him ever since they were children. In fact, he was her own dear and sweet childhood friend, whom she frequently used to play with. Plus, Walter was also kind, thoughtful and generous to her, too. Additionally, Maureen was convinced that in due time, Kassie would eventually grow to love him, in return. Furthermore, he was a rich and decent looking young man, whom many regarded to be dashingly handsome… so why did she still feel… so… well… empty? Empty, in the notion, that although her mind regarded him as an aimable sort of fellow; however, her heart was ice cold and frozen towards him emotionally. Perhaps, it was due to the fact that she considered Walter more as a surrogate brother, than as a husband or a lover? Maybe, their lack of romantic gatherings made her feel more friendly towards him, rather than anything else? It was difficult to say. Although Kassie very well knew that most young women in their village would have died to have taken her spot as his new bride; but the real truth was, that while those women might have died to trade places with her, Kassie, on the other hand, was willing to trade her own soul, if it meant that she could run away and escape from this unwanted union.

Would Kassie come to grow to love Walter? Only time could tell. But in the meantime, Kassie still couldn't help but feel… well… melancholy. But why? What was the big problem? Kassie still had her health and her home… at least, for the time being. Plus, hundreds of other young ladies, similar to her own age and stature, were also forced into unwanted marriages every day. However, they, unlike her, were probably and most likely more content with their new roles as wives. So why was it so difficult for Kassie to accept her own fate? Why did she wish for more? But most importantly, what precisely was she even wishing for, in the first place?

Suddenly, Kassie remembered the portrait of the Dark Horseman. Lord Henry Galloway. A portrait that she had stared at a million times over, ever since her childhood; but unlike before, as of recently, it started to haunt her. Lately, in her dreams, Kassie saw herself on horseback, wearing her white bridal gown and riding through the dark and gloomy forest. At first, Kassie was aware of her surroundings, but then, the further she rode out into the forest, the more she grew distressed and weary, along the way. Eventually, as more time came to pass, Kassie soon found herself lost in the woods. And just as she was right about to lose all hope, a dark and mysterious figure emerged from out of the shadows, galloping on horseback and coming straight to her rescue. But before Kassie could see his face, she suddenly awoke to find herself back inside her bedchamber and in her bed. Back to her normal life, awaiting a marriage that she dreaded with all the fibers of her being. Ironically, her dreams were her only blissful escape, while her reality remained her true nightmare.

Why was the Dark Horseman, such an intriguing character for her? Kassie wasn't entirely certain. Even after listening about his legendary tale from her grandmother, Kassie still knew very little about him, the former Lord Henry of Galloway Manor. But from what Kassie could gather and sense, he seemed like a complex man. If his legend was true and he was indeed cursed, then how would a man like him feel like, having lived or better yet, existed for the past hundred years in complete solitude? To have no one else around to speak or converse to? To have been denied the opportunity to venture outside of his cursed lands and experience life beyond this tiny and secluded village? To have witnessed everyone that he'd ever cared or loved, all perish away and die? But then, again, had the Dark Horseman ever experienced love, at all? After all, he, too, like Kassie, was once engaged. But did he actually love her? His fiancé? Did he miss being in the arms of another woman, after a hundred years of living within the constraints and boundaries of his curse?

For some strange reason, Kassie felt compelled to know. For in the end, she was immensely curious about the Dark Horseman; perhaps, a little too curious for her own good. After staring at his portrait for so long, Kassie was extremely attracted to her strange and mysterious gentleman. Although he was only a legend, Kassie still secretly wished to meet him. Even if it was only limited to merely her own dreams; for truly, she desperately longed to see him. To speak to him. To touch him. To kiss him. Ah, yes, Kassie was extremely attracted to the man, whose portrait hung above the walls of her family's estate. If only it could be…

Suddenly, Kassie reverted her attention back to reality and remembered that she was still, at this very moment, seated above her horse. In exactly an hour, she was destined to ride into church to marry Walter. Everything was ready. The priest was there. Her grandmother. His family. The entire village. The cake and celebratory decorations were all set. Even their home was already furnished with their new furniture, including Walter's personal chests consisting of his belongings having been recently delivered to the estate. Everything was set. Even Kassie, herself, was already dressed and prepared for the occasion, as well. With her long, fiery and red hair that was carefully arranged into a tight braid, adorned with fresh rose petals and various wildflowers, all woven into her hair and attached to her transparent veil. In addition, her new wedding dress was pressed and secured onto her petite and delicate figure. Last, but certainly not least, even her fresh bouquet of white daisies had already been delivered and carefully placed straight into her hands. Ah, yes, everything was prepared, delivered and ready to go. From here on out, Kassie's entire future had already been negotiated and meticulously planned, without her having any say in the matter. Sadly, this was it. Come this afternoon, Kassie was going to become a wife to Walter; a man, whom she considered as only a mere friend and nothing more. At this point, all that was left for Kassie was to ride along the straight path with her horse, and then, walk into the church. That was it. Nothing more.

Alas, the bride was on horseback and the deal was done. Now, it was time for Kassie to finally accept her fate, just as her grandmother, Maureen, had said so the day before. But the one thing that everyone else in her entire household failed to calculate was time… for Kassie was placed on horseback far too early. After all, she still had another hour or so, before she was supposed to arrive to the church. And so, out of her own better judgment, in a last-minute split decision— a decision that would ultimately come to alter her own destiny— Kassie decided to take one last tour around the property as a single lady, before going to the church to become a wife. Therefore, with one tug at the reins to her horse, both she and her horse, Faith, were off for a brief ride across the park.

CHAPTER 3

Riding through the woods was never an easy task, but lo and behold, this is where Kassie and her horse, Faith, now found themselves wandering about. After encircling a mile around the park at Wiltshire Hall, Kassie decided to ride a bit further south, towards the estate's outlying reaches. But soon after turning an unexpected corner, Kassie suddenly found herself exploring an entirely different part of the grounds, which were almost unrecognizable to her. Curiously, she ventured below into what appeared to be a hidden forest. To Kassie's amazement, the forest, in which she just so happened to stumble upon, was absolutely breathtaking and magnificent.

This newly discovered forest appeared to have been abandoned, with no visible traces of any other villagers dwelling inside. The original clean stone road that Kassie first ventured upon, was now replaced by a dirty and muddy path that was covered with several inches of mud and shriveled up foliage. As a whole, the entire forest appeared to have been surrounded by ancient oak trees. Based upon her initial impression, the trees looked to be aged hundreds, if not, thousands of years old, due to the sheer density of their trunks. Stretching far and wide, the trees' branches extended from one tree trunk to another. Furthermore, in-between them, were an endless amount of vigorous colored leaves that were all scattered about, exhibiting various sizes, shapes and shades— particularly, in the color of green. From dark emerald to light mossy green, to cool jade and even copper, the fallen leaves were all dispersed all around. Apart from these trees, there were also various other plants and fauna growing throughout the forest in great abundance, as well.

Along the path, there was also a wealth of ivy vines that grew and flourished everywhere, accompanied by their pesky long stems that extended and crawled about. In addition, found at every corner were hundreds of wildflowers, all in bloom. From white and pink daisies to yellow daffodils, to red poppies and bluebells, they were all perfectly blossomed, right in time for spring. But, out of all of the lovely flowers that grew within this majestic meadow, there was one particular set of flowers, which managed to capture Kassie's sole attention. It was there, right in the very heart of the forest, where a small field of wild purple violets grew, that shined and glowed, even from afar.

At first glance, Kassie could see them slightly off from her path and closer midway towards the other sets of trees. Although it was greatly unwise for her to leave Faith unattended as she wandered off into an unknown territory alone and unaccompanied; Kassie, nonetheless, still felt compelled to do so. Currently, as it stood, her own wedding bouquet was sadly, rather dull. Apart from the standard plain and white daisies that dominated her floral bouquet, Kassie had no other variety of colors to show for. Meanwhile, the purple violets right across from her were so incredibly vibrant and stunningly beautiful, that Kassie felt almost like a fool to not take advantage of this rare opportunity to collect them. Even from her own viewpoint, Kassie was simply mesmerized by their enchanting and magical beauty. Never one to be a coward, Kassie decided that she was willing to take a risk. Perhaps, this way, her bridal bouquet would have some spark of life and passion, in contrast to its current bland and unadorned state. Having quickly decided to go through with her decision, Kassie rode Faith down towards the direction leading up into the field of violets. Since she planned on only briefly stepping away for a short moment, Kassie jumped off from her horse, walked Faith over to a nearby tree and then, she tied her to the tree's trunk. Once Faith was safely secured, Kassie proceeded to slowly walk back towards the field and eventually, within a few short paces, she finally came face-to-face with the lovely patch of violets.

Much to her delight, the violets were everything that Kassie had hoped they would be. Up-close, they were far prettier and lovelier, than what she could ever have imagined. Unlike the other wildflowers that grew within the gardens at Wiltshire Hall, violets, in particular, were a pesky flower that she had often sought to grow there, but always failed to successfully do. Each winter, Kassie attempted to plant them in the soil to her garden; however, come spring, they never seemed to blossom. Rather than finding a lovely field of violets in May, Kassie found a flowerless bed of soil, instead. Apart from the other wildflowers that grew within her grandmother's gardens, violets were a long time favorite of Kassie's. In fact, it was the favorite flower of her own late mother, Daphne.

Even in her fondest childhood memories, Kassie recalled her home having always been filled and decorated with violets throughout the vast estate. Amazingly enough, back then, violets once bloomed in their very own backyard. However, ever since her parents' unfortunate deaths, sadly, violets never again grew within their estate. In truth, it wasn't because no one else cared to replant them— it's just that the soil, itself, no longer accepted them. Given that it had been well over five years and counting, since Kassie last laid eyes on a violet... at least not until today; she decided, at last minute, that apart from its sheer loveliness, that if she was also brave and bold enough to pick and add just a handful of them into her bouquet, then it was almost, as if, she was also honoring her own dear late mother in spirit, for her lack of appearance at her upcoming wedding.

And so, with much determination, Kassie approached the field of wild violets. As she slowly bent down, she began by picking just a few. Upon plucking her first one, Kassie stared down to simply admire the stunning flower in her hand. A treasure of nature, she thought to herself. Being just as soft as velvet, with its unique shade of dark purple being as bold and as regal as royalty itself; this violet was unlike any other flower that Kassie had ever previously gazed upon before. Curiously, Kassie brought the flower up-close to her face and gave it a sniff. To her surprise, the violet's scent was also unlike any of the other fragrances that she had previously ever smelt before. In truth, the scent was absolutely intoxicating— almost addictive.

"These violets will make a lovely addition to my bouquet," she remarked.

After picking her first flower, Kassie promptly picked a few more. Afterwards, she carefully arranged a total of five additional violets into her bridal bouquet. Once the violets were securely attached to her blue ribbon, Kassie stood back up. Since she was ready to return back to her horse, who was currently still waiting for her back at the road, she took a brief moment to admire the scenery.

"If only I could stay here forever," she whispered to herself aloud.

Now, whether or not this was a wish or not, it's rather difficult to say; for once Kassie uttered these very words, a small creature suddenly jumped straight out from a bush and landed near her.

"A bunny!" she happily exclaimed.

Sure enough, a small and furry white baby rabbit magically appeared right in front of her. Rolling around on the mossy green grass, the bunny managed to crawl up besides Kassie's white wedding gown, as it began rubbing itself against her leg.

"Aww, you're so incredibly cute!" Kassie joyfully exclaimed, as she quickly scooped the bunny up from the grass and straight into her caring arms.

Once within her possession, Kassie gently placed her bridal bouquet onto the grass and reverted her attention back over to the bunny. With its soft fur, tiny eyes, long ears and fluffy tail, Kassie was overjoyed by its sheer cuteness. As she continued to cradle the young bunny within her arms, she quickly noticed a small trail of blood encircling around its small foot. It was hurt.

"Oh no, you poor thing!" cried Kassie, out of concern.

Determined to help the injured animal, Kassie carefully placed the bunny back down onto the grass, as she promptly gathered a few loose leaves from the ground. Using the leaves, she gently wiped away the remaining blood and then, she moved to cover the wound by tying a piece of grass around its injured foot. However, right as Kassie was about to do that, the bunny unexpectedly managed to hop away. However, rather than escaping far, the bunny simply wandered off to her bridal bouquet nearby and began sniffing at her flowers.

"I see that you like my violets, too," Kassie remarked, with a smile.

But then, something truly remarkable happened. As the bunny inspected her bridal bouquet, its injured foot managed to rub against one of the petals to her newly picked violets. Amazingly enough, Kassie observed that somehow, the bunny's blood did not smear over onto the flower. On the contrary, the open wound now appeared to have been miraculously… sealed? Sealed… as in healed?

"What?!" shouted Kassie, in confusion.

Immediately, Kassie came running over to the bunny's side, as she scooped it back into her arms. Curiously, she promptly began inspecting the old wound and just as she had previously suspected, it was now fully healed. Healed, within an instant. But… how… how was this possible? Only but a mere moment ago, that same injured animal was previously bleeding through an exposed wound. However, as of now, it was completely healed. But how on earth, was this even possible?

Suddenly, Kassie recalled that right before this mysterious miracle transpired, the bunny was previously preoccupied with sniffing away at her bouquet of flowers. Somehow, in the midst of this small animal smelling her bridal bouquet, the bunny managed to rub its injured foot against… a violet… that was it! It was the violet! It was magical! It cured the bunny! It was a magical flower located right within this very forest! An enchanted forest!

"My goodness!" exclaimed Kassie, in blissful excitement.

One way or another, Kassie and her horse had managed to stumble upon an enchanted forest, near her own estate! While Kassie jumped for joy, she held onto the bunny tightly within her arms, as she danced along. However, her celebratory dance was short-lived; for shortly afterwards, she suddenly heard a vicious growl, coming straight from behind her. Almost immediately, Kassie completely ceased dancing and stood quietly still. Something was lurking inside of these woods and was now, making its way towards her direction. Seconds later, another similar growl was announced.

But this time around, Kassie suddenly felt fearful. Unlike this cute, adorable and most importantly, harmless bunny that came to playfully greet her; this time around, this new visitor did not sound too friendly. Not, at all. In fact, it sounded rather dangerous... and... deadly.

Time was of the essence; and so, Kassie stood still, as she tried her very best to devise a quick plan to safely escape. If she continued to remain standing still here in this same exact spot, then sooner or later, that evil creature was eventually going to make its way down and corner her. More likely, when confronted with this beast, it was going to ultimately attack and even, possibly kill her. Wearing nothing but her white wedding gown, Kassie was unarmed and completely vulnerable to the hidden dangers of the forest. However, recalling her previous studies back at university, Kassie remembered that when faced with an adversary in the jungle, it's best not to make direct eye contact with them and to slowly walk away from the confronting predator. Following this crucial lesson to heart, Kassie slowly bent down and grabbed her bridal bouquet. While holding the bunny on one hand and her bridal bouquet on the other, Kassie slowly began tiptoeing back towards Faith's direction.

For the next few steps, all seemed well and Kassie appeared to be rather successful. Fortunately, she no longer heard the animal's growls and Faith was only inches away. Eventually, soon enough, Kassie was going to get back on her horse and ride back to her village to get on with her wedding ceremony. A wedding that Kassie still at this very moment of terror, secretly wished with all her heart, would never ever, come to be.

Just then, the bunny, being the impatient creature that it was, suddenly wiggled itself straight out from her arms and leaped up into the air. As it landed back down onto the ground, it made a large thumping sound along the way. Soon afterwards, it bolted straight ahead and made its way back to the field of violets. Much to Kassie's horror, at that very same moment, a wolf suddenly emerged from behind the shadows. Within an instant, the wolf snatched the baby bunny from off the ground in the blink of an eye. In one swift move, the wolf viciously devoured the poor and defenseless creature, leaving nothing behind except its' remaining small bones. Horrified by this gruesome sight before her, Kassie screamed in terror. Unfortunately, her cries caught the attention of the hungry wolf and within mere moments, the wolf swiftly reverted its focus over towards Kassie. As the only remaining living creature standing within its near vicinity, the wolf was now determined to claim Kassie as his next victim.

Running for dear life, Kassie bolted straight ahead, as she desperately tried to run back over to Faith. However, after running for a few short minutes, Kassie soon realized that Faith was nowhere to be found. Somehow, in the midst of all this chaos, she managed to travel the wrong way. And now, she was completely lost. But, most importantly, she was also being hunted by a hungry predator, who was determined to make Kassie his next meal.

Confused on what to do next, Kassie just continued to run. As fast and as swift of a runner that the wolf was; so, too was Kassie. Luckily, her years of running and playing within the fields of Wiltshire Hall had finally paid off; for Kassie was able to swiftly leap across the forest, while maintaining a safe distance away from the wolf. However, the more that Kassie ran, she slowly began to grow tired. Eventually, with the physical limitations due to her irritable bridal dress, she could only run so far. Alas, this bride wasn't going to make it to her own wedding. Instead, she was going to be eaten alive by this detestable beast! Whether marrying Walter or being eaten by the wolf, both outcomes were not exactly ideal happy endings for Kassie. Acknowledging that neither one of her paths were roads that she wanted to walk down in the first place, Kassie suddenly stopped running midway. At long last, she was finally ready to accept her fate.

"If the wolf shall eat me, then let it be," she said, as she closed her eyes in defeat.

However, unbeknownst to Kassie, a third prospect was in still in store for her fate. A prospect that was soon going to become a new reality for her. While she closed her eyes and opened and extended her arms wide to surrender herself over to nature, Kassie patiently waited for the wolf to jump up and devour her, right there and then. But strangely enough, rather than hearing the howls of a hungry wolf, Kassie suddenly heard the trotting of a horse, galloping from afar, instead. A horse was coming. But how? Faith was still tied up to the tree somewhere, probably on the opposite side of the forest. Had she gotten loose? Did her horse sense that she was in danger? Was she coming to her rescue?

As the sounds of the galloping horse came closer, Kassie suddenly opened her eyes to witness as to what was actually happening in real-time. To her amazement, rather than seeing her horse, Faith, it was an entirely different horse, instead. In contrast to her own white horse, it was a black stallion. But more curiously enough, right above the horse was a man seated, whom Kassie had never met before. From afar, the man appeared to have dark hair and was dressed in a dark green petticoat, with black trousers and a pair of brown boots. As the man and his horse grew closer, Kassie squinted her eyes once more and to her sheer surprise, she finally recognized the man at long last.

"My God!" she exclaimed. "It's the Dark Horseman, in the flesh!"

CHAPTER 4

Within mere seconds, the Dark Horseman quickly leaned over and scooped up Kassie within his arms, as they rode off straight ahead. Riding through the forest with great agility, he valiantly galloped away, moving as fast as a speeding arrow having been recently released from a bow. Meanwhile, as the wolf continued to chase them down, the fearless Dark Horseman quickly retaliated by further increasing his speed even more, as he gracefully rode just as fast as the wind could possibly carry them.

With her eyes remaining closed, Kassie held onto dear life. As they continued through the forest, Kassie was seated right in front of the Dark Horseman on his horse. Meanwhile, as he rode along the darkened path, Kassie held on tightly to his coat, which felt like velvet. Although she couldn't see him, she could, instead, feel him. As her hands remained tugged along the inner rims of his petticoat, she could feel the traces of his blouse, which felt thin and sheer. Slowly, she continued to hold onto him tighter and as a result, she accidentally brushed her hands against his exposed and warm skin. Amazingly enough, his chest was firm, muscular and strong. He was certainly most fit and active to be sure. Curiously, Kassie reopened her eyes wide, as she attempted to stare at the mysterious rider's face.

To her awe, there right before her was none other than the man from her most beloved and cherished portrait. Miraculously, identical to his painting, he looked precisely as to how Kassie had always envisioned him to be. Similar to her own dreams, his eyes were as emerald as the forest, with his hair as black as the night, and his face as white as a ghost. As they continued to gallop down the path, his curly black hair floated against with the wind. But most fascinating above all else, was that his clothes were exactly still the same just as it last was when Kassie previously stared at his portrait no more than a few hours ago. Wearing a dark green petticoat, white blouse, black trousers and a pair of brown boots, the Dark Horseman appeared unchanged from his portrait that was painted at least a hundred years ago. However, unlike his portrait, the Dark Horseman was far handsomer up-close and in the flesh. And now, seated right underneath him, Kassie continued to admire the man, whom she spent most of her entire life fantasizing about.

From her viewpoint, his face was far more muscular, than what she had imagined him to be. His posture was strong and proper, while his face remained kind and mysterious. His lips were full and rosy, while his eyebrows were dark, thick and well defined. And his eyes... oh...his eyes.... were the deepest shade of emerald green, that simply sparkled and shined against the scenery. Furthermore, upon closer inspection, Kassie observed that his eyes alone spoke a thousand unspoken words, all on its very own. It was as if, after a hundred years of solitude, the Dark Horseman had witnessed a million mysterious tales of his very own, all seen through his magical and wonderous eyes.

As they continued to ride along, dashing through the forest, Kassie began to wonder as to what was going to eventually become of her. Was he really saving her from the wolf, or was he kidnapping her, instead? Did he actually come to rescue her, or was he here for her own doom? Was he her savior or was he, her failure? Was she truly safe within his arms, or was she off to meet her maker? At this very moment, Kassie wasn't entirely sure.

But this much she knew: the Dark Horseman was real! He wasn't just limited to being a mere myth or a legend, nor a figment of her own imagination. Instead, he was an actual real man. A person, who also existed in the living flesh. Another being, just like Kassie. But most importantly, he was a man, who continued to exist, even in this current century. Somehow, along her journey through the forest, Kassie managed to stumble upon a man, whom she longed to meet, ever since she was a child. After years of staring at his portrait and envisioning him in her dreams, Kassie finally came face-to-face with him. And to top it all off, Kassie not only finally saw him, but she was seated right near him, too. Holding him. Touching him. Riding with him. Whether he was a saint or the devil, himself, it didn't matter. At long last, Kassie finally met the one person in the entire world, whom she secretly wished to meet. Alas, now, if Kassie was intended to die out here in this enchanted forest, before making it to her own wedding, then she was perfectly content with her fate. For after a lifetime of wishing, Kassie finally met the man of her dreams.

As Henry continued to ride on, all seemed well. The wolf was beginning to grow tired and in a few more paces, they were going to reach Kassie's horse and all would be well. However, in a surprise twist of fate, as soon as Henry reached the path leading up to Kassie's horse, he noticed that two fallen tree branches were currently blocking their path. Unfortunately, these branches were so incredibly thick and long, that it was almost impossible to continue riding, without having to stop and move them. However, if Henry did that, then the wolf was most certainly going to catch up with them. And so, determined to beat the impossible, Henry gathered more speed and with one powerful command, both he and his horse, Midnight, leaped high up into the air and jumped over the enormous obstacle!

"My God!" exclaimed Kassie, as they landed back down onto land.

"My God, indeed," agreed Henry.

Suddenly, Kassie looked over and behind them. From there, she saw that not only had those broken branches served as their previous roadblock and obstacle, but as of now, it was also currently blocking the wolf's ongoing path, too. In a miraculous twist of fate, the fallen tree branches couldn't have come at a better time. Now, with the wolf far away from their trail, Kassie could finally sigh a breath of relief. However, her relief was only short lived; for almost immediately soon afterwards, they suddenly came to a complete stop.

"Is something wrong?" asked Kassie, curious as to why they had abruptly halted.

"We're here," he announced.

Looking straight ahead, Kassie saw that she was indeed back to where she first arrived. Back to the same exact area, where she had previously stopped to gather her violets for her bridal bouquet. The same violet fields, where she met the injured bunny and nursed it back to health…well… sort of. Not counting the fact that the bunny was technically cured by the magical violets, of course. Needless to say, Kassie was right back to where she first arrived to, near the path leading back to the front entrance to the woods. And in just a few short moments from now, Kassie was going to retrieve Faith and ultimately return back to her world, as if this entire afternoon had never happened in the first place. Back to the church to marry Walter, her fiancé. Sadly, this was how it was going to have to be. This was the end. The end of her adventure with the man of her dreams, whom she hadn't yet had the chance to properly converse with.

But alas, something unexpected and unpredictable was still yet in store for our heroine, Kassie. Gazing straight across at the tree, in which she last tied Faith to, Kassie noticed only but a loose rope still dangling alongside the tree's trunk! Somehow, during her journey, the rope that previously held Faith together, got loose and Kassie's trusted horse managed to run away! But where to? Where did Faith go? Furthermore, sadly, with Faith gone, what was to become of her? Was Kassie going to be left alone and stranded out in the forest, all by herself? Besides, it was approaching dark, and she was already far too late to attend her own wedding. Therefore, what was Kassie going to do?

"My God!" exclaimed Kassie, as she quickly hopped off from Midnight. "Faith is gone."

"Is something troubling you?" asked Henry, as he jumped down from his horse to join her side.

"My horse! She's run off!" exclaimed Kassie, in great frustration.

"I see," observed Henry, as he quickly took notice of the loose rope that was still tangled around the tree.

"Oh, what I'm I to do!" she exclaimed, once more.

"The village is not too far from here," he began. "There's still daylight. If you start walking now, then I'm sure you'll make it back home by foot in time for dinner."

"I can't…" began Kassie.

For a moment, Kassie deeply concentrated on his words. While it was true, technically, she could walk back home. Granted, given that she was still wearing her wedding dress, it was going to be a messy walk back; but the bigger question was, did she really want to walk back home? Did she truly want to return back into the village to marry Walter? Even though she was already late as it was to her own wedding; however, if she returned back now, then her wedding was still going to take place, either way. Whether tonight or tomorrow, it was still going to happen, regardless. No matter the circumstances, if Kassie did indeed return back home, then she was ultimately going to face her future as Walter's new wife. A future role that she so desperately wanted to divert; no matter how much her grandmother wanted her to fulfill it. Suddenly, Kassie got an idea. Maybe, by staying in the enchanted forest, she could build a new life here, independently and away from Walter. Perhaps, with Faith running away it was fate's way of helping her and was truly, the best possible outcome that could ever have happened to her. Without thinking any further, Kassie decided to cease this rare opportunity to plead her case with her rescuer.

"I can't go back," she forceful stated. "There's nowhere else for me to go."

"Are you sure about that?" he asked, with a raised brow. "After all, you're wearing a wedding dress, are you not?"

"Yes…" she began but damn it, he had a point! What was she to say? What was she to do? Somehow, one way or another, Kassie needed to convince him to take her away with him.

"Yes?" he repeated, with an amused smile. Having only just met her, Henry was already intrigued by her.

"I'm a…" she continued.

"A…" he repeated.

"I'm a…" she said, once more.

"A runaway bride?" he asked, with a playful smirk.

Although it was true, she was indeed a runaway bride; however, due to her pride, she was reluctant to admit this obvious truth. Furthermore, had she admitted to Henry that she was indeed a runaway bride, then perhaps, he would give less sympathy to her case. If Kassie was going to successfully run away from home, then she needed to find shelter, along with a trusted companion to protect her. And thus far, Henry checked all of the required boxes. Perhaps, if she told him that she was a jilted bride instead, then maybe, just maybe, he'd be more willing to agree to take her into his custody.

"I'm not a runaway bride," she proudly declared. "I'm a jilted bride."

"A jilted bride?" asked Henry, in confusion. "Do you actually mean that your groom ran off on you?"

"Yes, that's precisely what I'm saying," she lied. "And now, I've got nowhere else to go."

"Listen," he began, "I'm sorry about your horse, but it's getting late and you really should start walking."

"But I've got nowhere to walk to… I've… I've… got… nowhere else… to go…" she begged.

"Surely, there's someone who can take you in," he said, firmly. "Family, friends, neighbors or acquaintances? By now, I'm certain that your parents must be worried sick about you."

"I don't… I'm an orphan," she revealed. And then, she added, "Like I said before, I've got nowhere else to go… no one to turn to."

Although this was partially true, Kassie was indeed an orphan; but at the same time, she still had a legal guardian. After all, her grandmother was still alive and well. Plus, with this passage of time, Maureen must have been worried about her too, by now.

However, Kassie's specific choice of words surprisingly tugged away at Henry's heart. Although Henry was not one to have a soft interior; somehow, hearing that she was an 'orphan' certainly caught his attention. Having been an orphan himself, meeting another similar and unfortunate soul, brought an unexpected form of sympathy and compassion into his stone heart.

"Are you certain?" he asked.

"Certain about what?" she repeated.

"That you've got nowhere else to go," he clarified.

"I'm certain," she boldly said. "As I said before, I'm an orphan."

"Very well," he said, reluctantly. "Come with me."

Returning back to his horse, Henry offered his helping hand to her. Delighted by his generous offer, Kassie quickly grabbed a hold of his hand, as he lifted her back up onto his horse. Soon afterwards, he hopped on and together, they turned in the reverse position and rode straight back into the forest. As Kassie held onto Henry tightly, she silently watched him in admiration and smiled. In a day that was supposed to be one of the worst days of her entire life, actually turned out to be one of, if not, the best day ever. Or better yet, what began as hell, most fortunately, ended in pure heaven.

CHAPTER 5

By the late evening, they arrived to what appeared to be the remains of the once glorious and legendary Galloway Manor. From the outside view, the manor's architectural design and structure was extremely grand and extravagant, and it was by far, much larger in size and stature in comparison to Wiltshire Hall. In fact, it would take approximately three separate versions of her family's home, in order to equal to one property that was identical to this particularly horrendously enormous estate. Furthermore, based upon the visual views of the exterior alone, the property actually resembled more of an abandoned ancient castle, rather than a forgotten countryside manor by the edge of the sea.

As they slowly approached to the front of the manor, Kassie observed that the entrance, along with its connecting iron gated fence, were all covered up with vines of ivy. From top to bottom, the ivy wrapped around and encircled the entire exteriors, as a whole. However, once they crossed through the gate's threshold, Kassie soon realized that the vines didn't just stop there. Rather, the vines grew throughout the remainder of the estate, including the inside as well. From the mossy grounds to the red brick path, to the stone walls and clay rooftop that comprised the manor, the vines grew all around everywhere and anywhere, in-between. Furthermore, if there weren't vines, then there were plenty of other plants that grew within their place as well, including several wildflowers. All around, various plants and fauna thrived all throughout the estate. From the small patches of dirt with specs of tiny bluebells peeking through, to the red roses that crawled along the outer corners of the stone walls. Sadly, it seemed that this once grand estate was not only forgotten, but it was also neglected too. No gardener. No servant. No... anyone... was here to care and look after it.

"Is this... Galloway Manor?" she asked, in astonishment.

Impressed by this fair young maiden, whom he had only recently just met by chance and had already known the precise name to his own private estate and residence, Henry curiously inquired, "So you've heard of my manor, before?"

"Yes, I have," she admitted. "But I just didn't picture it... so... so..."

"Abandoned?" he asked, with a raised brow.

"I knew it was abandoned," she clarified, but then she added, "But still, I thought it was going to be a bit more... well... tidy."

Suddenly, Henry unexpectedly laughed. This was unusual, even for him. In all of his many years spent in solitude, he had not once come across such a young and innocent maiden, who thought ill of his dwelling. In fact, she was the very first person, whom he brought here, ever since his curse.

"Well, how do you suppose an abandoned manor is supposed to look like? Shouldn't there be vines and other plants and creepy creatures, just lurking and growing about?" he asked, in a sarcastic manner.

"I suppose that you're right. But still, I expected something more... more..." she began, but somehow, she couldn't find the exact words to say.

"Romantic?" he asked, with a smile.

"Perhaps," she admitted bashfully, while blushing and turning in the color pink.

Amused by her shy reaction, Henry soon parked Midnight by the front of the manor, as he proceeded to jump down onto the ground. Once his two feet reached the dirt again, he moved to assist Kassie back down to join him. With her by his side, Henry offered her his hand, which she, in return, gladly accepted. From there, he escorted her into the manor. Once they arrived at the front entrance, Henry slowly pushed opened the doors and thus, in the process, revealed yet another mysterious layer to his new guest.

As soon as the doors to Galloway Manor were fully opened, Kassie was left standing still and speechless. For as large and as grand as the exteriors were, the interiors were far more exquisite and extravagant, than anything else that Kassie had ever seen before. Upon entry, the manor revealed a huge gallery, which extended from one side of the estate to the other side of the property. Additionally, in the center of the gallery, hung a massive sized antique crystal chandelier, that was so elegantly refined, that it also sparkled and shined, just like the moonlight. Even through the several thick layers of dust, the crystals still found a miraculous way to take center stage, by shining like a bright star, located high above in the night sky. Furthermore, behind the chandelier, looked to be a grand staircase, that appeared to lead to an upstairs floor. But from where Kassie was left standing, based upon her immediate bird's eye view, she could see that the manor was decorated with several pieces of antique and baroque style furniture, made from the highest quality of materials that looked to be foreign. Perhaps, even German. Continuing on, located on the far corner of the room, Kassie saw an oversized antique curiosity cabinet, that appeared to display a vast array of numerous collectables, consisting of Victorian style porcelain teapots, teacups and other dishware, all neatly arranged and organized from the inside; while at the same time, also appearing untouched and unused for the greater part of the past century. In addition, to her far right, there also appeared to be an extended red velvet sofa, along with matching red chairs and a large oval coffee table made from oakwood. Apart from the grey stone floors, there were also numerous red carpets, all scattered throughout the property.

Although the manor was enchantingly regal, at the same time, the manor was also… well… spectacularly... dirty. Yes, dirty. Sadly, several decades of accumulated dust and debris were all evidently showcased all around, in every possible inch and corner of the given space. From above the grand staircase to the foot of the stone floors, to the crystal chandeliers to the wooden tables, to the reading chairs to the velvet sofa, and everywhere else, in-between. Truly, there most certainly, wasn't a dearth of dust that wasn't evenly spread all around to practically everywhere within the manor's far reaches. Furthermore, if there wasn't a heavy dose of dust consuming and eating away at the furniture, then there were also a healthy number of thick vines that were rapidly growing and crawling along the interior walls. Why, even the main chandelier in the gallery had a good share of hanging vines, that draped over it. Seriously, had Kassie been more daring, then she could have easily swung herself from one end of the estate to the other, simply just by holding onto that very vine alone; as if she, herself, were residing within the mighty jungle. But if that wasn't enough, then there were also hundreds of other dried foliage, all scattered across the floor and located all throughout the property. One way or another, Lord Henry had certainly allowed his manor to wither away into nothing more, than specs of dust and dirt! How tragic this truly was, too!

"My goodness!" she exclaimed. "You've certainly let this house go. Now, haven't you?"

Surprised by her unexpected reaction to his humble abode, Henry quietly walked over to his dusty red velvet chair and sat himself down. For a few short minutes, he remained completely silent, as he pondered about her question. Finally, with Henry comfortably situated within his chair, he stretched his arms and legs wide apart and then, he reverted his gaze back towards her direction. Looking straight into her eyes, he posed her a question of his very own.

"Aren't you afraid of me?" he boldly asked the million-dollar question, while at the same time, hoping to receive an honest and direct answer from her.

"What do you mean afraid?" she innocently asked, in surprise. "Why should I be afraid of you? After all, you saved me from that hungry wolf. I'd say, that makes you, my hero."

"A hero?" he asked, astonished by her sincere answer. In all of his years, Henry had been called many things, but never once, a hero.

"Yes, a hero," she boldly repeated. "You're my hero."

Touched by her kind and heartfelt complement, Henry couldn't help but admire her. Curiously, he decided to press her even further. After all, it wasn't every day that he had an honored guest visiting his grand manor.

"What do you know of me?" he asked her, point blank.

Without a flinch, she simply responded, "Why, you're Lord Henry, the Dark Horseman, of course."

Hearing his actual birth name spoken by another, certainly caught him off guard. For a century, he was only known and referred to as the 'Dark Horseman.' From the wandering vagabonds to the pesky thieves, to the lonesome hermits and lost youths, all stumbling upon his dark woods, Henry was always referred by his cursed title, the Dark Horseman, by them. Ever since the first night, when his curse was originally cast, Henry roamed across the enchanted forest, each and every night, as he patrolled and protected the forest away from any potential threats, including intruders and foreign enemies. Whenever another soul stepped a foot into the enchanted forest, Henry was the first to know at the precise moment of their entry. Amazingly enough, it was his curse that enabled Henry to telepathically sense, as to who came and left within his dominion. For those who were fortunate enough to arrive with a kind and gentle heart, along with a good soul, Henry always came to their aids to serve as a saint; as he sought to help guide them through their journey out of the woods and leading them back onto the correct path, towards civilization. But for those unfortunate souls, whose hearts were evil and cruel, then Henry was there to serve as their punisher, here on earth. And if the wolf had been scary to Kassie, then little did she know of the actual truth; for Henry, whenever faced with an adversary, he could be far worse and more terrifying, than that of a harmless mere wolf, in comparison. But unlike everyone else, Kassie was the first person, in well over a century to have actually referred to him by his given name. After years of being called the 'Dark Horseman,' Henry almost forgot his own name. Somehow, now, hearing his actual birth name spoken aloud, it brought an unexpectant smile to his face. A smile, that he had seldom exhibited before; at least, not until today.

"Interesting," he said, most intrigued. "You seem to know a lot about me, already. Come now, enlighten me. Tell me, all that you know."

"Well," she began, "I've been told about your origin story."

"Really?" asked a surprised Henry. "Please, humor me. Tell me more," he said, as he folded up his arms and leaned his legs across the coffee table.

"But first," he interrupted. "Come and take a seat with me. Make yourself more comfortable."

Following his command, Kassie walked over to his side of the room and sat down on the empty chair, right across from him. Like everything else in the room, the chair was also dusty and dirty. However, this didn't matter to Kassie; for she, herself, was already covered in inches of mud and dirt, from her head and all the way down to her feet. Sadly, her once newly pressed and ironed white bridal gown was now covered with patches of brown dirt, all scattered about; along with traces of green mossy grass, attached to the hem of her dress. Needless to say, Kassie quickly took a seat and once more comfortable, she proceeded to answer his question.

"As I was saying," she continued, "Come yesterday, I learned that—"

"Wait," he interrupted, once more. "Do you mean to tell me, that you've only come to learn about me, only just of yesterday?"

"Well, not exactly," she admitted.

"Really? How so?" he asked, more curious than ever.

Now, dear reader, how was Kassie ever going to confess to Henry the complete truth? The fact that she's known and loved him, ever since she first laid eyes on his portrait, as a young girl? Or, that she's stared at his portrait, every single passing day; as if he were a real-life celebrity? Or better yet, that when she was previously told that he wasn't real and only just a figment of her imagination, that deep down within her heart, Kassie always secretly knew otherwise? That for years, he haunted her in her dreams and as a result, she wished for nothing more but to meet with him? To actually touch him? To feel him? To be with him? To belong to him? To love him? No, she couldn't tell him everything. Not now. Not ever.

"Well," she continued, "As of yesterday, I finally came to formally hear of your tale. You're a legend back at the village, just so you know."

"Oh," he said, most amused. "Is that so? Tell me, what do they say about me? Are they utterly fearful and terrified of me?"

"I wouldn't know," she admitted. "Honestly, I don't know too many people back in the village."

"Interesting," he said, amazed by her lack of socialization with polite society.

Back in Henry's time, solitude was frowned upon. All respectful families were expected to either host or attend balls, regardless of their backgrounds. In fact, everyone was required to attend a ball, especially young debutantes, such as this mysterious young lady, seated right across from him.

"Somehow," Henry continued, "I find that rather hard to believe. A young maiden, such as yourself, must have been very popular at social gatherings. Tell me, do they still hold balls at the village?"

"Yes, they do. But truthfully, I detest them all," she shamefully admitted.

"Hate balls?" asked Henry, in complete confusion.

For the first time in his life, Henry met an actual debutante, who not only hated balls, but that, she also detested them, too. Although Henry lived the majority of his existence in solitude, this wasn't due to his own choosing. Rather, this was a consequence of his curse. However, this particular young lady, now an invited guest at his home, actually preferred solitude, based upon her own free will. Alas, Henry was most perplexed and curious about this strange, but yet, humorous young woman.

"Yes, I hate balls," Kassie boldly clarified, once more. "With all honesty, I hate everything about it. From the gowns to the people, to the dancing and everything else in-between."

And then, as if she was forced to relive another unwanted memory of dancing at a ball, Kassie frowned and then folded her arms. Clearly, she was upset and Henry was absolutely fascinated by her reaction. Had he been away from society for far too long? Had people, especially, young women, changed so much over the past century? Or, had this particular young woman been an exception to the rule? In all honesty, Henry simply could not tell.

"May I ask, why do you hate balls so much?" Henry inquired.

Truthfully, Kassie hated balls, because at every single one of them, she was always forced to dance with Walter. From the moment she first debuted into society, as a young and eligible debutante, Walter was right there and waiting for her. Given the lack of male representatives in their small village, Kassie really didn't have too many options for other dance partners and suitors. Although Kassie tried her best to attempt to persuade her grandmother to spend at least her introductory season in London; somehow, it just never came to be. By then, Kassie had already left for university and by the time she finally returned back home after graduation, the entire inheritance crisis posed by Douglas, came into being. And so, Kassie, already aged twenty-one, was soon approaching spinsterhood. Given her lack of options and Walter's availability, a marriage deal was made between her grandmother and her fiancé. And so, because of these reasons, Kassie hated balls and everything else, associated with them. However, with that said, she couldn't honestly tell Henry the truth about all of this. No, it was far too soon. As far as he was concerned, she was a jilted bride and not a runaway bride. There was a big difference between the two, after all.

"Oh, nothing in particular," she innocently lied. "It's just that I much rather stay at home and read a good book, that's all," she added, which in truth, wasn't exactly a lie, either.

"Books, well," he began, most excitingly, "I have a huge library here at the manor, filled with an endless collection of various books. You're most welcome to read them, anytime that you'd like."

"Really?" asked Kassie, thrilled at this new and exciting prospect.

"Yes," he said. "But first, tell me more, as to what else you know of me."

"Like I said before, you're a legend back at the village," she began, "From what I've been told, you're Lord Henry, Earl of Galloway, and ever since your evil stepmother, Vera, cursed you as the Dark Horseman, you've been wandering through the forest for over the past one hundred years and counting."

"Is that what they say? Interesting," he reflected.

"Also, some regard you as a saint; but for others, you're the very devil, himself," she added.

"True," he said, with a smile across his face.

Wanting to learn more, Henry suddenly placed his legs back down onto the ground, sat straight up and while looking into her eyes, he finally asked, "But most importantly, what do *you* think about me?"

The intensity of his stare, made Kassie feel weak in her knees. Alas, she was now incredibly nervous. Although she previously felt extremely comfortable speaking to him earlier in the evening; however, seeing him look so incredibly handsome up-close, Kassie suddenly felt extremely vulnerable and insecure. The man, whom she long admired and loved for most of her life; was now, seated nearby and actually conversing with her in real life.

"Umm..." she began, as she gulped.

"Yes?" he said, with a raised brow. From the looks of it, he was impatient and determined to have an answer.

"Well," she continued, "I think that you're a rather good fellow. After all, you've taken me in, haven't you?"

"I'm still debating on that one," he admitted.

"Wait, you can't have me go back there! Please, I'll do anything!" she cried.

"Anything?" he asked, most amused.

Luckily for Kassie, Henry was a man of honor and a true gentleman at heart; therefore, he would never compromise her against her will— not now, not ever. However, after a hundred years of solitude, had she offered herself willingly to him, then he would be most inclined to accept such a proposal. After all, he was still a man, in the end; and truthfully, he hadn't been with another woman, in well over a century and counting.

"Well, almost anything," she clarified, after realizing that by saying 'anything,' he might inadvertently get the wrong impression. Although she was greatly attracted to him, she wasn't yet ready to compromise her virtue, either. At least, not yet.

"Don't worry," he clarified, too, on his part. "I'm a gentleman and you, I take it, are a gentleman's daughter. Am I correct?"

"Yes, that I am," she agreed.

"In either case, you're safe here with me. For however long that you decide to stay," he announced.

"Do you mean that I can stay here, with you?" she happily asked.

"Yes, you can. But I should admit, that you'll probably find me to be a rather complex companion," he warned her.

"Really, how so?" she asked, most curiously.

"Well, given that you're already aware that I'm cursed, you must also know that nothing can kill me. No poison or weapon can ever bring me down," he revealed.

"Does that mean that you're immortal? That you live forever?" she asked.

"So far, that's how it seems. As such, I don't sleep or eat. My only duty is to guard the forest. Apart from this, that's all there really is to know about me," he said, as if his entire existence was really just that simple.

"Wait, so you've lived like this, for the past one hundred years?" she inquired.

"Pretty much," he sighed.

"What about servants? Does anyone come to clean or…" she started to say, but then she trailed off.

"Does it look like I have servants?" he laughingly asked. "No, no servants. I've outlived them all. Sadly, it's just me. That's why the manor is in the current mess that it's in. Truthfully, I've never had any reason to clean it.

No balls. No parties. No honored guest. At least, not until tonight."

"I see, so I'm your honored guest," she said, with a smile.

It was the first time that Henry had ever seen her smile before. In fact, it was the first time that he had seen another person smile at all, in the past one hundred years. Even amongst the lost travelers stumbling upon the forest, no one else had ever smiled in his presence. In fact, everyone else that he had previously encountered, were either fearful or terrified around him. Not one person, in all this time, ever actually looked so... well... happy. How incredibly strange and odd, that this peculiar young maiden just so happened to wander right into his realm and appear so incredibly happy. Suddenly, it finally occurred to Henry that he didn't even know her name.

"Yes," he said, "And as my honored guest, I believe that you should tell me your name."

"Ah, yes, introductions should be in place. After all, I already know your name," she replied.

"Yes. Now please, kindly state your name," he asked, once more.

"Lady Kassandra Stanton," she proudly said. "But everyone calls me Kassie."

"Kassie," he repeated, with a smile. "That's a lovely name."

"Thank you," she graciously replied.

"Well, Kassie, you can stay here, for as long or as little as you like. But, for your own welfare and safety, I'd recommend that while you're staying here, you might also want to consider helping me by tidying up this place just a bit, don't you think?" he suggested, hoping that she'd willingly agree to his proposal.

Looking around the manor, Kassie couldn't help but agree with him. After all, the manor was in a complete mess. A dreadful state. Sadly, it most likely hadn't been cleaned in well over the past one hundred years. Why, the house probably hadn't had a woman's touch, ever since the time

Henry's stepmother last resided in here. Since Henry had already been so incredibly kind to allow her stay with him, Kassie felt compelled to agree to his terms, wholeheartedly. If cleaning this haunted and dirty manor meant that she could live here and far away from home, and thus, delaying and even possibly terminating her impending marriage to Walter, then Kassie was most willing to clean and do whatever Henry wanted her to do, without question! After all, any fate was a far better fate than being Walter's wife! Plus, this way, Kassie had her chance of a lifetime to be around her ultimate dream man, Lord Henry of Galloway Manor, in the flesh!

"I agree," she said enthusiastically. "I'll help clean your house, in exchange for my food and shelter."

"Very well," he said, sounding most pleased. "In that case, you can take up residence in any room of your choice upstairs with the exception to mine, which is the one located on the west wing. Apart from there, you're most welcome to claim any of the other rooms, as your very own."

"Thank you," she said, most happily.

"As for clothes," said Henry, as he stared at her dirty and torn bridal gown. "There should be plenty of other fine dresses and gowns available upstairs. You're free to have them all. As for food…"

"Yes, food…" she repeated. By now, it had been hours since Kassie last had a real meal; and given that it was now approaching nightfall, she was so incredibly hungry, too.

"Given that I don't eat or sleep," he reminded her, "Starting tomorrow, I'll resume my hunting in the forest. I promise to bring home game for you and from there, you can cook and eat it."

"Ah, yes, I see," she said, feeling a bit disappointed. While it was true, as an immortal, food wasn't a priority for him. However, Kassie, on the other hand, was a mortal and sadly, she wasn't going to be able to eat again in the near future… at least not until tomorrow morning.

"Very well, I think I shall retire now," Henry announced, as he rose up from his chair.

"But I thought that you don't sleep," Kassie asked, innocently.

"I don't," he laughingly replied. "But still, I like to relax and enjoy the privacy of my bedchamber."

"Very well. Goodnight, Lord Henry," she said.

"Oh, Kassie," he said, wanting to add one last thing.

"Yes?" she asked, in return.

"Henry, will be fine. No need for any formal or... even... legendary titles. Just Henry, will do," he kindly said.

Afterwards, Henry exited the room and retired upstairs, leaving Kassie alone to admire the rest of the manor. Rather than spending her wedding night with Walter back at Wiltshire Hall, Kassie was now whisked away to the historical Galloway Manor, underneath the same roof as her childhood crush; who already seemed to be everything that she had ever wished for him to be. Not only did he offer her his home, but he also didn't take advantage of her virtue, either. Plus, Kassie now had the freedom to live in any room of her preference! With this much freedom, Kassie was sure that now, at long last, she'd finally have enough time to write her first novel, in the near future. Oh my, had the gods been good to her, after all!

CHAPTER 6

An hour later, Kassie found herself settled into what appeared to be a master suite. Located upstairs on the east wing, was an unoccupied bedchamber that was so incredibly luxurious, grand and spacious, that it could fit at least four versions of her own bedchamber back at Wiltshire Hall, all inside this one single dwelling. While there were several other available bedchambers to choose from; however, in the end, Kassie opted for this particular bedchamber, due its inclusion of a connecting balcony, along with its breathtaking and spectacular scenic view overlooking the outside garden.

Surprisingly, her journey traveling upstairs was already quite an adventure; for along the way, Kassie was forced to fight against a whole host of cobwebs and spiders in the process. But if that wasn't enough to deter her, Kassie had to walk through piles of dirt and debris, including a vast collection of dried-up leaves that were all scatter on the floor, starting from the staircase and leading up into the hallway. In fact, the leaves were so incredibly dried out, that they almost practically turned into dust just by stepping down upon them.

However, once Kassie made it successfully up the stairs; she somehow, managed to automatically divert herself to the direction leading into the east wing. Knowing that the west wing belonged solely to Henry's domain, Kassie concentrated on the available east side. As she walked down the never-ending hallway— which was so impressively extravagant, that Kassie actually counted a total of at least a dozen pairs of French style crystal chandeliers, all hanging above on the ceiling. Furthermore, the ceilings themselves, were a true work of art. A masterpiece of their very own. Similar to the artwork painted above the Sistine Chapel— by the one and only Michelangelo, himself— the ceilings at Galloway Manor were just as equally exquisite and pristine.

Painted in the baroque style, the mural displayed an artificial sky, including a sun located in the center, followed by the moon on the far right, along with various clouds and stars all spread across. From the front entrance leading into the hallway, it initially looked dark and gloomy— with the darkness overpowering the entire scenery. However, the further one traveled down into the hallway, the moon eventually, found its way to shine and light up the wandering path. Furthermore, traveling a little further down, a few stars were painted above, in order to help shed some additional light to the otherwise, darkened background. But, as Kassie continued to walk down the hall, she noticed that about midway down, the ceiling art began to transition from pure darkness into light. Somewhere, somehow, in the middle of the hall, there was a significant shift, where the dark sky was eventually, replaced by an illuminated sky, which included a bright sun, along with white fluffy clouds. It was here, in this particular area, where Kassie finally decided to stop and take a peek at the available rooms.

At first, the initial room that Kassie originally opened wasn't actually a bedchamber; but rather, it appeared to be an abandoned ballroom. Based upon what Kassie could actually see through the deep layers of dust, it seemed to be a room filled with mirrors on all sides. Again, like all of the other rooms before, there was yet another grand chandelier hung up, high above in the center of the ceiling. Meanwhile, the floors below appeared to be white marble made from the highest quality of craftmanship imaginable. Based on the looks of it, one could only presume that back at its height, Galloway Manor must have held some of the most impressive and lavish balls in the entire history of their village!

Continuing on, Kassie closed the ballroom doors and moved on to the next room. Upon opening its door, to her amazement, she discovered on what appeared to be a home library. However, this was unlike any home library that Kassie had ever seen before. In fact, this particular library was far larger, than even the public library back at her village. But to make matters more impressive, the volumes of books appeared to be endless. The bookshelves, themselves, appeared to stretch from one end of the room to the other. Furthermore, the height of the bookshelves was most impressive by far, and they appeared to range from the very top of the ceiling and down to the floor. At first glance, there looked to be at least a million copies to various titles. Curiously, Kassie entered straight into the library and using her hands, she pulled out a few random books from off their shelves and began to dust them off using her fingers. To her surprise, Kassie found copies to various books relating to philosophy, science, history, languages and even fiction. Why, everything that any person could have ever hoped or wished to read, was all here.

Unfortunately, like all of the other previous rooms; this too, had sadly been greatly neglected, as evident by the several layers of dust. However, Kassie simply refused to accept this cruel injustice. One way or another, she was determined to restore this grand library. One polish, at a time. Eventually, in due time, Kassie was going to transform this sleepy and forgotten library back into its original glory, as one of this country's most exquisite libraries that was home to some of the rarest collections of books that she had ever had the pleasure to see and admire, firsthand.

Moving on, Kassie continued onwards with her journey down the hall, in her search of finding a decent bedchamber to retire in. As the midnight hour grew closer, Kassie began to grow tired; and with that, her patience also started to dwindle down rather thinly. After opening a few more doors into random bedchambers that all appeared to have previously belonged to other special guests and residents, Kassie finally came across a room more suited to her own liking.

Upon entering the last vacant bedchamber, Kassie immediately noticed that unlike the other rooms before, this one had a balcony. Excitingly, Kassie quickly ran inside and made her way over towards the terrace. Once there, Kassie peeked across outside on the ledge and to her amazement, she saw that the view overlooked an outside garden. Although Kassie had previously arrived at Galloway Manor from the front entrance, based upon this new bird's eye view from the balcony, there seemed to be yet another hidden garden at the back of the manor. But truly, a garden did not do it justice. No, it certainly did not. Rather, this was paradise. A real-life Garden of Eden.

Absent of a gardener, somehow, this magical garden still found its own way to grow and flourish, without any human assistance. Although there were several wild and overgrown vines, here and there; but overall, the scenic view was still absolutely magnificent. Throughout the garden, there were several hundreds of roses, all in bloom. From crimson red to white roses, each flower could be seen, all growing sporadically throughout the yard. While their thorns might have also dominated the same scenery; however, the specs of red and white colored petals peeking through was still a beautiful sight to behold. Unlike the roses that grew back at Wiltshire Hall, the roses that blossomed here at Galloway Manor, were far more superior in both color and vibrancy. Overall, the textures of these roses appeared to be much more refined and regal; but yet, it was still soft and delicate, at the same time. While Kassie was unable to simply reach over and touch them— for they were too far away from her given location— but from what her eyes could directly see, these roses were magical.

Apart from the roses, there also appeared to be a small pond, right in the center of garden. Although it wasn't a very large pond; it was still, nevertheless, a decent sized pond that also appeared to be more decorative, rather than functional. However, given the late-night hour, it was rather difficult to see the water so clearly. But apart from this fact, Kassie could still detect from the moonlight that the pond had several small lily pads, all floating above. Additionally, seated right above those lily pads, looked to be several tiny sized toads and other small creatures, that were lounging away. And in between those lily pads, also appeared to be several strands of floating moss and mold, all scattered about.

Further down the garden and beyond the pond, there were several rows of tall oak trees. Zooming in with her eyes, Kassie realized that these oak trees were also the entrance, leading into the enchanted forest. The very same forest, in which she had previously stumbled upon and met Henry.

"Ah, so this is where he enters into the forest," she deduced.

Suddenly, Kassie diverted her attention away from the forest and looked up at the sky to stare at the moon. There, shining right in the center of the night sky, illuminated by its surrounding stars, was the moon. While Kassie had often stared at this very same moon a million times over back at Wiltshire Hall, tonight was the first night, that she had ever stared at it from a new residence. How funny, she thought. Within the blink of an eye, her entire destiny had altered its natural course. From riding out with Faith in her white wedding dress, to being chased by the hungry wolf and rescued by Henry, everything in her life had already changed. And from the looks of it, there was no turning back, ever again. After abandoning Walter at the altar and disappointing her grandmother's ambitious desires, Kassie now found herself alone in an abandoned manor, with a man living with a curse. Oh my, how much had her life changed, indeed! Why, the only thing that continued to remain constant in her life right now, was the guarantee that no matter where she was in this world, that same moon was always going to follow her, wherever she traveled to. And in many ways, this brought a great sense of comfort and satisfaction to her. It was as if, her own deceased parents, were somehow still watching over her from up in heaven.

Truly, there was no reason to continue on dwelling on her past any further; for Kassie needed to move on with her life. At this point, there was nothing else to return to. Eventually, in due time, Walter would remarry another woman, her grandmother would move elsewhere and Wiltshire Hall would revert back to Douglas. And that was that. Case closed. Now, Kassie needed to reinvent herself. She needed to enjoy this newfound freedom and her new life, here at Galloway Manor. Grateful to God's miraculous intervention on her unwanted wedding, Kassie was content with her newfound and present circumstances. Although she was still uncertain about her own future; but at least for now, she had shelter, a bed to sleep in and clothes to wear. And come tomorrow, she was going to have food to eat. Ah, yes, life was very good!

In the meantime, Kassie was growing tired and a goodnight's worth of rest was in great need. And so, she walked back into her new bedchamber to head off to bed. However, along the way, she managed to briefly catch a glimpse of herself in the mirror. Although the mirror, just like everything else in the manor, was covered in dust; miraculously, through the tiny open specs that weren't plagued by dust mites, Kassie could slightly still see an image of herself, peeking through. Walking over towards the mirror, Kassie used her hands to wipe the dust away from the glass. Once she cleared most of the layers of dust and debris off, she saw a full view of herself. There standing in front of the mirror, she saw that her once pure white bridal gown was not only dirtied by the outdoor elements; but rather, it was also badly torn and ruined, in the process. Meanwhile, her hair was now undone. The flowers that were previously adorned in her hair were now, all practically all gone— most likely, blown away by the wind, during her previous run through the forest. Sadly, Kassie was a complete mess. Although she was far too tired to take a bath, she was still, at the very least, determined to tidy up and change into a fresh pair of clean clothing.

Since Henry previously mentioned that some of the bedchambers had already been furnished and stocked with clothing, Kassie quickly rushed over to the armoire, as she hoped and prayed to find a collection of women's clothing within it. Much to her delight, Kassie certainly won the jackpot. For the bedchamber that she had chosen was most definitely, once occupied by a woman. Upon opening the drawers to the armoire, Kassie found numerous dresses, gowns and other female garments, specifically designed and tailored for a lady. And from the looks of it, not only did these clothes remain so incredibly well preserved and in pristine condition, but they also appeared to have never once been worn before, either. Curiously, Kassie placed one of the dresses to her side and much to her joy, the dress seemed to perfectly match her figure. Truly, this was really too good to be true!

Searching through the remaining drawers, Kassie found plenty of other accessories, including several hats, pairs of shoes and even gloves. But even more intriguing was that along her search, she managed to stumble upon a drawer that contained bras, undergarments, corsets and even… night lingerie. However, these night lingerie were nothing like what Kassie had ever seen, or worn before. Unlike the plain oversized white undergarments that she often wore to bed back at Wiltshire Hall, these sleeping wears were much more revealing and form fitting. Why, there were several opened areas that exposed the female skin! How could any woman sleep comfortably in these sorts of clothes!

Unfortunately, Kassie was far too naive; perhaps, even too

innocent for her own good. While she was intended to be a bride, her grandmother had neglected to educate her about the matters concerning the wedding night. Having failed to think beyond her own wedding ceremony to Walter, Kassie never once put a second thought in her mind concerning their first evening alone together, as man and wife. Had she done so before, then perhaps, she would have held a much better understanding and an appreciation to what she had just stumbled upon. Furthermore, due to the hasty marriage arrangement between Kassie and Walter, Maureen also failed to secure any sort of lingerie inside of her granddaughter's hope chest. Therefore, due to all of the above reasons, Kassie thoroughly remained innocent and naïve about the entire matter concerning post-marital relations.

In the end, Kassie opted to wear a simple violet colored daydress to serve as her nightgown for the evening. As she removed her tattered wedding dress from off her body, she quickly threw it over into the fireplace, nearby. Come tomorrow, she intended to light a fire and burn the remainder of her tattered wedding gown— that most fortunately, never came to be!

Once changed, Kassie walked over to her new vanity table, sat herself down and grabbed a hairbrush that was conveniently previously left above the table. After wiping it clean, she noticed that on the brush was listed the initial "J." Curiously, Kassie wondered who this mysterious "J" might have been. Suddenly, having recalled her grandmother's previous tale about the Dark Horseman, Kassie remembered that he too, once had a fiancé named Julia. The "J" must have stood for Julia. This must have been her room. No wonder there was so much female clothing in here!

Realizing that Kassie had unintentionally taken up residence in Henry's former fiancé's room, she also recalled that long ago, Julia had previously run away with his half-brother, Phillip.

"How dreadfully terrible that must have been," she uttered to herself.

Like Kassie, Henry, too, was once inches away from the altar. He, too, almost became a husband, but sadly, it never came to be. Somehow, this runaway bride came to meet another fellow runaway groom; and now, together, they were living inside this abandoned and forgotten manor, as two free and unmarried individuals. How interesting had fate been!

However, while Kassie was thrilled at the prospect of not marrying Walter, she also couldn't help but wonder if Henry had felt much of the same. In all of his years spent alone, did he ever come to miss Julia? Did he regret not marrying her? Was he devastated to later learn that his own brother had married her, instead? Did he feel betrayed by their forbidden love? Or, did Henry not care at all, due to his curse? There were so many questions running through Kassie's mind, as of now. However, Kassie still had much to learn about Henry and of Galloway Manor; and so, for now, she decided to think no more of it.

After brushing and arranging her hair, Kassie walked over to the bed and pulled out the blankets. As she suspected, the bed was, of course, covered in dust, dirt and debris. But, after today's unplanned events, Kassie was still grateful to have this rare opportunity to sleep inside a bed—regardless of its uncleanliness state. In fact, at this point, any condition was most entirely welcomed. And so, Kassie did her best to dust away the remaining particles and after doing so, she climbed up into her new bed, closed her eyes and went to sleep.

CHAPTER 7

On the opposite side of the estate, Henry lay wide awake inside of his bed, as he silently stared away up at his ceiling. For the past one hundred years and counting, this is how he spent his eternal evenings, in total and complete solitude. After wandering through the woods by day, Henry often returned to briefly retire into his empty bedchamber to look above and stare away at… nothing. Ah, yes, this was Henry's lonesome existence. To live forever, but to live alone. Cursed to wander the earth, forever more. Neither death nor hunger, can ever suppress him. Sadly, Henry hadn't eaten an actual meal in more than a century. Not only did he no longer crave for any food, but he hardly remembered as to how it even used to taste like, in the first place. Unfortunately, even the mere thirst for water meant nothing more to him, than a distant and forgotten memory from his former life.

Was he a ghost? Or a vampire? Or even, a werewolf? Sadly, in fact, he was neither of the above. Instead, Henry was something entirely unknown and unclassified. Something that lacked in any documented fairy tale or legend, or even in a horror story. Unlike the other creatures from myths and folklore, Henry was still technically a man; a man that just so happened to be frozen and trapped in time. A man who never aged. Whose face, body and appearance still resembled that of a thirty-year old. But apart from his physical appearance, could he still bleed? Well, yes, actually, as a matter of fact, he could— just like any other man did. But unlike others, Henry's wounds always healed naturally on their own and within mere seconds. In fact, whenever his body sustained an injury, his wounds were instantly retransformed back into his original state, as good as new and without evidence of a scar or even a blemish.

In the span of a hundred years, numerous men and criminals alike, had wandered into his land within this past century. Some good, others bad. For the good and kindhearted souls, who accidentally stumbled upon his forest, Henry took compassion on them as he guided them back onto their journey through the woods and into civilization. But for the men, whose hearts were tainted and evil, Henry made sure they felt the wrath of his being, well before they exited his domain. As he wildly chased and terrorized them through the forest, Henry made it his quest to install as much fear, as he possibly could within them. Over the years, he developed the reputation as being the legendary Dark Horseman; and with that, came the birth of his own famous and mythical legend embedded into local village folklore, along with an endless amount of tall tales foretold about his deeds that were shared across a late night's fire, as a form of entertainment spoken by the villagers, as they gathered together at their local inns and pubs.

But how could Henry distinguish between good and evil? How could he judge a man's inner character by a simple glance? Well, the answer is that Henry was simply born with this talent. Prior to the enactment of his curse, Henry already had the natural talent and good sense of detecting one's true character. Dating back to his early youth, Henry was an excellent cards player and part of that very talent, relied upon his rare and keen ability to read people. And so, from the time when Henry could first count cards, he could also count people, too. Just by looking at a man, Henry already detected their entire life story; from their economic and social backgrounds, to their education and political views, and much more. Most of the times, Henry's presumptions about them, generally turned out to be mostly true. Overall, Henry was an excellent judge of character and that trait continued on with him, as he entered into eternal existence. In hindsight, the curse only heightened his ability to sense people's true personalities; rather, than having been simply born out of thin air, as a consequence of his curse.

Furthermore, as part of his curse, Henry was forbidden to leave the grounds of Galloway Manor and the enchanted forest that surrounded it.

For decades, Henry tried to venture outside of the forest's forbidden boundaries; but every time he attempted to do so, there was always some invisible electrical force that prevented him from exiting. In the early years of his curse, Henry tried several more times to defy the rules of his doomed state; but alas, to no avail, he always managed to fail. From attempting to jump and hop over that invisible boundary, through hitchhiking a horse or carriage ride with one of the traveling vagabonds; Henry's ongoing plans to escape constantly failed, each and every time. However, one time, Henry did manage to miraculously come as so close as to reach the far outer edges of the forest; however, once his fellow traveling vagabond exited the forest's forbidden boundaries and crossed over into civilization, Henry was immediately pulled and sucked back in. And so, after several more disastrous attempts, countless battles and failed missions to escape, Henry was reluctantly forced to accept his ultimate and most unfortunate fate.

Sadly, acceptance didn't come so easy for Henry. No, it simply didn't. At least, not without a fight. And so, throughout this past century, Henry voluntarily threw himself into harm's way. From allowing armed men, thieves and knights alike to fight him directly, head-on; each time, Henry closed his eyes, as he dropped his sword onto the ground and surrendered himself over to his opponent, while secretly hoping and praying that maybe... just maybe... this time... the blade of his enemy's sword would finally pierce and kill him... once and for all.

Unfortunately, this never came to be. As the blade entered into his body and as he fell down onto the bloody ground, by the time his enemy fighter escaped, Henry was instantly healed and restored back into his original form— just as if, the previous battle fought had never even have happened, in the first place. But if others couldn't kill him, then that still didn't stop Henry from trying to kill himself, as well. Attempt... after attempt... after attempt... Henry tried to drown himself, throw himself off his horse, hang his neck with a tight rope, stab and shoot himself… even going, as so far as to force lethal poison down his own throat… but again... nothing seemed to work! Alas, Henry was truly of the undead... and of the unliving. No matter what he did, Henry simply couldn't escape his reality. Tragically, Henry learned the hard way that neither death nor any other humanly matter, could ever release him from this godforsaken curse!

But apart from death as a form of release, was there another possible cure to his curse? Rather than trying to end his own life, wasn't there a better way? A reversal of this looming spell? Unfortunately, for Henry, it seemed rather hopeless. Having previously acted upon his lust for revenge, Henry prematurely killed his stepmother, before he had the chance to discover a cure to his curse. Sadly, through her death, Henry now had to endure the consequences of his rash actions: to accept his doomful sentence to forever wander these lands, while stuck in the body of a thirty-year old man for the rest of eternity.

Ironically, even with his impressive library that hosted an endless supply of various books, Henry still couldn't discover a cure to his curse— a curse, which truly, felt more like a disease than anything else. In the span of a hundred years and counting, every single person that Henry had ever known or loved, had all either deserted him or they died. Even his own fiancé and half-brother abandoned him. His own flesh and blood. As for the few remaining loyal servants, who were employed at Galloway Manor during the time of his stepmother's reign, they all eventually, in due time, came to taste the sweet offerings of death.

Thus, after the deaths of his remaining servants, Galloway Manor ultimately grew into oblivion. With each passing year, Henry sat back in despair, as he watched all of the estate's surviving plants, trees and vines grow and consume the outside of his once grand and upscale manor. With no gardeners, housekeepers and other vital servants needed in order to upkeep and maintain his large estate, Henry silently watched as his inheritance, his estate and his family's legacy fell apart. Although in hindsight, Henry, who neither slept nor ate, probably could have tried much harder to keep Galloway Manor in better shape with his own two bare hands; however, somehow, Henry lost all motivation and desire to do so. Truthfully, in all honesty, what was the point? He no longer welcomed any guests. No visitors. No family. No friends. No brother. No wife. No children. No servants. No one. Absolutely, no one, at all.

And so, Henry did nothing. As the dust grew and consumed the entire manor, he simply sat back, watched and did nothing. Absolutely, nothing. Sadly, the only source of a companion that he still maintained was his beloved horse, Midnight; who, just like himself, was also a prisoner to this same curse. Meanwhile, as Henry and Midnight galloped away and rode into the forest by day; come evening, they would eventually retire back into the manor with Henry returning into his old bedchamber. However, being the restless spirit that he was, remaining within the narrow constraints and enclosure of his secluded bedchamber was far too much for him to bear. After spending a few hours... mostly by being preoccupied with staring up at his ceiling... Henry eventually grew impatient and restless, and was eager to reunite with his beloved horse once again, to ride outside into the forest until daybreak. And so, Henry came to embody the very persona behind his own legendary title, the Dark Horseman— not only by name, but in action as well. Throughout the night and leading up into the midnight hour, Henry, along with his trusted horse, rode through the forest in complete darkness— and thus, ultimately, transforming into one of the many creatures, who resided within the enchanted forest.

Although there were several other creatures, who also lurked inside of these woods— from the innocent rabbits to the swindling foxes, to the curious squirrels to the serene fawns, to even the bumbling bees and the sleeping bears— all of these fellow animals lived and thrived within Henry's domain. But apart from these known creatures, along with the other plants, trees, wildflowers and other fauna that comprised this enchanting land, the forest still remained overwhelmingly mysterious and terrifying— especially, in the dark. Furthermore, although there were a great many things to be afraid of in the enchanted forest, from the dark shadows to the treacherous wolves; Henry, by far, was probably the scariest of all… at least, when he wanted to be.

But, even with this rare ability to install fear into the hearts of others, what was the purpose of it all? Of his own existence? Why was Henry even cursed, in the first place? Well, it was rather complicated. But to make matters short and simple: Henry was a wealthy earl, with a grand estate and his evil stepmother, Vera, wanted nothing more than to selfishly claim it all for herself. Plain and simple. And so, as a result of her envy and greed, a curse was enacted. But what wasn't supposed to happen… was… well... for Henry to have actually lived to tell the tale.

Had things gone according to plan, then the curse was supposed to claim Henry's life, from day one. With her own son, Phillip, fleeing the scene with Henry's fiancé, Julia, Vera expected Henry to die that fateful night. But alas, fate had other plans in store for Henry; for his late mother, Sarah, arrived to earth as an angel sent from heaven above, in order to help in his greatest time of need. And so, rather than dying from suffocation caused by the crawling vines that sought to strangle him into oblivion, Henry was freed, instead. However, although he was spared, it also came with a hefty price, too. While mother nature may have forfeited their claims to his body, a debt was still owed to the forest... Henry's soul, in exchange for his services to protect and safeguard the forest from the outside world. Even though this life sentence seemed like a bitter end, Henry's mother, Sarah, still held out hope for a miracle. A miracle, that one day, Henry's spell would be broken. But they needed time. Time to discover a cure. Time, in which one day, Vera would eventually have a change of heart, to see the errors of her ways and to reveal the remedy to this curse. However, this option was only feasible, if no harm was to befall upon her. Although Sarah begged Henry not to seek revenge on the very woman who cursed him; the youthful man was nevertheless, blinded by his own rage, along with his consuming desire and quest for his revenge. Ultimately, Henry gave into those desires and as a result, his fate was tragically sealed. Unfortunately, by slaying Vera, Henry was now forced to wander the ruins of Galloway Manor and the enchanted forest, for all eternity.

As the years passed by, Henry slowly grew accustomed to his life in solitude; for what other choice did he have? Apart from Midnight, he had no other companions. No friends. No family. No wife. No mistress. No one. Had he missed his old friends and family from before? Yes and no. While he missed his father and his former servants who worked at the manor, but apart from them, he cared for no one else. Sadly, long ago, he did once care for his half-brother, Phillip, but that was well before he betrayed him by running off with his fiancé, Julia. Although their engagement was prearranged by their families, eloping with Julia was still a mark of betrayal and a wound to his honor. Had Henry loved Julia? Well, in truth, Henry couldn't hardly remember. Having lived so long in complete solitude, had Henry actually cared about Julia at one point in time, he honestly couldn't recall. But even if he had loved her, what was the point?

But now, in a twist of fate, a new young woman suddenly entered into his life and this was most unexpected by far, even for Henry. In all of his years, no one else had ever come so close as to even step one foot into Galloway Manor, let alone reside and sleep in here. Apart from Kassie, not a single soul had ever bothered to engage and converse with him, as a regular man. Over the years, for all of the lost men, who wandered into his woods, never before had anyone sought to befriend him. Why, no one else had ever once considered him to be a hero, like her.

In the past, after guiding the lost travelers to the main road and back towards civilization, they were always grateful to hurry home with the intent of never returning into the forest, ever again. But in truth, that was also a part of the secret to the enchanted forest: not everyone was destined to find it. For those who managed to accidently stumble upon it, the enchanted forest was always meant to serve a specific purpose for them; almost as if, the person-in-question's visit was designed to teach them some sort of a valuable and moral lesson about life. Whether it was Henry scaring the evil folks back into living more decent lives through his dark and scary persona as the Dark Horseman; or by guiding the kindhearted souls safely back home, as a friendly reminder that they were good hearted people, on the righteous path and doing God's kind work, here on earth. The reality was that everyone and everything, that walked, crawled and moved along through this forest, all served a purpose— including Henry. Eventually, once their purposes were fulfilled, most were designed to never return— let alone, discovering the enchanted forest, ever again.

Therefore, finding Kassie in the enchanted forest was not a pure accident. She was summoned here for a reason. What that specific reason was, Henry was still not too sure. Was it possible that she was here to help break his curse? For a brief moment, Henry was hopeful. But alas, even she couldn't possibly possess the power to break his curse. Why, no one could. Honestly, if someone was meant to break his curse, then they would have come long ago within these past one hundred years by now, wouldn't they?

But regardless, either way, Henry was already greatly fascinated and intrigued by her. Just what was a young bride doing here, wandering inside of his forest? Pray tell, why wasn't she at her own wedding? Did her groom really jilt her? Abandoned her, right at the altar? Somehow, Henry found that rather difficult to believe; for based upon what his eyes could see, Kassie was quite a stunning and beautiful young woman.

With her long, shiny and fiery red hair, that gently floated down her back, Kassie was a classic and elegant beauty, with fair skin and blue eyes. Being tall, petite, large chested, and with curves that were proportionate to her body, Kassie certainly possessed a very attractive figure. Truly, in Henry's humble opinion, she was by far, one of the most beautiful women that he had ever seen before— even, prior to his curse.

But apart from mere beauty alone, Kassie also seemed to be a rather humorous character. From hating balls to freely offering her domestic services to actually clean his polluted manor in exchange for her shelter, brought an unexpected smile to Henry's face. Sadly, it had been several years, since Henry last smiled. In fact, had he not done so today, then Henry would have almost all but forgotten as to how to even properly smile, in the first place. From what Henry could already tell, Kassie was of a good, kind and sweet nature sort of lot.

Furthermore, to top it all off, she thought him to be a hero. But not just any hero, *her* hero. A fine complement to a man, whom many considered to be the very devil, himself. But how long would she stay here? A day? A week? A month? Forever? No, forever wasn't possible; for Kassie, unlike him, was a mortal. But even if she stayed for as long as she could, it would only equal to one humanly lifetime... which was what... eighty... or... ninety years, at most? Hardly enough time to serve as a companion to a man destined to live forever!

Eventually, in due time, Kassie would leave soon. Whether it was tomorrow or even a year from now, it was going to inevitably happen. Whether she left voluntarily or died along the way, it really didn't matter. After all, everyone else in Henry's life was destined to leave him— one way or another. Sadly, this was the tragic reality of his curse.

Suddenly, at last minute, Henry decided to look out of his balcony and stare up at the moon. Tonight, out of all nights, for some odd reason, the moon looked exceptionally large, as it brightly shimmered and shined against the darkened night sky. Sadly, while Henry had experienced much loss over the past century, the only thing that remained forever constant in these past one hundred years and counting was the reappearance of the nightly moon. And just like him, that very same moon was also destined to remain up here, as a prisoner of the sky, night after night, for the rest of all eternity.

CHAPTER 8

The next morning, Kassie awoke to find herself in the most peculiar predicament: staring back at a furry, black and eight-legged creature, which was conveniently seated right above her. But how pray tell, did this come to be? Well... it all began... when the sun first rose up into the morning sky during the early hours of dawn, while Kassie was still fast asleep. After her busy adventure from the day before, Kassie was reluctant to awaken so early in the morning; for truth be told, Kassie had never really been much of an early bird to begin with. Meanwhile, as she remained within her state of slumber, a tiny creepy, crawling, furry and black animal found its way into her bed. Eventually, when Kassie finally awoke from her deep sleep, as she peeked opened her eyes, she most unexpectedly caught sight of the lurking animal. Sadly, given that Kassie was still half asleep, she incorrectly presumed that she was still busy dreaming away and that the animal that she had just seen, was nothing more than a mere figment of her wild imagination. However, as the creature continued to crawl forward and approach closer to her, it soon eventually reached her side. Not long afterwards, the creature began crawling up along her arm and moving towards her chest.

A few seconds later, Kassie finally opened her eyes; but shockingly enough, as soon as she did, she saw that seated right along the edge of her nose was none other than a spider!

"Yuck!!" screamed Kassie, in horror, as she immediately hopped out of her bed, just like a traveling grasshopper.

"My God!" she exclaimed again, as she violently pushed the spider off her face and back down onto the floor.

Once Kassie and the spider were a good distance apart from one another, she stared across at it. Unlike the night before, the darkness had prevented Kassie from seeing the true condition of the room. But now, in the daylight, it was abundantly clear that this room was also in desperate need of attention. If Kassie was going to live here for the near foreseeable future, then she also required a clean, sanitized and habitable room that was free of any spiders, cobwebs or anything else that affected her overall sanity and health!

Determined to put her thoughts into action, she quickly changed into a fresh pair of clothing, braided her hair and was soon, off to work. Although Kassie was limited with any decent cleaning supplies, she was still determined to transform the room— even if she needed to get creative, in order to make up for these inadequacies. Since her new bedchamber already had a balcony, Kassie decided to take advantage of the open fresh air. After quickly gathering all of her beddings, Kassie walked them over to the edge of her balcony and with one large shake, she shook the dust from off her belongings and onto the ground.

On her first try, a huge cloud of dust surrounded her and as a result, she began to cough and sneeze. However, regardless of Kassie's ongoing allergies, she was still determined to have a clean room. And so, using her right hand to cover her mouth, Kassie used her left hand to shake the remainder of her beddings, including her pillows, blankets, bedsheets and everything else in-between. After a few long minutes of shaking, in the end, much to her delight, her beddings looked almost practically brand new. Determined to continue on, Kassie grabbed the rest of the decorative furniture from inside of her bedchamber, including a pair of oval sized cushions seated above a small chair near the window. Additionally, she also grabbed a few throw rugs and embroidered hand towels, which were located inside of her connecting bathroom. One by one, Kassie shook them outside of her balcony, as if there was no tomorrow. Indeed, her hard work certainly paid off, because by the end of the hour, her room was practically dust free. Well… almost.

Taking a handkerchief out from the drawer inside her new armoire,

Kassie took a deep breath as she spit her wet saliva onto it. Although there wasn't any current available water inside of her room, Kassie was still determined to add some wet moisture onto her handkerchief to continue on with her dusting. Once the handkerchief was fully moist, Kassie proceeded to use it as a cleaning rag. Moving in the direction of her mirror, she wiped the mirror, as if this was the first time that it had ever been thoroughly cleaned before. Slowly, layer by layer, the decades of dust that had accumulated over the years, finally came to end. One by one, Kassie wiped and scrubbed off all of the dirt and grime, until the once dusty and spider-cobweb infested mirror was no more.

An hour later, the entire mirror, along with the room's surrounding windows, were now all shiny and sparkling clean. Determined to finish the rest of her bedchamber, Kassie tried her best to wipe down the remainder of the furniture. From the tables to the chairs, to the stools and chests, to the decorative objects and their respective shelves, Kassie dusted every nook and cranny. In the end, Kassie tackled just about everything, with her last and final task remaining being the floors. Although the floors were going to prove to be challenging, Kassie still didn't shy away. Instead of using another wet rag to wipe them down with her knees, she decided to cleverly use her own two feet, instead. Wearing a new pair of her slippers, Kassie spit two more times onto another pair of handkerchiefs and then, she tied them down to underneath each pair of her slipper. Once done, she began to dance and glide across the floor, almost as if she was actually skiing outside above frozen ice. Luckily, much to her credit, the wet rags underneath her slippers managed to suck up all of the left-over dirt, dust and grime from off the floor. Creative thinking at its finest, indeed!

Another hour later, Kassie's room was at long last transformed. Although it wasn't as sparkly and shiny as she had originally hoped it would be; it was still, nevertheless, far more decent and vastly improved from its previous condition. However, after exerting so much physical labor in one day; by now, Kassie was overwhelmingly tired and desperately hungry. Having not eaten a single bite since yesterday morning, she was now in great need for food. And so, in a desperate attempt to find some food to eat, Kassie quickly changed once again into a new yellow colored dress, along with a matching yellow ribbon that was tied to the bottom of her long braid. Once she was cleaned, dressed and prepped, she exited her room and made her way down the stairs.

By the time Kassie arrived downstairs, the grandfather clock, which was located near the front entrance of the manor, suddenly rang. Looking straight ahead, she saw that it was now noon. Lunch time. After a busy morning spent cleaning, she was extremely hungry. Borderline starvation. Practically famished. Suddenly, a large growl came from the pits of her stomach. Was her stomach... actually rumbling? This was certainly a first!

Determined to locate any bits and morsels of food, Kassie promptly searched throughout the first floor, in the hopes of finding a kitchen. Along the way, she passed by several other rooms, including: another ballroom, dining room, banquet room, salon and an outside terrace. However, it took several long minutes to even locate anything that remotely resembled that of a kitchen; but sadly, neither one of these rooms were it. Eventually, after traveling across the estate for at least another half hour or so, Kassie finally arrived at the far end of the hall. It was there, along the southeastern wing of the first-floor, where she found something that resembled a kitchen.

Happily, Kassie pushed through the doors and just like all of the other rooms before, this kitchen, too, had long been neglected. Although at first glance, the kitchen appeared to be yet another grand and spacious room, that was filled with the most expensive and high-quality furniture and kitchenware imaginable; however, the overall condition of the space was not surprisingly, rather poor. Sadly, just like everywhere else in this manor, this entire room was once again consumed by dust, dirt, grime and cobwebs, alike. Furthermore, even the windows couldn't do this kitchen any justice; for they were all, sadly, covered with so much mold and residue, that it was rather difficult to see through them clearly. Suddenly, Kassie's stomach growled yet again and with each passing minute, she was growing desperately hungrier than ever before!

Hoping to find something to eat, Kassie quickly ran over to the pantry and opened the first cabinet that she saw. Unfortunately, much to her disappointment, upon opening the cupboard she found more cobwebs, instead. Even though Henry didn't require any food to eat; but at the same time, surely, he must have had some company over at least within these past one hundred years, didn't he? Granted, Kassie was aware that it was probably highly unlikely that she'd ever find any decent ingredients to use to prepare a gourmet meal for herself; but still, surely, there must have been something in here that she could eat? Even a cracker or better yet, a piece of fruit? Hell, at this point, Kassie was willing to eat dried leaves and unripe berries, if she had to!

Suddenly, Kassie felt something move and touch her hand from inside of the cupboard. Whatever it was, it was large and… furry. Furthermore, whatever it was it somehow managed to rub itself against her. After this morning's terrifying encounter with the spider, Kassie quickly pulled her hand back from out of the cupboard. Relieved by her quick action to avoid another pesky little furball, Kassie sighed a breath of relief to herself. However, her relief came a bit premature; for after having done so, Kassie slowly took a step back and to her horror, she actually stepped on that very same creature!

Immediately, Kassie jumped up into the air and hopped onto a nearby chair. As she stood up on the chair and looked down below, Kassie quickly noticed that what she had stepped on was none other than a small baby squirrel. Although the squirrel was remarkably rather cute, Kassie still didn't feel quite comfortable with touching it. After all, she was dreadfully terrified of mice, and a squirrel was only one step below from being equal to a mouse. Hoping to avoid any direct contact with the squirrel, Kassie curled her entire body up into a ball, as she remained in that position while up on the chair, as she quietly prayed for the squirrel to quickly exit the kitchen and return back into the yard. However, her patience for silently waiting for the animal to disappear seemed to make no difference; for the longer she stayed quietly curled up on the chair, the longer the squirrel stayed in the room, rolling back and forth over the floor. Determined to have it leave, Kassie began clapping her hands and stomping her feet against the wood of the chair; but sadly, this too, proved unsuccessful. Suddenly, she began to grow curious as to why the squirrel was so interested in remaining inside of this kitchen.

Unfortunately, at that very moment, Kassie's stomach growled again. At this point, her own stomach was starting to hurt due to extreme starvation. Even though Kassie was terrified of this small but harmless squirrel, she also knew that she needed to overcome her fears in order to survive this ordeal. Mustering up all of her inner courage, Kassie jumped back down onto the floor. However, once she did that, her landing managed to scare away the squirrel. In a sudden bolt, the squirrel quickly dashed off and exited the room through a tiny crack in the back door, which led outside into the garden. Following his trail, Kassie noticed pieces of what appeared to be some sort of a broken nut… perhaps, an acorn? Or an almond? But whatever it was, it was most certainly a nut. A nut, that even she, as a human being, could eat. Realizing that the squirrel was going to lead her down to her only source of an actual meal, Kassie swiftly followed the squirrel's footsteps into the garden.

"Wait!" she cried, as she ran after the squirrel.

As the squirrel ran down the lawn, Kassie hurried along to chase after it. Eventually, after much running, the squirrel stopped in front of a large tree, overlooking the pond, nearby. Soon afterwards, it quickly climbed up the tree trunk, as it attempted to flee away from her. However, by then, Kassie had already gotten her answer: for there, standing right in front of her, was none other than a glorious walnut tree. A very large, overgrown and plentiful walnut tree that at this very moment, was currently filled with an endless supply of walnuts!

Happy about her new discovery, Kassie immediately pounded against the tree with her hands and legs, so that a few walnuts could fall back down onto the ground. Luckily, Kassie's plan worked and in no time, a handful of walnuts managed to tumble down. Hurriedly, Kassie rushed over to collect them. Once in her hands, she sat down underneath the tree and began cracking open the hardened shells with her bare hands. Afterwards, she silently ate them, while she peacefully watched the pond and listened to the beautiful sounds of nature. At long last, Kassie was finally able to eat and put an end to her hunger. However, her somber and peaceful moment was short lived; for at that very moment, a gunshot was fired loudly from afar!

74

CHAPTER 9

“Is this what you brought back from hunting?” asked Kassie, in confusion.

“You might as well get used to it, because it’s dinner,” Henry boldly proclaimed.

“But how am I supposed to eat it, if I don’t even know what it is?” she asked again.

“Come now, Kassie, have you never seen quail before?” he asked, most amused.

“As a matter of fact, no I haven’t,” she admitted.

“Pray tell, what have you actually seen before, then?” he asked, curiously.

“Well, back at Wiltshire Hall…” Kassie began.

“Wiltshire Hall? Is that where you’re from?” Henry asked, wanting to learn more about her old life.

“Yes,” she replied. “Anyways, as I was saying before, I’ve never encountered this sort of animal at the dinner table, back at Wiltshire Hall.”

“Then, what have you previously encountered at the dinner table? Kassie, please do enlighten me,” Henry pleaded, as he sat down on an empty chair in the kitchen.

"Very well," she began, "We've had chicken, duck, meat, lamb, and fish… and eggs… lots of them… naturally, of course."

"Well, now, you've got quail eggs here, too," Henry reminded her, as he pointed at the small pile of tiny eggs that he recently brought back with him from his latest hunt.

"Yes, but I still don't know what quail even is…" she also reminded him, in return.

"A quail," he began, "Is another type of a small bird. They're quite common here, in these woods."

"Ah… a small bird, so that's why it has all of these feathers," she remarked, innocently.

"Yes, I suppose that's probably as to why it does," he replied, laughingly.

"Well, I can make do with this. The quail, plus the eggs, that should keep us full, at least for a while," Kassie concluded.

"Correction, it will keep *you* full. Not me, remember?" he asked, with a devious smile.

"Ah, that's right. You don't eat, do you? Why, I, personally, don't think that I could ever survive a hundred years, let alone, a single day without eating something," she confessed.

Amused by her admission, Henry couldn't help but laugh even more. Somehow, even in the most mundane of situations, Kassie tickled him. In all of his many years of existence, Henry had never met anyone else, who was so sincere and innocent as she.

"Well, like I said before, I don't eat. But given that you, on the other hand, still do; I promise to continue with my daily hunting and to catch game for you. Furthermore, from here on out, since I'll be preoccupied with hunting, it will be up to you to prepare your own meals. Now, if you don't need anything else, I'll be on my way," said Henry, as he got up from his chair.

"Wait, you're leaving now? So soon? But you've only just got here," she said.

Intrigued by her surprising plea, Henry secretly wondered as to why she wanted him to stay behind with her so badly. Did she possibly want company? Specifically, *his* company? Was she also lonesome and in dire need of companionship? Or, was it remotely possibly that she was simply interested in being around him?

Turning around, he asked, wholeheartedly, "Do you honestly want me to stay?"

"Yes, actually, I do," she said, with a smile.

And that very smile of hers, sealed the deal. In the past one hundred years, Henry hadn't seen another human smile like hers before. Perhaps, even more than a hundred years. Maybe, the first in his entire existence. For in that exact moment, her smile brough a warmth to his chest. What was this odd feeling that he was beginning to feel? Was this… joy? Or… happiness? Is this what it felt like, when being around another person and actually interacting with them?

"Very well, if you please. As my honored guest, I shall oblige with your request and stay," he agreed, as he returned back to his seat.

"Wonderful!" she said most excitingly, as she clapped her hands together.

"In that case," Kassie began, "I'll need your help to pluck these feathers off from that… umm… what do you call it again?"

"Quail," he reminded her.

"Ah, yes, quail," she said. "Now, please do hurry, as I'm practically starving to death!"

"Wait a minute," he interrupted. "Are you honestly telling me, that you purposely asked me to stay behind with you, in order to have me pluck all of these feathers off from this quail? Do I stand correct, by this assumption?"

"Why, yes, of course, I do. I mean, I've never actually plucked feathers before. Honestly, I don't even know where to begin," she admitted.

"Interesting," he reflected. Looking straight at her, he said with an amused smile, "From what I recall from last night, I thought that you previously mentioned that you already knew how to cook."

"Well, I do. I just don't know how to prepare quails, that's all," said Kassie, hoping that he'd agree to her request.

"Alright, since you asked, I will help you," said Henry, as he stood back up, picked up the quail and walked over into the garden to clean the bird outside.

A few minutes later, Henry returned back into the kitchen with the cleaned and prepped quail in hand. Not wanting to further delay her, Henry handed the quail over to Kassie, as he took a seat back at the kitchen table. Once seated, Henry watched on, as Kassie placed the quail down onto the counter and walked over to the stove. Looking at her, Henry was simply fascinated by Kassie. After many long years, his kitchen finally had a cook. But upon carefully studying her actions from afar, Henry couldn't help but notice that this new cook of his appeared to be more of an amateur than anything else, and at this precise moment she seemed to look... well... rather... confused...

"Is something troublesome?" he asked.

"Oh," she said, feeling a bit startled and surprised that he had even bothered to ask her, in the first place.

"Do you need help with anything?" he asked, once more.

"Well..." she began, "If I'm being honest, then maybe..."

Standing back up from his chair, Henry walked over to her side and then, he further inquired directly, "How can I be of service?"

"Well, Henry," she said, "Truth be told, I'm not really certain, as to how to start this... this... cooking thing of yours."

"Do you mean, the stove?" he asked, with a raised brow.

"Ah, is that what you call this? A stove?" she asked, with her eyes beaming as wide as it possibly could.

"Interesting," he said to himself. "After the past one hundred years, I naturally presumed that this equipment must have since evolved from my time. However, I'll admit, I also did not suspect that it would change by that much over the years, either. Tell me Kassie, what do you use now back at Wiltshire Hall?"

"Umm… truthfully... I'm not really sure," she bashfully admitted.

"What do you mean? Don't you cook?" he asked, confused by her statement.

"Well, normally, no, I do not. Generally, I do the eating and seldom the cooking, as we already employ a professional chef back at Wiltshire Hall. Besides, I'm a lady. It's not my job to cook," she proudly stated.

However, her excuse of being a 'lady' wasn't going to get by Henry, so easily.

"Whether or not, you're a lady, a duchess or a princess, is completely irrelevant. Everyone, at some point or another, must learn basic survival skills, including cooking," he boldly stated.

Furthermore, he added, "You cannot live your life, solely by depending upon the charity of others. Kassie, for your own welfare, you must learn to adapt and become more independent."

"That might be true, but…" she began; however, midsentence, Henry interrupted her.

"Tell me Kassie," he began, "What sort of culinary tasks, can you do?"

"Well, apart from arranging salads and decorating tables —"

"Decorating tables? Is that how you classify cooking?" he interrupted, astonished and surprised by her mere suggestion of such a thing.

"But decorating tables, counts as kitchen décor. Therefore, yes, I do include them," said Kassie, firmly.

For a long moment, Henry just stared at her in amazement. Did she really consider decorating tables, as a form of culinary skills? Or the simple act of chopping vegetables, as another dish for a wholesome meal? At this point, Henry was beginning to wonder, if she even knew how to perform basic domestic chores, in the first place.

"Tell me, Kassie, do you even know how to clean?" Henry asked, most curiously.

"Clean? Why, of course, I do. I mean, a few wiping and dusting, here and there. Plus, a decent run through using a standard broomstick. Honestly, Henry, that's really all there is to it," she plainly admitted.

"Fascinating," Henry said, as he tried his best to imagine her doing such domesticated tasks. However, for some reason, he struggled to actually picture her doing such domestic chores successfully.

Curious, herself, as to why he had even asked her, Kassie inquired, "Henry, do you presume that because I'm a lady, that I'm unable to properly clean and straighten out this haunted manor of yours? I'll have you know that back when I was at university, I also did my share of cleaning at our ladies' dorms."

"A haunted manor?" asked Henry, in sheer surprise. His manor might have been many things, but it certainly wasn't haunted.

"I'm sorry Henry, haunted is not appropriate. I didn't mean to offend you. After all, it's not your fault, that... you're... well... cursed," she confessed.

"Kassie, I'll have you know that this manor is not haunted nor cursed. My lady, it is *I*, and *I alone*, who's the cursed one," he corrected.

"Again, I didn't mean to offend. Oh dear, I suppose we've gotten off on a bad foot! Truly, I am sorry!" exclaimed Kassie, in her attempts to apologize, after much defeat.

"That's quite alright," he quickly stated. "It's just that for a young lady, such as yourself, to offer your domestic services to my manor… well… naturally, I just presumed that you already knew how to cook and clean, that's all."

"But I can cook and clean!" Kassie shouted. "Here, I'll prove it to you. If you can turn this… this… thing…on… then I can cook this darn meal!"

"Thing? As in the oven?" he asked.

However, this time, Henry was growing rather amused by her lack of culinary skills. Surprisingly enough, he found her unexpected naivety to be yet another sweet and endearing trait of hers.

"Yes, oven!" she huffed, out of frustration.

Being the true hero that he was, Henry immediately stood up and walked over to the oven. Upon opening the black iron rod door, he pulled out a match from his pocket and lit a fire inside. Using a small wooden spoon that was kept above the counter, Henry poked around the small pieces of wood inside. Once the fire was safely settled down, he asked Kassie to hand him the quail. Unfortunately, because Kassie was previously too preoccupied with her own conversation with Henry, she neglected to prepare the quail in advance for cooking. However, not wanting to delay him any further, Kassie hurried and threw the quail into a pan, quickly drizzled a few spices on top of it and then, she promptly handed the bird over to him. Upon receiving it, Henry placed the quail straight into the oven to cook. Afterwards, Henry, having fulfilled his obligation to her, was about to exit the manor and return back into forest for good; when alas, Kassie called him back in yet again.

"Wait," she cried. "Where are you going?"

"Well, as it's still daylight outside, I'm returning to the forest, of course," he replied.

Naturally, by now, she, of all people, must have already well understood that the forest was his primary domain, after all.

"But aren't you going to eat what I've cooked?"

Amused by her growing concern for his welfare, Henry replied, "But *I don't* eat, remember?"

"Ah, yes, that's right," said Kassie, while at the same time, appearing gravely disappointed by his soon-to-be lack of company.

Not wanting to disappoint her, Henry decided that for once, he was going to stay behind this afternoon and humor her. Even though a well-balanced meal was no longer a necessity for him; however, if he stayed with her for the remainder of the day, then that decision wasn't going to cause harm to anyone, now, would it? After all, he was her host, was he not? In fact, weren't all good hosts expected to do everything in their power to accommodate and entertain their guests? Especially, a guest like Kassie?

Staying true to his word, Henry briefly stepped away to return his horse, Midnight, into the stable, before returning back into the kitchen to join Kassie at the table, an hour later. Given that the quail was a small bird, an hour was more than a sufficient amount of time to cook the meat. Furthermore, Kassie also had the eggs and table to prepare, too. After years of an unoccupied kitchen, Henry was excited to see what Kassie had produced. Unfortunately, although he was aware that he couldn't enjoy and relish the taste of her dish; Henry still could, at the very least, try to remember from the far reaches of his own memories on how a delicious meal was supposed to look and taste like when freshly served, straight out of the oven.

Upon entering back into the kitchen, Henry saw Kassie already seated at the table and waiting for him. Much to his delight, the table was elegantly decorated using a soft lace tablecloth that covered the wood. In addition, above the table, included his late mother's delicate and fine porcelain plates, crystal glasses and polished silverware, all carefully arranged. Excitingly, Henry walked over and took an empty seat beside her.

"Shall I serve you?" asked Kassie, almost in a hesitant tone, as if she were asking him more for permission.

"You can. But Kassie, I should forewarn you that as a result of my curse, my tastebuds have all but vanished," he revealed.

"But you can still eat, can't you?" she asked, most curiously.

"Technically, yes, I can consume food; but I cannot actually taste it," he said.

"Aww, that's too bad," she said. "I was so hoping that you'd like it."

"Don't worry about me, Kassie. You just go on ahead and enjoy your meal. I'm sure that whatever you made, it will be absolutely delicious," he said. And then, he added, "But Kassie, I'll tell you what, while I eat and chew away at this gourmet food of yours, I'll try my very best to remember as to how my favorite meals used to taste like, back in the day. Sounds good?"

Thrilled by his offer, Kassie happily nodded her head in agreement. Afterwards, she walked over to the kitchen counter, grabbed a tray consisting of the main course, and then, she gently placed it down onto the table in front of him. Once it was safely secured on the table, Kassie walked back over to the kitchen counter to retrieve the rest of her side dishes. Meanwhile, as Henry lifted up his fork and knife in preparation for his first meal— which was truly, his first meal in the past one hundred years— he waited in great anticipation for her arrival. A minute later, Kassie returned back to the table and after much wait, she was now ready to lift up the lid from off the tray to reveal the star of the show.

"Are you ready?" asked Kassie, with an innocent smile.

"I've only waited the past one hundred years for this precise moment," he said, jokingly.

"Oh, that's true, isn't?" asked Kassie, as it suddenly dawned on her that his joke was actually, very much the truth.

"Okay, here it goes. Hope you like it," she said, as she quickly pulled the lid from off the tray.

Expecting to see a tender, juicy and brown-crisp roasted quail, Henry saw an ashy, black and burnt quail, that was almost the same texture and color as coal. Areas that should have normally been white and moist, were instead, black and hardened. Sadly, Kassie's attempts to bake this quail proved to be disastrous; for this delicate and small bird was simply and kindly put: overcooked.

"What do you think?" asked Kassie, most excitingly. Unfortunately, the young lady was completely oblivious to the fact that on her first try, she had inadvertently and practically torched the bird into total ashes.

"Well," began Henry politely; but truly, even he was a bit lost for words.

But in all honesty, how could he tell her the truth without injuring her pride? Or her feelings? After all, this was probably the first real meal that she'd ever actually really cooked before. Luckily, at least, for Henry's sake, given that he had no sense or use of his own tastebuds, whether or not this quail tasted like heaven or hell, it really was irrelevant; for truly, they all tasted the same to him, either way.

"It looks absolutely delicious," he lied.

"Oh, I'm so glad!" she happily exclaimed, as she took a seat beside him.

Curious about her own feelings about her dish, Henry silently watched on, as Kassie began to service them with their upcoming meal. After slicing and separating the bird, she distributed the meat onto each one of their plates evenly. Then, she proceeded to serve the side dishes, which included the quail eggs that Henry had also previously brought back with him this morning from his hunt, along with a few vegetables and strangely enough, a very odd choice of walnuts that appeared to be used as a form of garnish.

"Walnuts?" he asked, confused on how this strange nut was now, somehow lumped in together with this meal.

"It's from the tree outside. It's a great source of protein," explained Kassie.

"Ah, I see," he said.

Still curious as to whether or not, Kassie was even aware that her quail was burnt, Henry silently watched on as she took her first bite of her meal. To his complete surprise, she seemed to be actually enjoying her meal! Not only was she enjoying it, but the young woman was practically devouring it like a beast! My goodness, was she so starving that she failed to notice that she was practically eating rubber!

"I take it that you like quail, after all," Henry said, as he finally took his first bite of the fire torched bird.

"I suppose I do," she admitted, in all honesty. "It's probably one of the best dishes that I've eaten in these past two days."

"Interesting," he said to himself aloud. Perhaps, Henry had been out of the kitchen for far too long. Was it possible that people nowadays ate their meals… well… overdone?

"Are the meals nowadays cooked, in this particular way?" Henry asked, hoping that Kassie could further help shed some more light into this matter.

"Cooked in which way?" she asked, innocently.

Not wanting to offend her, he politely asked, "Well… cooked in… a matter of being… let's just say 'well done'?'"

"Oh, the fact that I've overcooked this quail, you mean?" she bluntly said.

Much to his relief, he replied, "Well, yes. I'm glad that you're aware."

"No, the cook back home at Wiltshire Hall, doesn't burn our food like this. The chef tends to serve our meals medium rare. But truthfully, I don't mind a few burnt pieces, here and there. At least this way, I know that its thoroughly cooked," she admitted, as she took another bite of her quail.

"I see," he said, laughingly.

Even though Henry had no appetite, having already tasted the quail, he decided to move onto the quail eggs. Reaching over his plate to grab one of the tiny eggs, he gently tapped against the bottom of the egg with his spoon, in the hopes of cracking the hardened shell to reach the boiled contents inside. However, much to his surprise, after tapping his spoon, nothing seemed to have happened.

"What's wrong?" asked Kassie, who, at the same time, appeared to have been observing him at the table, as well.

"I'm trying to crack open this hard-boiled egg," he said, in concentration.

"Oh, here, let me help you," Kassie offered.

Immediately, she got up from her chair and walked over to his side.

While standing behind him, Kassie took the egg from his hand and in one large smash against the table, she cracked the egg open, exposing the dripping yolk from within. Afterwards, she poured the yolk over the burnt quail and then, she returned back to her seat.

"Kassie, this egg isn't cooked," Henry remarked, realizing that what he had previously presumed to be a hard-boiled egg, was in fact, not cooked at all.

"Was I supposed to cook it?" asked Kassie, in utter confusion. "Does it not come precooked, already?"

"I take it that you've never prepared eggs before, have you?" he asked her, in return.

Not one to be ashamed, Kassie simply nodded her head in agreement.

"Very well, next time, I'll personally teach you how to prepare and cook food more properly. Starting with eggs, as our first lesson," Henry said, with much determination.

"Really? That would be absolutely wonderful!" she joyfully cried.

Suddenly, Kassie jumped up from her chair, ran over to his side and gave him a big hug. Although this was entirely unexpected, Henry couldn't help but be touched by her warmth. Kassie was going to be a handful for sure; but at the same time, she was also great company, too. At least with her around, Henry was always going to be entertained. Plus, the feel of another human body against his, surprisingly felt… well… rather good.

CHAPTER 10

For the past few weeks or so, Kassie tried her very best to tackle her quest of restoring each room inside of Galloway Manor, in the hopes of rehabilitating the once beloved and famous manor. Starting from her own bedchamber located upstairs in the east wing, Kassie slowly made her way down the hall, as she tackled each room by dusting, polishing and sweeping away one floor, table and window, at a time. But along the way, she couldn't help but catch Henry occasionally walking by and watching her. Somehow, for some peculiar reason, it almost seemed as if he was actually staring at her, even from afar. Whether she was wiping a window or dusting the furniture, he was always around and studying her. Did she mind? No, not really. Especially, not initially. After all, it was his manor and she, his invited guest.

Although Kassie didn't think twice about it at first; but after a while, she began to grow nervous. How strange this was, too! Even though Kassie spent most of her youth pining away over Henry, but now, she suddenly felt shy around him. It made absolutely no sense! I mean, Kassie never felt anxious by anyone before; so why now? Why with Henry? Of, all people?

And now, to make matters much worse, after living alongside with Henry, underneath the very same roof as him for the past several weeks, Kassie wasn't so entirely certain, as to how she was supposed to properly act and engage with him, whenever he was around her. Was she required to smile back at him, whenever he looked at her? Especially, with those dreamy green eyes of his? Was she meant to hug and kiss him, every time he brought back game from his latest hunt? For most certainly, his strong and muscular arms could easily do with some extra loving care. After all, wasn't it incredibly rude not to thank him, after each and every cooking lesson that he so kindly offered to her?

Even though Henry never asked for anything in return from Kassie; somehow, she, herself, began to feel… well… rather disappointed by his lack of requests. For some odd reason, Kassie wasn't entirely satisfied with their current relationship. Were they friends? Yes, they probably were. However, at the same time, they were also both unmarried and living together within the same household and dare I say it, dear reader, unchaperoned. But was this it? Was this a real-life preview on how regular married couples interacted together, well after the exchange of their wedding vows?

Although they were definitely not man and wife; Kassie, was unfortunately, rather ignorant as to how a husband and wife were supposed to act and behave together… physically. Previously, having been so preoccupied on fleeing her own wedding to Walter, Kassie sadly, neglected her rather important 'the birds and the bees' conversation with her grandmother. Due to this particular omitted yet very important discussion, Kassie remained completely blindsided and ignorant about the actual facts as to what precisely takes place physically between a man and a woman, well after their wedding ceremony.

Furthermore, Kassie was never interested in the subject of biology at university; therefore, she simply elected to take yet another philosophy course, instead. Tragically, due to these reasons, Kassie had absolutely no clue as to what actually went on between a man and a woman, beyond friendship. Although she heard of the terms 'desire,' 'lust,' and 'passion' from various books and romantic novels that she had previously read back at her university's library; but sadly, she failed to fully comprehend, as to what those precise terms actually meant in action. As far as she was concerned, Kassie was already Henry's friend, even though she wasn't his wife. But at the same time, she was also beginning to feel certain strange and foreign emotions that exceeded beyond playful glances and innocent admiration. Instead, Kassie began to feel things that made her… well…

crave Henry. Crave him in the same manner that she craved for food. But unlike food, to crave a man... what did that mean exactly? At least with food, a craving meant eating; but with a man, one couldn't simply eat him, or could they? And if so, then is this what desire... meant?

Loving Henry was already a given; for Kassie had loved him her entire life. But apart from love, she started to feel and experience newfound emotions, that she honestly and truly could not comprehend. It all started the day Henry gave Kassie her first cooking lesson. As promised, the day after her first dreadful attempt to prepare quail, Henry taught her the fine art on how to properly boil eggs. While demonstrating to her on how to safely start a fire over the stove, he gently grabbed her hand and helped her to light a match. That simple act of his hand touching hers, made her tingle with delight. Afterwards, upon releasing her hand, Henry leaned over towards the stove; however, as he did that, he managed to pass by her side and thereupon, Kassie got a large whiff of his own personal scent— which was so incredibly addictive and intoxicating, that she was left utterly speechless! Just like the oak trees outside in the forest, Henry had the freshest of scents. Unfortunately, for Kassie, this unique aroma sent her into a maddening state; for after that very moment, she wanted nothing more than to bathe and roll herself in the very same water as he!

But if that wasn't enough to drive her emotions into insanity, then her next encounter with him a day later was the true icing to her cake! It all happened, while she was busy wiping away the dust from the mirrors, inside of the ballroom. Being the gentleman that he was, Henry decided to pay her a surprise visit to check on how she was doing. However, having recalled her previous great distaste for balls, Henry decided to take a chance and seek to personally change her opinion regarding this matter. Therefore, Henry was absolutely convinced that, if she could properly learn to dance the waltz correctly with him, then perhaps, her opinion about dancing and balls would change.

Not wanting to deny him this simple request, Kassie reluctantly agreed. However, when the time came for them to finally come into direct contact, with his one hand around her waist and the other leading her hand, this close proximately to Henry was really too much to bear! Although he seemed unmoved by their closeness; Kassie, on the other hand, had to fight each and every ounce of her nerves, in order to remain still within her posture.

Day by day, hour by hour, minute by minute, and second by second, Kassie's emotions and feelings about Henry were on a constant roller coaster. With each stare, smile and touch, Kassie thought of nothing else but him. For the first time in her entire life, she began to feel this burning sensation growing inside of her chest. With each passing hour, she adored him more and more. Not only was he as handsome and dashing like his portrait, but his personality and kind character was something entirely unexpected and very much appreciated.

Furthermore, to make matters more complicated, after their brief dance lesson, Henry soon left her side to return back into the forest. Unfortunately, his sudden departure, left her feeling rather lonesome and wanting more of him. However, later on that same night as Kassie was retiring off to bed, she managed to stumble upon him in the hallway. Like her, he too, was retiring up into his bedchamber. But, as he spoke about their next cooking lesson the following morning, Kassie paid little attention to his words and instead, she simply stared away at him, looking straight into his eyes by the light of her candle. With just one glance into his dreamy eyes, Kassie found herself completely lost within his company. In that exact moment, as he was busy speaking away, all she could think about was following him down into his own bedchamber and surrendering herself over to him, once and for all. But, what did it mean to 'surrender' to a man? Although Kassie naturally felt these strange urges, she also wondered as to what this all really meant, too.

Next, Kassie decided to tackle the library as her next assignment for restoration. After spending a few extra days combing through the thick and heavy layers of dust and debris that had accumulated inside of the library after a neglected century, Kassie finally got a chance to take some time to review the vast collections of books in there. Determined to find answers about these strange and new emotions stirring up inside of her, she decided to tackle the one subject that she had always avoided at university just like the plague: biology. Although Kassie hated biology— for the very thought of dissecting an innocent animal hit her nerves in the most unpleasant sort of way— she also knew that if she was going to thoroughly understand these new emotions growing within her own body, then she needed to read it directly from a book. And so, after retrieving a copy to a textbook involving the human anatomy, Kassie came to discover as to just what happens between a man and a woman, after mating. Suddenly, it all began to make sense!

All of these feelings, attractions, and yearnings… these were all just nature's way of forcing Kassie to mate with Henry! Although they weren't married, it honestly didn't seem to matter to her; for she already loved Henry and now, she just wanted to explore this new physical side with him. After all, marriage didn't stop the other animals inside of the forest from mating with each other, either. It was just nature. It was natural. And now that Kassie finally understood what 'desire' actually meant, she was ready to pursue the act of love wholeheartedly with Henry.

But did Henry feel the same way about her? It was hard to say, for this entire time, he always behaved in such a well refined and gentleman-like manner around her. But perhaps, if she made herself more attractive and available to him, then maybe he, too, was willing to give into her growing desires. Besides, she had nothing to lose, right? With Walter out of the picture, Kassie now freely had the opportunity to pursue a new romantic relationship with Henry. After all, he did invite her to stay here at Galloway Manor; surely, he must have developed feelings for her by now, shouldn't he? Plus, after a hundred years of solitude, Henry must have wanted to make love to another woman after so long, didn't he? But somehow, the very thought of Henry being with another woman pained Kassie immensely. And so, she decided right then and there, that if Henry was going to lay with another woman, then it might as well be her!

After reading a few more books on the 'art of romance,' Kassie understood that in order for her to seduce Henry, then she needed to start wearing clothes that were more appealing to the opposite sex. Recalling the lingerie that she had previously discovered on her first night spent in her bedchamber, Kassie decided to give them a try. Previewing them in the mirror, she was delighted to see how they magically transformed not only her figure, but the lingerie also managed to reveal certain parts of her body that were normally disguised underneath her day clothes.

And so, one night, after a long day spent busy working away on her ongoing restorations and he busy riding outside in the forest; come that nightfall, Kassie decided to finally make her move. After Henry bid her a final goodnight and retired off into his bedchamber, Kassie quickly ran upstairs into her own bedchamber and changed into one of her lace lingerie. And then, with much courage, she exited her room and started walking down the hallway, in the direction of Henry's bedchamber.

CHAPTER 11

As Henry lay in his bed, he stared up at his ceiling… which was typical of his nightly routine for the past one hundred years and counting. But unlike previous years, this time it was different. Far different. Incredibly different. Vastly different. A whirlwind of a difference. Alas, for as Henry rested there, he thought of nothing else but Kassie…

Kassie, her very name brought a gentle ease to his troubled and stone heart. For the man, who lived the majority of his existence in complete solitude, having such a kindhearted and sweet natured woman so near, meant everything in the world to him. More than he could have ever hoped or imagined. In fact, Kassie was the very air that he breathed. A sonnet to his poetry. The melodies to his songs. The gentle breeze to a warm summer's day. In essence, she was graceful, elegant, refined, delicate, proper and breathtakingly beautiful. She was everything good and wonderful in this world. But most importantly, she was *real*. Not just another figment of his imagination or a whimsical fantasy, but an actual and true person who was right here with him. Standing before him. Acknowledging him. Greeting him. Smiling at him. Dining with him. Dancing with him. Conversing with him. Engaging with him. Living with him. Here, inside this once lonesome manor— which ironically, was no longer lonesome anymore. It was truly a miracle. It was as if Henry was living within a dream... but strangely enough, it wasn't and instead, an actual reality.

With regards to his opinion of her, Henry certainly respected and thought very highly of her. Kassie was brave and fearless, as evident by her willingness to blindly opt to live besides him, a mere stranger, within this dark and isolated manor. Furthermore, Henry also found her to be highly intelligent, kind, generous and ever so patient; for anyone willing enough to take on the enormous responsibility of restoring his manor simply had to be. But most importantly, Kassie was also determined, focus, reliable and based on what he observed thus far, she constantly stayed true to her every word to him.

In these past few weeks, Kassie's relentless hard work and dedication to restore Galloway Manor had already spoken volumes for itself. Henry's bleak, deteriorated and abandoned manor was already, ever-slowly, transforming back into its original grand state and looking more and more similar to how it once used to be during the height of its old glory days, prior to the curse. Gradually, everything around him was changing. The once dusty grand staircase was now shiny and sparkling. The kitchen, that was previously infested with rows of cobwebs and loose ivy vines, had since been removed. Furthermore, all of the various mirrors inside of the ballrooms were currently polished and shined; and surprisingly now, as a direct result, Henry could finally see his own reflection projected through them. Even the books within the library were now also thoroughly dusted, cleaned, and dare we admit... readable. Alas, everything was changing... and for the better. Even Henry, himself, was starting to change, too.

After a hundred years of neglect, Henry was starting to care about his own humble abode; for unlike before, he, at long last, finally had a reason to care. Remarkably, it took one woman to change his entire outlook, regarding his environment and even, his own existence. After witnessing just how hard Kassie strived each day to oversee the restoration of his home, her relentless efforts ultimately came to inspire him in the process. Rather than kicking back and doing nothing at all, this time around, Henry started to put in more effort. From helping her to put away the dishes, to returning a borrowed book back into its proper place on the bookshelf in the library, to wiping away a stain from off the table, Henry was slowly changing his ways. Surprisingly, he actually began to care about his manor and the condition of it. Finally, after all these years, his manor was starting to look and feel more like an actual home, rather than another historical and abandoned ruin. A home that was actually lived in. A home that was, dare we say, even cherished.

Meanwhile, as his manor slowly began to blossom and evolve... so did his own feelings, in the process. No longer was he unmoved and unaffected by the affairs of Galloway Manor. Instead, Henry took a key interest in both the estate and of his honored guest. Steadily, Henry grew more affixed and enchanted by Kassie's every passing move. After a century of darkness, she was the light that had long been missing in his lonesome life. Furthermore, her overall cheerful persona and positive attitude was highly contagious. It was as if her own soul and inner light lit up each and every room that she walked into, even in the darkest of rooms. Miraculously, somehow, her inner light also managed to shine and spread right through onto him, as well. Yes, everything around Henry was most certainly changing... including, his own heart.

Just like a bar of frozen ice that melts when positioned underneath the sun, a similar diagnosis can be also said with regards to the condition of Henry's heart. After a century of darkness, he had finally stumbled upon a bright and shining star in Kassie. From her smiles and her laughs, to her dancing and her cooking, to her stories and her ideas, Henry grew more fascinated by her with each passing day. She was by far, the most fascinating of all the living creatures and beings that existed within his domain... and luckily, for Henry, she was here, right by his side. Willingly. Freely.

Although Henry never had that much experience with the matter concerning love in the past; however, by now, he already well knew that what he felt for Kassie was beyond affection and admiration. It was love. Love, in its truest of forms. Ah, yes, Henry was truly, desperately and madly in love with Kassie! But pray tell, how did it happen and when did it come to be? Well, truthfully, Henry had already fallen for her long ago, at first sight, in fact... but it just took him some time to recognize it.

From the first moment he saw her running through his woods, Henry was immediately captivated by her. After spending the past century alone inside of the forest, Kassie was the first woman that he had ever seen frolicking down his dirt road before. Not only was she so incredibly beautiful, with her stunning red hair flying against the wind, as she so bravely fled away from that hungry wolf; but her relentless and courageous spirit, ultimately drew him to her, like an invisible magnetic force that summoned him in. Even from across the forest, he could feel her arrival. Although at first, he couldn't see her; but still, he could sense her. Her scent, her aroma, her aura... her soul. Alas, she was a good soul, too, at that. After all, Henry had the talent of detecting one's inner character; and luckily, for Kassie, she was from amongst the good.

Similar to the wolf before him, Henry also tracked her down using his superior senses. Hearing the footsteps of the predator wolf from afar, Henry was compelled to save her. Therefore, with one tap against Midnight's reins, Henry and his horse were off to rescue Kassie from the hungry wolf. Luckily, Henry arrived right on-time, before catastrophe struck. And upon his arrival, he swiftly lifted her up into his arms, as they rode off into the sunset.

With Kassie safely secured within his arms, Henry secretly smiled to himself. For as beautiful as she looked from afar, Kassie felt even more desirable up-close, when pressed against him. However, once he gazed directly into her eyes for the first time, Henry immediately recognized her strong and courageous spirit that was equal to his own. A perfect match to his own wandering immortal self. And in that instant, Henry already knew at once, that she was the one for him. The woman, whom he had long waited for. His mate.

However, his opinion about her further elevated, once she proclaimed him to be her hero. Most surprisingly, her unexpected complement instantly melted his heart. Although Henry was already extremely enchanted by her from the very beginning, it was her overall charm and rare ability to see past all of his faults, that finally sealed the deal for him. Ultimately, in the end, he no longer saw her just as a mate, but as an actual soulmate, instead.

Now, that Henry was fully aware about his own true feelings about her and that he indeed loved her; but at the same time, he was also grateful to have her in his life. In fact, Henry was secretly beyond grateful to her former groom, for having previously abandoning her back at the altar. Ironically, due to his selfish actions, his abandonment allowed Kassie to escape and accidentally stumble upon his forest. Furthermore, having lived with this curse for the past one hundred years and counting, Henry was almost thankful to Vera for having placed the curse on him, in the first place; for had she not, then Henry would never have lived long enough to meet Kassie in this current era.

Kassie, her name was already written deep within his heart. From her failed cooking attempts to their dance rehearsals in the ballroom, Henry found himself enchanted by both her beauty and charm. For as beautiful as she was, Kassie was also a clever lady, with an impressive mind. Truly, all of her long hours spent studying away in his library, thoroughly impressed him. Never before had he met a woman so inclined to read.

Even though Henry had his fair share of women back in his time, strangely enough, he never previously felt these strong desires and yearnings for another woman before. But apart from love, what else did Henry feel for Kassie? Well, he certainly was attracted to her. But more than that, he desired her. Yearned for her. Like the wolf in the forest; he too, wanted nothing more than to consume and devour her. To tear off all of her clothes and impose himself onto her. To kiss her sweet and delicate skin, as he entered her. To feel her underneath him, as he claimed her as his own. To taste her sweet body with his lips, as he explored all inches of her body. Ah, yes, Henry was hopelessly lost in his desire for her!

But did Kassie feel the same way as he? Did she too, wonder what it would feel like to explore a romantic relationship with him? Sadly, Henry doubted that she would; for she was a lady and noblewomen like her, were born and breed to marry men from within their own station. After all, he had almost done much of the same. Had he ever loved his previous fiancé, Julia? No, he did not. Like most men in his time, Henry agreed to their union, purely due to his family's wishes and nothing more. While Henry might have previously agreed to marry Julia, he did not love her. In truth, he never loved anyone before, apart from his own family. But they were not of a romantic nature. And in these past one hundred years, Henry had never loved anyone or anything else before… not until Kassie came along. And now, because of her, he was already changing. Evolving. Transforming.

Although Henry was cursed to forever remain as an immortal and to never savor the sweet taste of death, nor enjoy the joyful sensations of biting into a sweet apple; he, was nevertheless, learning how to care for someone, other than himself. Apart from Midnight, Henry thought of nothing more than Kassie. Was she happy, while he was away? Or did she miss him? Did she approve of Galloway Manor? Was she content with the game that he brought back from each hunt? Did she find his cooking lessons useful? Or, was she impressed by his dancing skills? Henry couldn't help but wonder. If Henry had been a mortal man, then he would have already proposed marriage to Kassie long ago. By now, they would have been married, and he would have spent each of his living nights together with her, while he slept in her loving and caring arms as his wife. But alas, Henry wasn't mortal. He wasn't anything but a cursed 'being.' A 'being' that neither died, nor truly lived. Sadly, Henry, at his fundamental core, was really... well... *nothing*.

While he was *nothing*, she was *everything*. Therefore, how could a woman like Kassie, ever want to be with someone like him? Truly, she deserved so much more. However, at the same time, Henry still held out hope. Hope that somehow, Kassie would reciprocate his romantic feelings. That miraculously, she would walk straight into his bedchamber, proclaim her love for him and then, surrender herself willingly over to him. But that was only but a wish...

Alas, it was hopeless to ponder about what could never be! Hoping to clear his mind, Henry decided to walk outside onto his balcony to get some needed fresh air. It was there, as he stared up at the bright moon in the night sky— the only thing that had always remained constant these past one hundred years— that Henry came to finally realize that this nightly routine of his was no longer enough to sustain him. No, it certainly was not. It wasn't enough to just get by, as if he was riding a train down through eternity. Just 'existing' wasn't enough; he needed more. Even though he was cursed to live in these lands and forest for the rest of time, he still craved for more. Truly, he wanted her. He wanted Kassie. As far as Henry was concerned, he already loved her and now, he wanted nothing more than to be joined by her. Even if she was a mere mortal, fated to live only for the next eighty years on earth, that was plenty enough for him. For Henry was willing to live the rest of eternity in hell, if it meant that he could spend the next eighty years of heaven with her. In fact, he was willing to sell what little was left of his own wretched soul in exchange for it.

CHAPTER 12

As nervous as Kassie was, she was still determined to go through with it. Having walked about a mile, traveling from the east wing and over to his side of the manor along the west wing, she was most certainly not going to turn back had Henry decided to reject her. But would he reject her? Was that even a remote possibility? No, he couldn't, could he? Even if he wasn't interested in her, then at the very least, surely, he'd take pity upon her, wouldn't he? As a gentleman at heart, he'd be inclined to offer his bedchamber to her to sleep in at least just for the night, right? For God only knew that Kassie was far too exhausted to even attempt to walk all the way back to her bedchamber.

Luckily, to her relief, Henry opened his door. However, his reaction to her unexpected and revealing outfit was even more surprising. Perhaps, her worries about him rejecting her were all in her head; for at this very moment, he looked rather… well… happy.

"Kassie? What are you doing here, so late in the night? Is something wrong?" he asked half concerned but yet, also secretly half delighted to see her too, all at the same time.

"No, nothing's wrong," she admitted. "I'm here to see you."

"To see me? But why?" he asked, with a sparkle of hope in his eyes.

"Henry… I… I…" she began, but somehow midsentence, her nerves got the best of her, and she started to feel weak in the knee.

"Do you want something?" he asked, with high hopes.

"I want…" she continued.

"You want…" he followed after her.

"I want… *you*," Kassie finally revealed, as she pushed her way straight through his door.

Then, suddenly, the most wonderous thing happened: they kissed! Upon entering into his bedchamber, before Kassie even had a chance to make it passed him, Henry grabbed her immediately and before she knew it, they had already locked lips! At long last, his lips were finally pressed against hers. Meanwhile, his tongue managed to push through against hers, where it patiently remained intertwined with his. However, if that wasn't enough to melt her burning heart, then his arms did the trick by securely wrapping them around her waist, while she held on tightly to his shoulders. After spending a few minutes engaged in a heartfelt embrace, Henry reluctantly pulled himself away from her.

"Kassie, are you certain that you want to go through with this?" he asked. "Because, if you do, then there's no turning back. Once we start, I can't promise that I'll be strong enough to hold back and stop."

"I'm certain. I'm ready, Henry," she spoke softly, with a smile.

Upon her permission, Henry immediately acted directly on his impulses and swiftly scooped her up into his arms and then, he carried her off and over to his bed. As he gently placed her down above his mattress, Henry looked at her in fascination. While staring at her fiery long red hair that was currently loose and tangled across his entire bedspread, Henry was bewitched and hypnotized by her breathtaking beauty. It was if, a wild flame had recently been lit and was now, burning a bright blazing fire, right from his own bed. Gazing upon her wonderous and delicate face, Henry observed that Kassie appeared to be enjoying herself, while lost in a blissful state. With her eyes closed, her lips remained open and ready for his reunion. Meanwhile, her body was stretched across, and her lingerie was practically screaming for him to do the honors of removing them. For a brief moment, Henry looked at her with admiration. By far, she was the single most beautiful and enchanting creature that he had ever had the pleasure of seeing in all of his time spent here on earth. And within mere seconds, she was going to be his. In every possible way, humanly imaginable. At long last, Henry was completely lost to her seductive spell and at this very moment, he was ready to invade her. To devour her. To conquer her.

Not wanting to delay a second more, Henry began to remove all of his clothes. One by one, Kassie watched on, as he removed his shirt, then his trousers, and then finally, his breeches— revealing his very large and aroused maleness. Having seen him, in all of his glory, for the very first time, Kassie's blue eyes immediately widened, as she suddenly came to realize that very soon, his enormous maleness was going to invade her fragile and petite body. Although Kassie was aware as to what was about to take place between them— given the heavy biology textbook that she had recently read in the library— but at the same time, Kassie wasn't so entirely certain, as to how he was supposed to fit into her. Suddenly, out of a brief moment of fear, she gulped. Detecting her hesitancy, Henry smiled and quickly sought to reassure her.

"Don't worry," he said, with a reassuring smile. "I promise to go slowly."

Although his promise to 'go slowly' was meant to be comforting, Kassie still questioned it, given his enormous size. But either way, she was still determined to go through with their act of love. As far as she was concerned, Kassie already loved Henry, even though she still didn't openly admit this to him as of yet. But eventually, when the time was right, she was going to tell him the truth. Hopefully, by then, he'd admit much of the same to her, in return. But for now, Kassie was going to enjoy this rare and romantic moment with the one man in the entire world, whom she adored so very much with all her heart.

"Are you ready?" Henry asked, as he finally approached her side.

Silently, Kassie nodded in agreement, as she closed her eyes and surrendered herself willingly over to him. Not knowing how to engage in the next intricate steps of their lovemaking, Kassie voluntarily let herself loose and over to Henry's more capable and experienced hands. Following his lead, Kassie welcomed and embraced Henry's advances, as he joined her in bed and then, slowly, he proceeded to remove the remainder of her clothing.

One by one, Henry peeled off Kassie's lingerie. First, he removed her stockings and then, he discarded and threw them over to the opposite side of the bedchamber. Once her soft skin finally became exposed to him, Henry leaned down and slowly, he began to kiss each and every inch of her bare skin, starting from her legs and moving upwards towards her inner thighs. Delighted by the warmth of his plump lips pressed against hers, while his sturdy hands moved and traveled against her own delicate figure, Kassie moaned from utter pleasure; which, in return, made Henry hungry for more. Having waited for a woman for more than a century, Henry was eager to enjoy this new romantic liaison with the one woman, whom, at this very moment, held his entire heart within the palm of her hands.

Determined to see her naked body, Henry continued to undress Kassie. After removing her bra and corset, he finally came into direct contact with her large and voluminous breast; which at this very moment, were just as pink and as juicy as the tastiest of apples that's ripe and ready in spring.

"Mmm... delicious," Henry noted with a wicked smile, as he leaned down and began licking and sucking Kassie's nipples with his wet tongue.

Surprised by this new intoxicating sensation, Kassie moaned from excitement, as Henry squeezed her breasts tightly with his hands. Afterwards, he placed his head in-between in her breasts, as he continued to lick the outer rims of her breasts and then, ever so slowly, his tongue traveled over to her pink and hardened nipples. Meanwhile, Henry's hands moved further down below her body. Once his hands discovered her undergarments, he tightly held onto her, while he tugged them down. After removing them off completely; much to his delight, Kassie was now left entirely stark naked. Gradually, Henry moved his hands down to her most private of areas and as he grabbed a hold of it, he could feel that she was already wet and ready for him. Having touched her most sensitive region in her entire body, Kassie almost immediately, screamed for joy. Henry, in return, smiled. She was ready; and he, as a true gentleman at heart, had absolutely no intention of ever leaving her disappointed. Especially, not now. Not, ever. Alas, the time had finally come for them to join together and become united, as one.

Slowly, Henry rolled on top of Kassie, as her naked body lay right underneath from his. As he continued to kiss her lips and caress her buttock with his hands, he finally asked her, "Kassie, are you ready?"

Even if she wasn't, at this point, Henry wasn't very confident that he could even pull back, had he wanted too; for right now, he was already far too much invested in her. Although Henry had spent the past one hundred years not craving anything, from food to sleep; for the first time in decades, he finally craved for something or even... someone: Kassie. Even the mere mention or thought of her name, brought a joy to his heart. And now, at long last, she was here, right underneath him and most importantly, ready for him.

Much to his satisfaction, Kassie silently nodded, as she closed her eyes shut and held onto him with all of her might. Was she nervous or afraid? Given that this was going to be her first time alone and intimate with another man, Henry didn't fault her. After all, it was normal for a virgin to feel nervous. Although Henry would have much better preferred that she lost her innocence to him as his wife; however, at this point, he was willing to take her and have his way with her, in any possible shape or form. Even though she wasn't legally his wife, Henry vowed to himself, right there and then, that on this night henceforth, that for however long she lived on this earth, he intended to remain by her constant side, always. This way, even as an immortal, Henry could still continue to honor and respect her, as if she was his real wife in spirit; if not in the flesh.

Wanting to make her feel more comfortable, Henry whispered into her ear, "Don't worry Kassie, I promise to be gentle with you."

Instantly, Kassie smiled, in return; and Henry was now ready to make his move. As he placed his warm and sweaty body over hers, he gently pushed her thighs further apart, until they were expanded to as wide as they could possibly stretch. While Henry continued to kiss and caress her, he slowly positioned himself even closer onto her. Once their bodies were pressed together, skin to skin, Henry gently lifted his body partially up, as he got ready to invade her.

"Whatever happens Kassie, please don't be afraid. It might hurt at first, but I promise that it will feel more enjoyable, as we progress," he explained.

Having agreed to move forward, Henry was now ready to claim Kassie as his. With one sudden thrust, Henry entered into Kassie, as gently as he possibly could. At first, she was briefly startled; however, as he slowly began penetrating inside of her, back and forth, she strangely grew accustomed to it. Although he had promised to go slow with her, the more he moved inside of her, the faster he began to thrust into her. Sensing his hesitation, Kassie urged him not to hold back.

"Don't worry Henry, my love," she spoke, softly. "I'm alright. Please do as you wish. I'm not afraid anymore."

Her words, spoken right there and then, sealed the entire deal for him. If Kassie wasn't in pain and she was alright, then Henry was going to take advantage of her kindness and lose himself in this moment… which, dear reader, is precisely what he did, too!

Upon hearing her confession, Henry decided to take full advantage of her proposal. Having previously fought so hard to keep a slow pace with her, Henry finally gave into his carnal desires and allowed his body to roam free, in place of his mind. And so, Henry determined to make Kassie his woman, gave full permission to his body to move at the speed of light. Now, rocking faster in-between her legs, he moved back and forth within her, as fast as he possibly could… without any fear or hesitation on his part.

Faster and faster, he pushed further and deeper into her, as he continued to spread her legs wider apart. As he penetrated and moved forward into her, she screamed louder and louder, as she tugged and clawed at his back. After years of being alone, Henry was enjoying every last inch of her. Finally, as he pushed his final thrust into her, Kassie climaxed and yelled so loud from pleasure, that even Henry was highly impressed by his own ability to excite her so much.

As their lovemaking continued well into the late hours of the night, Henry claimed her as his, over and over and over again… until finally, they both gave up due to pure exhaustion. Eventually, as Kassie fell asleep within his caring arms, he watched over her with loving eyes. Surprisingly, for the first time in this past century, Henry did not wander off into the forest to ride during the midnight hour. For once, he stayed back home inside the comfort of his own bed, while he watched the moonlight shine against the woman, who now not only claimed ownership of his body but of his heart, as well.

CHAPTER 13

"**Y**ou're aiming too high," Henry forewarned.

"But I'm only doing what you previously told me to do," replied Kassie, as she remained still and in full concentration.

"Not quite," he said. "You must lower your aim."

"Lower my aim? But why? If I do, then surely, I'll miss," she protested.

"No, you won't," he confirmed.

"Are you sure?" she asked.

"Positive," he boldly proclaimed. "Have I ever given you bad advice, thus far?"

"No, I suppose that you haven't," Kassie reluctantly admitted.

"Now, get ready," Henry instructed, as he leaned over above her shoulders and tried his best to adjust her grip.

"Get ready," he repeated again, as they together, took a step forward. Afterwards, once the coast was clear, he finally yelled, "Fire!"

Upon his command, Kassie immediately released her hold on the trigger to her shotgun and fired straight away, up into the air. Unfortunately, the thrill and excitement of it all, was far too much for Kassie's nerves to bear. Truly, she preferred staying quietly at home in the comfort of Galloway Manor, rather than journeying outside into the cold and windy woods to hunt for wild critters. However, Henry was determined to teach her the fine 'art of hunting;' and so, Kassie reluctantly agreed to his persistent request and as a result, she soon found herself standing out in the chilly forest with a heavy but armed shotgun, as they hunted for game.

"Did I hit it?" she asked, curious as to whether or not, her first attempted shot was a success.

Briefly, Henry politely excused himself from her company and walked over to inspect the grounds onsite, directly. About five minutes later, he returned but only to deliver the bad news to her.

"Unfortunately, my dear Kassie, it appears that you've missed," he admitted, while hoping that her first failed attempt wouldn't deter her from trying again.

"I see," she said, with much disappointment. "I suppose that quail won't be on tonight's menu, after all."

"Perhaps," he joined, "But, that doesn't mean that we still can't try again."

"Try again? Do you mean that we're going to continue to stand here and just wait for another flock to fly by us? Honestly, Henry, we've already spent the past hour waiting for the last flock!" Kassie whined, out of frustration.

Truly, waiting for another flock of quails to pass by was far too much for her own nerves!

"Alright, if you prefer not to wait, then we can try hunting for something else," Henry advised.

"Henry, must we really hunt at all? As far as I'm concerned, I'd much rather have us return back to Galloway Manor, so that we can preoccupy ourselves with *more enjoyable* activities…" she suggested, most deviously.

Of course, Kassie highly preferred Henry's intimate company in the comfort of his bedchamber than any other tedious outdoor adventure. Ever since their first glorious night together, they spent almost every waking hour of each day playing and exploring their newfound romance inside of Galloway Manor. What originally began as foreplay in his bed, soon carried over to the chairs in the study, then the table in the library… and then the walls in the ballroom… and then the floors in the kitchen… and then, the sofa in the salon. Room by room, Henry and Kassie made love, as if their very lives depended upon it. From sunrise to sunset, he kissed and caressed her, endlessly. For the past several days, she found herself completely lost within his kisses and embrace. While she was beyond blissfully happy and enchanted by her new lover, the only real challenge that they now faced was of Kassie's constant hunger for food. With all of the physical activities associated with their lovemaking, Kassie eventually, found herself exhausted and in desperate need of food for more energy. While Henry was an immortal and unaffected by their lovemaking marathon; Kassie, in contrast, was growing weak, tired and famished. And so, in order to recharge his new lover, Henry decided to take this opportunity to teach Kassie the fine art of hunting.

"Kassie," he began, "You very well know that if we're to carry on with our *activities* back home, then I also need to ensure that you've got enough food and energy to do so."

"But surely, I can eat something simpler," she innocently suggested.

"Kassie, you need protein. Besides, you've already mastered the art of cooking, dancing, cleaning, and given that you're already a highly trained equestrian, it's high time that you learn hunting, too," he boldly proclaimed.

"But why should I bother learning about hunting, when I already have you?" asked Kassie.

"Listen Kassie, I want you to learn as much as you possibly can about everything, so that you can be self-sufficient. In these past one hundred years, I've had to learn the hard way to do everything myself. This world is a mysterious and sometimes dangerous place; therefore, I want to make sure that you're trained on all of these essential skills in order to survive out here, curse or no curse," said Henry, in a serious tone and manner.

"But Henry," Kassie began, as she walked over to him. Carefully, she grabbed a hold of his hand and then, while looking directly into his eyes, she vowed, "I will never leave you."

"And I will never leave you," he promised her, in return. "But, in the meantime, if you plan on staying here with me in this forest, then you've also got to learn how to survive living within it, too."

"And surviving is hunting, eh?" she asked, with a raised brow.

"Precisely," he agreed. "Now, are you ready to move onto your next task?"

"Very well, I suppose," she said.

"Alright, that's more like it," Henry said, as he swiftly pulled her right behind him and then, taking five steps forward, he led them away from the open and airy fields and down into the dark and murky woodland areas.

"If you don't want to wait around for another flock of quails, then I highly suggest we aim for one of the other smaller land creatures that are currently frolicking away inside of this forest," he advised.

As they walked together down the muddy dirt road that brought them deeper into the forest, Henry stopped midway along their journey, in order to direct Kassie's attention over to a tiny fox that was currently lingering away underneath a fallen log. Unlike most foxes, this particular one was bright yellow, almost sun-like in color. Although its stature was rather small; however, its petite size failed to deter itself from having the motivation to crawl underneath that overwhelmingly much heavier log— a log, that was practically triple the weight of its own tiny size. At first glance, Kassie found the animal to be remarkably cute. Had she not been out and about hunting with Henry, then Kassie would have much rather have stopped to play with it, instead of continuing on with her lesson.

"Look over there," Henry slowly whispered into her ear, as he pointed towards the tiny fox. "If you stay quietly put, then we might be able to catch it."

"The fox?" asked Kassie, in complete horror. Although she was open to the idea of hunting for small game, killing this small and defenseless animal seemed just too cruel… even for her.

"Yes, the fox," he clarified; however, seeing her dissatisfied reaction, Henry immediately sought to comfort her. Sympathizing with her current conflicted nature, he further added, "Kassie, don't be afraid. Take it from me, you'll only be doing it a favor. Don't be fooled by its apparent innocence. You must kill it while you still can, before it becomes an even greater threat later on in the future."

"A threat? Why Henry, pray tell, whatever sort of threat could this poor and defenseless animal possibly be?" she asked, in astonishment.

In all truth, Kassie struggled with the idea of harming such a lovely creature; which ironically, had the same precise shade of yellow that was so incredibly similar to her former fiancé Walter's hair coloring. No, thought Kassie, this animal wasn't going to be a threat or even, a problem later on. She couldn't kill it. It was simply too cruel. If she was going to have to starve tonight, then so let it be!

"I can't," Kassie finally admitted. "Henry, I'm sorry… but I can't… I won't do it!"

"Very well, Kassie, I can't force you. We'll just try to find something else," he said, in a calm and reassuring manner, that surprisingly brought much relief and comfort to her own conscience.

Ultimately, after deciding to let the fox freely go, Henry and Kassie continued onwards with their journey, as they quietly tiptoed across the forest. After passing by several rows of fallen trees and broken branches, they finally stumbled upon a red-haired rabbit lying down along the dirt road. Similar to the white rabbit that Kassie previously saw when she first stumbled upon the forest, this particular rabbit had a bright fire-liked coat that resembled Kassie's own vibrant reddish hair. The red-haired rabbit also appeared to be preoccupied, as he ate all of the overgrown moss and clovers that were currently spread alongside the dusty pathways. Just like the fox before, Kassie was also hesitant to claim the life of another small and innocent creature.

"Kassie, if you aim now, then you might be able to shoot it," Henry quietly whispered to her.

However, Kassie couldn't find the heart to kill it. No, it would be too cruel. She couldn't find the means nor motivation to do it. However, regardless of her own personal feelings, mother nature found a way to intervene. Ironically, in a twist of fate, the fox that she had previously set free, somehow managed to wander off and followed them into their part of the woods. As Kassie and Henry silently stood there, the fox, as cunning and as sly as he was, swiftly crept its way towards the log and was now, mere inches away from snatching the rabbit all for himself!

"Kassie, if you don't act now, then that fox is surely going to claim that rabbit for himself, before you even have the chance to mourn for it," Henry forewarned her.

Much to her disappointment, Henry was right. In a matter of seconds, this sneaky fox was going to attack and kill this innocent rabbit for its dinner. Sadly, Kassie's decision to spare this fox's life also meant that this little rabbit was going to become its next victim, due to her foolish pity over the fox. It was truly the cycle of life, in action. Suddenly, Kassie realized that if she simply stood there and did nothing, then not only was she going to sleep hungry, but that, she was also going to allow this innocent rabbit to be killed by this ruthless and devious fox. No, it wasn't right! It wasn't fair! She had to do something to intervene!

Mustering up all of her courage, Kassie decided to act upon both her instincts and her sense of justice. Raising her shotgun high up into the air, she positioned herself, just like Henry had previously instructed her to do so, the day before. Now, with her hands tightly held against the trigger, she took a deep breath. Finally, as the fox leaped straight up into the air, Kassie released her trigger and shot a bullet straight across.

"My God, you got it!" Henry proudly exclaimed, as he ran over to the site.

As Kassie stood there, frozen with her gun now resting below and above the ground, she stared straight ahead as Henry lifted the dead animal up into the air. Even though Kassie desperately sought to avoid committing this cruel and gruesome act of killing; however, had she not pulled the trigger right there at that moment, then that poor innocent and defenseless red-haired rabbit was going to be viciously torn into shreds by that evil fox. While Henry dangled the yellow-haired fox into the air, Kassie silently watched on, as the red-haired rabbit gracefully hopped away— ignorant to the fact that due to her quick actions, it had inadvertently survived yet another day in the forest.

"Well, done Kassie!" exclaimed Henry happily, as he returned to her side.

Placing their new game onto the ground, Henry pulled Kassie towards him and bestowed a kiss upon her lips.

"I'm so incredible proud of you," Henry began, as he pulled his lips away from her. "So far, you've managed to master everything that I've taught you!"

"Are you so surprised?" asked Kassie, with a devious smile and a raised brow. "After all, I've had an exceptionally fantastic teacher."

Touched by her sincere complement, Henry immediately grabbed a hold of her and together, they tumbled down onto the ground, with Kassie landing right on top of him. As they nestled together side by side on the grassy field, they took in a few minutes to quietly enjoy their embrace, as they peacefully listened to the pleasant melodies of nature. Looking up at the clear blue sky, Henry held tightly onto Kassie, as he reflected upon their newfound romantic relationship.

"I should have married you, before we started this relationship," he admitted, with much shame.

Being the true and sincere gentleman that he was, Kassie understood his inner conflict and sense of guilt about taking her innocence away, outside of marriage. Under different circumstances, she would have agreed with him; however, at the same time, being that she lost her innocence to the one man in the world, whom she loved, admired and respected so dearly, it didn't matter that much to her. She had no regrets. No second guesses, or remorse. For as far as Kassie was concerned, Henry was the only man, whom she intended to ever make love to from now until death.

"Don't be ashamed Henry, because I'm not," Kassie boldly stated, without a shadow of a doubt nor with any hesitation.

"But I should have claimed you as my bride first; a lady like you deserves so much more," Henry reflected, as he pulled her closer to him and then, leaned her head against his chest.

"Henry, it doesn't matter... I... I...," began Kassie, but before she could even finish her sentence, Henry scooped in and locked her in another passionate kiss.

"We should be married Kassie," he interrupted her. "But," he added, "What priest or church would allow for such a union to even take place between us? A mortal married to an immortal? A human married to a cursed being? Heck, I can't even leave this damn forest, due to this dreadful curse! Hell, our marriage would be condemned, before we even stepped a foot inside of the church!"

Sensing his frustration, Kassie was determined to bring his heart at ease. Staring at the white daisies growing along the grass, she suddenly had an idea. If they couldn't marry inside of the church, then she intended to bring the church over to them. Picking two daisies from off the ground, she slowly tied one end to the other to form a circle. She repeated the same steps again with the second flower, and then afterwards, she had two rings of daisies held within the palm of her hand. Reaching over to grab his hand, she slid one of the flower rings against his finger, while she did the same for herself.

"If the church won't wed us, then I shall," said Kassie, determined to legitimatize their love as best as she could.

"What do you mean?" asked Henry, in confusion.

"Just repeat after me," she began, "I, Henry, take thee Kassie, as my wife..."

Following her instructions, he repeated just that.

"Very good," Kassie said, as she continued on, "And I, Kassie, take thee Henry, as my husband. To love and honor, for all eternity."

"You're leaving the death part, aren't you?" he asked, most amused.

"Yes, and now, my love, we are married in the eyes of God," Kassie proudly proclaimed, with the brightest of smiles that touched Henry's heart and burned his soul.

As Kassie leaned down and sealed their vows with a passionate kiss, Henry held onto her with all his might. After years of waiting, he finally found the love of his life. For however long or little their lives together were meant to be, at this very moment in time, he was content and did not question it any further. Although he had much rather preferred to have sealed their marriage in a more traditional church, the church of Kassie was good enough for him.

Looking deep into her sparkling blue eyes, he admitted, "I love you Kassie, with all my heart."

"I love you too, Henry," she admitted, as she bent down to kiss him.

And for the remainder of the afternoon, the happy couple enjoyed their honeymoon outside in the comfort of nature.

CHAPTER 14

With Henry peacefully lying down above the mossy evergreen grass, Kassie decided to take it upon herself to make her first romantic leading move, as an active partner to their newly self-proclaimed husband and wife status. Plus, after several days of practice, Kassie was eager to take the lead in their next round of lovemaking. And so, with Henry comfortably resting, she slowly pulled herself away from him and began to undress herself.

"What are you doing?" asked Henry, disappointed that she had so abruptly pulled herself away from him, without a proper explanation.

"What does it look like I'm doing?" she asked in return, with a devious smile.

Lifting his head up from off the ground, Henry saw that Kassie had already unbuttoned the front of her dress. Seeing the traces of her breasts from her exposed chest, Henry couldn't help but smile. Although they had practically made love in almost every room inside his manor, this was going to be their first time together, outside in nature.

"Very well, carry on," Henry replied, with an approving smile; as he, too, joined her in unison and began removing his own clothes as well.

Afterwards, they were both undressed and left standing, stark naked in the middle of the forest. Meanwhile, as Henry was right about to pull her down onto him, Kassie managed to stop him midway.

"Wait," she cried. "Please, let me lead this time, instead."

Amused by her sudden interest to dominate them, Henry played along with her request, as he reclined back down onto the grass. Once he was comfortably positioned, Kassie slowly climbed above him. After reading a new book that she had recently discovered in the library entitled "Kama Sutra," Kassie was ready to explore a few new moves with her lover. Since most of the time, Henry made love to her while on top, Kassie wanted to see what it would feel like if she was the one on top of him, in reverse. And so, once Henry appeared more peaceful, Kassie swiftly made her move.

After climbing above Henry, Kassie seated herself right above his manhood. Stretching her legs as far apart as she possibly could, Kassie tried her very best to make herself as wide and as available for him to enter into her. Slowly, she lowered herself onto him, until finally, they came into direct contact with each other, skin to skin. But before, she entered into him, Kassie grabbed his right hand and gently placed it right behind her buttock, so that he could feel her soft bottom. And then, she lifted up his left hand, brought it directly to her face and slowly, she brought it directly into her mouth, where she began to lick and suck it. Pleased by her unexpected move, Henry immediately moaned from pleasure and Kassie, in returned, smiled.

Excited by their new foreplay, Henry grew more aroused. Meanwhile, Kassie, being equally as excited as he, grew wet from down below. And in the process, Kassie's breast grew more plump, round and pink. Pleased by the sight before him, Henry was determined to claim her exquisite breasts as his own. Gradually, moving his hands away from her mouth and buttock, Henry reverted his attention and care over to her breasts, where he cupped both pairs within the palms of his hands. Slowly, Henry began to touch and caress them and eventually, out of intense desire, he squeezed them with all his might; which in return, forced Kassie to scream loudly due to the extreme pleasure she felt, emerging from deep within her. Afterwards, she bent down to give him a kiss and upon doing so; within mere seconds, the couple found themselves locked away in another passionate kiss. As Henry's tongue explored the traces of Kassie's soft and delicate lips, his desire and appetite for her grew more and more intense; and she, the same, in return. Alas, the time for them to unite was soon approaching!

After a while, Kassie couldn't wait no longer. The time finally came for her to practice the new moves that she had previously studied. And so, stretching as far and as wide as she possibly could, Kassie pressed herself down and pulled Henry's manhood right into her. Immediately, upon entrance, they both released a huge sigh, as Kassie positioned herself to continue onwards. Following the same rhythm as riding her own horse, this time around, Kassie gave her best efforts to ride Henry.

Slowly, she began rocking back and forth, bouncing above him. At first, it felt a bit strange and odd to have been seated on top of him; but at the same time, she rather liked it. It was a nice change to be the one on top this time, in reverse. Plus, it felt a bit different, too. Instead of lying still underneath him, being on top was surprisingly more liberating. Strangely enough, it felt as if her own body felt more alive; for she was required to do more work as the driver, seeking to earn his pleasure. As the primary person leading their lovemaking, Kassie was determined to do her best to please him.

As she rocked back and forth, she could feel all of her inner nerves begin to vibrate, with such dominating intensity that she herself, was quite ready to explode from this new blissful state. It was truly ecstasy, in the making! Exercising in this new position, Kassie experienced a brand-new wave of happiness and pleasure, originating from in-between her legs, as she pressed and vibrated herself against his body. Meanwhile, as she rolled her head back and screamed from delight, Henry followed her and moaned aloud, too. Determined to encourage her even more, Henry pulled her further down onto him, as he reached over to her legs and then, he stretched and pulled them even wider apart.

Inspired by his eagerness to assist her, Kassie decided to thrust even harder and faster above him. As she moved up and down on him, Henry placed his hands behind her soft and delicate buttock, while she continued to lead. Meanwhile, Kassie's large round pair of breasts shook and jiggled, along the way. Mesmerized by her voluminous breasts, Henry decided to move his hands away from her buttock and over to her breasts, where he gently cupped them with his hands. While Kassie concentrated on her swinging rhythm and moves, he watched her with excitement. From this position, he saw everything. Her precious soft, delicate and petite body over his; her wild, untamable and long red hair flowing against the wind; and her eyes closed as she moaned and screamed from pure desire. Ah, yes, Henry was certainly most pleased by the stunning mirage playing right in front of him. And to top it all off, her breasts were now pink, plump, wet and most desirable. While their joint sweat excretion helped them to slide against one another, Henry decided to graduate their lovemaking to the next higher level.

With Kassie busy riding him from above, Henry gently lifted his buttocks and hips up from the ground to help enter into her even deeper. Upon doing so, Kassie yelled happily aloud, due to the sheer intensity of him being buried deep within her. Looking straight into his eyes, she leaned in and gave him another passionate kiss. While their lips were intertwined by their growing desires for one another, Henry's hands wandered across to her breasts, where he squeezed them yet again, with as much force as he possibly could. Surprised by the sudden tug of his hands, Kassie burst into moans of pleasure, as she slowly progressed into her climax. Rocking harder and faster than ever before, she concentrated as she tried her best to finish her ride on him. Moving at a quicker speed, she thrusted faster and faster and faster… until finally, she yelled one last and final scream, as she quickly collapsed directly onto his chest.

Although their most recent lovemaking affair in the forest was already a lengthy experience, their session was still not quite done. Determined to have his way with her, this time around, Henry decided to take the lead. Taking advantage of her already lying down above the grass, Henry rolled over to his side and slowly, he made his way to place himself right above her. With Kassie comfortably lying underneath him, Henry pushed her legs further apart, until they were as wide and as far apart as they possibly could be. Once she signaled to him that she was ready, Henry positioned himself and in one swift move, he entered into her with as much force and intensity, as he could. After much practice, the lovers were now extremely comfortable and relaxed with one another. By now, Kassie was already a well experienced lover, having slept with him several times before. As a result, Henry was no longer afraid to embark upon all of his wildest desires with her. Therefore, alas, his inner beast was unleashed! And unleashed he most certainly was; for Henry was now more determined than ever to enjoy his heart's delight with her to the fullest extent!

Upon entrance, Henry thrusted himself back and forth within her, while she screamed and clawed away at his back. Faster and faster, he pushed, thrusting and vibrating within her, as he surrendered his entire body over to the passionate force of their mutual desires for one another. While his body moved at an incredible speed, Henry bent down to kiss Kassie. As his mouth came into direct contact with hers, he slowly pushed through her lips with his and eventually, he was reunited with her tongue. Finally, with their tongues intertwined, Henry reached down from below, grabbed Kassie's buttock and then, he pulled her body even closer to his. Meanwhile, as Henry continued to penetrate within her, Kassie tried her best to move and slide along with his rhythm. With the sun shining against their hot and wet bodies, they both reached their climaxes at the same time and afterwards, they collapsed together back down and onto the grass.

Sometime later, a very naked Henry and Kassie nestled together on the grassy field, as they looked up at the sky. On this particular day, the sun was shining high above, while the white clouds floated above the clear blue sky. Meanwhile, the birds, bees and other small creatures were busy enjoying the beauty and the resources of the forest, as Henry held Kassie tightly within his arms.

As far as Kassie was concerned, life right now, at this precise moment was perfect. She did not desire, nor want anything more. Not wealth. Not status. Not anything. Here, in this exact moment, she was perfectly content with the man, whom she loved dearly with all her heart. The man of her dreams. The man, whom she secretly dreamed and wished for, almost all of her life. And now after everything, she was here with him in the enchanted forest. But sadly, dear reader, sometimes our own happiness isn't meant to last forever; and in Kassie's case, while staring deep into Henry's loving eyes, she was once again made aware that while she was a mortal, he was an immortal… and because of this mere fact alone, their fates weren't meant to last beyond a short season. Although Kassie was previously told that Henry's curse was irreversible, she was still determined to find a cure… even, if it meant that she had to uncover that mystery for herself.

"Henry," Kassie began, as she leaned over and rested her head against his chest.

"Yes, my love?" he asked, in return.

"Whatever happens, I'm going to find cure to your curse. This much, I promise you," she vowed, with all her heart.

Touched by her sincereness, Henry smiled on as he hugged her even more tightly within his grip. While he had previously spent the past one hundred years trying much of the same; this time around, for some reason, he trusted Kassie. Maybe, after all these years, she was the missing link to his curse. Perhaps, this feisty redhead of his was going to cure him, after all. Besides, his life had changed so much already just by being around her; for this lonely man finally found his soulmate, who was equal to him in every possible way. Even if Kassie failed to find a cure to break this spell, then, at the very least, it was still worth a try if it meant being with her for however long as time would permit. Meanwhile, as Kassie slept away within his arms, Henry closed his eyes and pretended to join her in her sleep. And surprisingly, for the first time in over a hundred years, Henry could almost swear that he too, had briefly managed to doze off and enter into the dream realm, when he reopened his eyes several hours later.

CHAPTER 15

For the past several days, Kassie found herself overwhelmingly busy and preoccupied in the library, roaming through a host of various books, ancient manuscripts, scrolls and encyclopedias. While her evenings were dedicated to Henry, curtesy of his bedchamber— which to be fair, was by now, also her primary shared bedchamber as well— her days, in contrast, were spent alone in complete solitude. It was during these long and lonesome hours, where Kassie found herself in full concentration, as she quietly sat and studied in the library. With Henry busy away in the forest and hunting for her next meal, Kassie remained behind at the manor with the sole purpose of continuing on with her research. Keeping true to her vow, Kassie was determined to find a cure to Henry's lingering curse, one way or another.

But pray tell, how was this even possible? How could Kassie discover the cure to an unbreakable curse? A curse that was never meant to be broken? A spell enacted by a wicked witch; who, ironically, had long ago, met her doom by the hands of her own victim? Her stepson, nonetheless? The one woman... nay... the only soul in all of existence, who knew the precise remedy to that very curse? Sadly, dear reader, one couldn't help but wonder: was Kassie's quest already a hopeless cause?

Alas, Kassie simply refused to accept this! No, she absolutely refused to give up on Henry! After all, he was her true love; the love of her life. Regardless, as to how difficult and hopeless their obstacles were, Kassie still intended to save him. No matter how long or how little time it took, she was determined to discover a cure to his curse. His life... her life... their very futures together stood at the balance. Everything she did or didn't do at this point, it all mattered. If Kassie was going to have a happy ending, then she needed to break Henry's curse, once and for all.

Drawing upon past histories, legends, myths, folklore, fairy tales and all of the alike, Kassie knew that at the very least, her answers lied somewhere within the pages of these written texts. Somewhere, hidden away within these books, ancient manuscripts and scrolls, were words of wisdom, as expressed by those who lived before her and were much more experienced than she. Truly, there was an answer somewhere concealed in there, just waiting to be discovered. As an avid and keen reader herself, Kassie was well aware to the fact that books and other written materials, were often the key to answering some of life's most mysterious pursuits. Had more people taken the actual time to read them, then perhaps, the world might be a much safer and happier place to live in.

Starting from collections pertaining to various key figures from legends and folklore, Kassie gathered as many books as she possibly could on this subject. After searching through a whole host of several bookshelves in the library, she had well over a hundred books or so, at her desk. One by one, she reviewed each and every one of them, in the hopes of uncovering a clue. Meanwhile, wanting to record her findings, she kept a notepad and pen handy nearby, in order to write everything and anything that captured her attention. Reflecting back to her past days spent at university, she understood the value of trial and error. Furthermore, in order to find a solution to a given problem, Kassie knew that it was imperative for any true scholar or scientist to formally document their experiments and findings onto paper, so that they can have tangible evidence and information to use and reflect upon later on. And this, dear reader, is precisely what Kassie did, too.

From fictional novels to autobiographies, folklores to legends, fairy tales to gothic horror stories, Kassie read them all. But as she quietly sat down at her desk and pondered away about finding a cure, she had to ask herself this one important question: what exactly *was* Henry? If she was going to find a cure to his curse, then she needed to start by better understanding as to what he really was, in the first place. After all, how can a remedy be prescribed, if one fails to fully understand the actual disease? So, therefore, what precisely was Henry afflicted with?

Was he a vampire or a werewolf? Did he crave the taste of blood like Dracula; or did he wander through the night in search of prey on a full moon, like a werewolf? Or was Henry a zombie, sentenced to wander through earth, until the end of time? Although Henry was cursed with immortality, he was neither of the above. Unlike Dracula, Henry never craved blood; in fact, he craved for absolutely nothing. Furthermore, after spending the past several nights together, Kassie was absolutely convinced, without a shadow of a doubt, that he wasn't a werewolf either; for if he had been, then surely, she'd have witnessed his transformation into a beast during the last full moon, wouldn't she? As for a zombie, well… Henry might have been cursed to wander about; however, it was only exclusively limited to the borders of the enchanted forest and tragically, as a result, he was unable to freely leave his domain for the outside world.

While legends and folklore might have failed to provide the answers that Kassie was so desperately searching for, she decided to revert her attention over to fairy tales, instead. However, much to her dismay, most of her fairy tale research pertained to damsels in distress and not the other way around. According to tradition, men were not supposed to be the ones cursed; no, generally, it were the females, in reverse. From Sleeping Beauty to Snow White, it was the prince, who was destined to kiss the sleeping princess, in order to break their curse. In fact, according to these fairy tales, it was true love's first kiss that was ultimately designed to break all of these famous spells. After all, it was regarded by many scholars and storytellers over the years that true love's first kiss was the one universal cure to break a wicked curse. And while true love's first kiss was almost always guaranteed to serve as the prelude to an inevitable happy ending; Kassie, most unfortunately, found herself at a complete loss. For in her unique case, they had already kissed… in fact, they had previously kissed about a million times over, among many… many… other things. Ah, yes, not only had Henry and Kassie passionately kissed, but they already did almost every possible thing imaginable that was associated with the act of love… and yet, Henry was still cursed. If the rule pertaining to true love's first kiss was indeed still accurate, then this very rule somehow failed to apply to them. Sadly, either Kassie wasn't Henry's true love; or, this classical rule simply didn't apply to his unique curse.

But if true love's first kiss wasn't the cure, then what was it? Although one could argue that perhaps, their love wasn't true; however, Kassie simply refused to believe this. Deep down within her own heart, she knew with all of her inner being that Henry loved her. Endlessly. And she, in return, loved him, too. In fact, she had always loved him, practically her entire life. While their love was unconventional, with she being a mortal and he, an immortal; Kassie was still determined to make their romance work, no matter the cost.

Therefore, what was Henry and how did his curse affect their love and relationship? While Henry wasn't a vampire, nor a werewolf, nor a zombie, he wasn't a monster, either. Nor a ghoul or even, a ghost; for she could touch and feel him, as if he were a real man. No, she thought to herself; Henry was indeed a real man. Yes, a real man, who neither aged nor decayed. Trapped at the age of thirty, Henry was a regular man, who was simply frozen in time. A man, whom, for over the past century, no longer craved the same humanly desires that normally befalls the rest of mankind. Neither death nor injury, can harm him. Sleep nor hunger, cannot overtake him. As far as Kassie knew, Henry was simply cursed to remain in Galloway Manor and to wander the enchanted forest, for all of eternity. And that, plainly put, dear reader, was the summary to his curse.

By analyzing and recording as to what his curse even was to begin with, the next question that Kassie asked herself was how did his curse negatively affected his overall, existence? While Henry was immune to any plagues, diseases and other humanly afflictions, he was unfortunately, also cursed to live alone, while the rest of his family and friends all perished throughout the past century. Apart from his horse, Midnight, Henry had no one… not, until Kassie came along. Now, with Kassie by his side, what had changed for him, so far? Well, for starters, he was no longer alone. In fact, not only did he have company now, but he also had a new lover, too, in the making. Furthermore, by taking Kassie into his home, Henry's gloomy and abandoned manor had gradually transformed from a dusty, dirty, cobweb infested estate into a pristine, sparkling and shiny property that almost resembled its original state back in the manor's glory days. And slowly, through his interaction with her, Kassie deeply reflected and eventually, came to the conclusion that Henry, himself, was already changing.

As promised upon her arrival to Galloway Manor, Henry resumed his daily hunting and began bringing home game for Kassie's meals, each and every day. After previously ignoring the humanly value and necessity associated with dining and eating a proper meal for over the past century, Henry humored her and reluctantly, he decided to join Kassie at the table, as she eagerly ate away at one of the many delicious meals that she prepared for them, in exchange for his hunting services. While Henry might have lost his sense of taste, along with his general craving for food, he still graciously ate her meals, in appreciation for her efforts. However, although Henry insistently claimed that he no longer possessed any tastebuds and couldn't savor not one bite to any one of her dishes; as of recently, on a few rare occasions, Kassie could have sworn that based upon his own facial expressions, that he appeared to have actually liked and enjoyed her most recent batch of dishes. In fact, exactly one week ago, he even went so far, as to actually complement her on using a new spice! Without saying another word, Henry already well knew that her new secret ingredient was indeed, cinnamon.

While some may argue that Henry might have only been polite to her; but somehow, his face spoke otherwise. Unlike before, when Kassie first arrived at Galloway Manor, Henry's usual unemotional and poker face, was gradually transforming into the face to a man, who could no longer conceal, nor lie to her directly. Whether or not her cooking was less than ideal, his face ultimately told her the truth. If something was delicious, then he looked happy and smiled; but if something was foul and ill tasting, then it showed plastered across on his face, as well. Furthermore, how did Henry know that she had added a new spice into her dish? She hadn't told him before. Plus, how did he know that it was cinnamon? It wasn't so easily detectable to the naked eye; for the brown powered substance generally blended in with the rest of the meal. Therefore, how did he know? How else could he know, if he couldn't taste the spice for himself?

Somehow, slowly, it was as if, the quality time that they spent in each other's company was changing him. Gradually, Henry was slowly regaining his tastebuds and senses again… but this wasn't supposed to happen, now, was it? At least, not according to the rules of the curse.

But if that wasn't strange enough, then their nights spent together were even stranger. While Kassie often fell fast asleep right after their nightly lovemaking routine, Henry usually stayed up late in bed and watched over her for a good while, before he eventually, left her side to wander back into the forest. However, these past few nights, Kassie awoke in the middle of the night to a large sound hovering right above her head. The sound was so incredibly loud that it even managed to awaken her, during her deep sleep. As she opened her eyes to her surprise, she actually found Henry lying down beside her with his eyes closed and... snoring? But how was this even possible? In order for one to snore, then one must sleep... and Henry was cursed never to sleep. However, somehow, Kassie swore that he did just that: sleep. Between tasting her cooking and sleeping besides her, Henry was evolving right before her eyes. Strangely, it was almost, as if, by being with her, Henry was almost... well... turning back into... a human.

However, Henry was technically, already a human; well, almost. After all, he was an immortal; whereas, regular men are just mortals. And thus, this differentially between immortality and mortality was the root to Kassie's problem. While Henry was an immortal, she was a mortal; and this mere indistinguishable fact, ultimately served as a roadblock to their happy ending. Eventually, in due time, Kassie would grow old and perish away, while Henry would continue to live on, alone. While nothing on earth could separate them from their love; death, on the other hand, was their only obstacle. Even though Kassie was perfectly content on spending the rest of her mortal life with Henry; however, secretly knowing in the back of her mind that one day, she was ultimately going to die and thus, leave him behind, pained her immensely.

For most couples, death served only as a temporary separation; in which eventually, the earthly couples would once again be reunited in heaven. A promise of the hereafter. While this promise might have served as a comfort to many couples throughout the centuries, the same could not be equally said for Kassie. For if Henry couldn't die, then that also meant that they could never again be reunited together after death in heaven. Furthermore, unlike a vampire or a werewolf, his curse couldn't carry over to her. There was no vampire's or a werewolf's bite that could transform her into an immortal. Sadly, in the end, she was a mortal; therefore, she was still fated to die. Tragically, because of this unfair disadvantage and inequality that distinguished them, between a mortal woman and an immortal man, this was now an obstacle that negatively impacted both of their lives. As it currently stood, if Kassie failed to find a cure to his unbreakable curse, then she was doomed to also suffer a terrible fate of her own: being separated from the love of her life at the time of her death.

Ironically, the real truth was that Kassie wasn't afraid of death nor of dying, for she had already been well accustomed to this very subject, due to the untimely deaths of her own parents. A time to be born and a time to die; Kassie was well aware of mother nature and the cycle of life. All beginnings have an end and all endings have a rebirth; and so, on and so forth. However, in Henry's case, there were no endings. His existence continues to carry on, for all eternity. While Kassie might not have troubled herself before with this subject; but now that she was a part of his life, she desperately needed to find a solution to their looming problem. In fact, her very own happiness depended upon it!

And so, Kassie thoroughly documented her thoughts, findings and reflections into her handy notepad. While Henry's situation might have been unique and possibly hopeless, she still needed to do her part and write it all down. As an aspiring writer, Kassie now found herself in the center of her own fairy tale and she, at the same time, the very author and heroine of it.

Looking outside the window, Kassie admired the view of the forest from up in the library. While Henry was probably away and hunting as of right now, she noted that apart from his standard daytime routine activities, she wasn't entirely certain as to what he did exactly out in the forest, during the night. Of course, their evenings were almost guaranteed to begin with dinner and end with their lovemaking; but afterwards, once Kassie fell fast asleep, she was never truly certain as to what Henry did precisely, when riding outside and alone in the forest with Midnight. Was he guarding the woods, or hunting for midnight prey? She honestly did not know. While Kassie was aware of his general affairs in the day; his nights, in contrast, were so mysterious. However, if Kassie was ever going to get to the bottom of this curse, then she needed to know everything. She needed to know what Henry did, whenever he snuck out into the forest so late into the night. And so, determined to find answers, Kassie decided that tonight she was going to have to enact a plan of her very own. Although Henry had previously warned her not to step a foot into the enchanted forest so late at night by herself; however, Kassie couldn't turn a blind eye to this matter. As it currently stood, Henry would never willingly allow her to come with him into the dark woods. And so, because of these reasons, she decided that tonight, not only would she pretend to fall fast asleep after their romantic time spent together; but that, as soon as he stepped out of their bedchamber, she was going to follow him from behind. Ah, yes, come tonight, dear reader, Kassie was going to discover for herself, as to what precisely goes on in the dark woods, during the midnight hour.

CHAPTER 16

Upon opening her eyes, Kassie found herself alone inside of Henry's bed. Just as she predicted earlier in the afternoon, right after their lovemaking and upon closing her eyes, Henry soon dressed and left her side to wander back into the forest. As Kassie rose out of bed, she looked outside of her window. There, from across the manor, she saw Henry ride into the dark forest, with only the moonlight serving as his only source of light. Although Henry was most likely going to be gravely upset with her decision to follow him into the forest so late at night and all by herself, she ultimately decided that she still needed to take that risk. After all, if she was ever going to discover a cure to his curse, then she needed to understand everything about him, both the good and the bad.

Determined to go through with her plans, she quickly dressed into her clothes and then, she hurriedly exited his bedchamber and ran down the stairs. A few minutes later, Kassie, now fully dressed, wearing an emerald green cloak and carrying a small traveling lamp, found herself wandering outside of Galloway Manor and entering into the woods. Following Midnight's horse tracks, she walked their same trail, which in the end, led her further down the road and moving deeper into the heart of the enchanted forest.

While the environmental conditions might have been intimidating for some— with the weather being a bit chilly and the creatures of the night busy croaking and chirping about along the way— Kassie still, nevertheless, continued onwards with her journey. After walking for about ten minutes or so, she suddenly heard some commotion from afar. Curiously, she quickly ran and hid behind an oak tree to listen in on the conversation taking place from right across from her.

It was there, from behind that oak tree, that Kassie saw Henry conversing with a lost traveler. The traveler was an elderly gentleman, who was dressed in old and tattered clothing. He appeared to be traveling with a large wooden caravan as his mode of transportation, that was pulled by two medium sized horses. From the looks of it, it seemed that the elderly gentleman had been lost and was asking Henry for assistance. Listening in, Kassie overheard Henry provide the elderly gentleman with directions on how to exit the forest. According to Henry, if he followed the northern star and continued riding along the straight path, then eventually, he would reach the village by daybreak. Grateful for his generous assistance, the elderly gentleman reached into his pocket and was about to gift Henry with a gold coin. However, Henry stopped him midway and instead, he reached into his own pocket and gave the elderly gentleman a piece of bread that Kassie had recently baked, earlier in the day. Touched by his sincere generosity, the elderly gentleman gave Henry a warm handshake and then, he bid him a final farewell, as he departed the scene to continue on with his journey through the forest.

Based on what Kassie had just witnessed, she was truly impressed by Henry's kindness, generosity and patience. Not only did he help the elderly traveler, but he also rejected his offer of payment. Furthermore, Henry even graciously bestowed him bread, in return; to a man, who most likely, probably hadn't eaten a proper meal in several days. Curse or no curse, Henry was most genuinely, a good-hearted man with a kind and generous soul; because at the very core, he wasn't obliged to help the lost traveler, in any shape or form. Instead, Henry willingly helped him, because he truly wanted to do so. It really was just as simple as that.

Suddenly, Kassie understood Henry's true purpose, with regards to his presence in the nightly forest: for all the lost travelers wandering through his land, Henry was their guide. Their helper. Their aid. For all of those men, who were so desperate enough to pray for a miracle in the gloomy hours of the darkened night, Henry was their savior. Their saint.

Their guardian angel. Just as he had saved Kassie from that hungry wolf all those weeks ago, Henry was also just as equally important to them, as he was to her.

After watching Henry's interaction with the elderly gentleman, Kassie decided that it was best that she turn around and return back home. After all, she already got the information that she needed. Plus, if Henry ever discovered that she purposely went against his wishes and secretly followed him into the forest so late into the night, then he was going to be terribly angry at her. Whether or not, his previous request was meant to serve as a direct warning to her that something evil and dreadful lurked inside of the nightly woods, or if, it was just another general cautionary deterrence; in truth, Kassie really could not tell. However, either way, it was in her overall best interest to simply leave and quietly return back into his bed. But just as she was about to exit, she heard a howling sound come from behind her.

To her horror, the howling was loud and widespread. From what Kassie's ears could detect, this wasn't the sound of a single wolf, but of a pack. One after the other, she listened to the howls of the hungry beasts; whom, by now, were most likely ready to devour their prey. Although Kassie knew in her mind that it was probably best that she run immediately; however, at the same time, she suddenly grew concerned about Henry's welfare, along with the growing fear of leaving him behind to fend for himself. Even though Henry was an immortal; but surely, even he had his own limitations, didn't he?

However, before Kassie had the time to react, the pack of wolves soon descended down the hill and arrived at Henry's area, where they quickly encircled him. With her heart beating rapidly inside of her chest, Kassie watched on from behind the oak tree in fear, as she witnessed the five vicious wolves surround her beloved Henry and his horse, Midnight. With their red eyes and hungry mouths wide open, all covered in drool, along with their sharpened and razor blade teeth exposed through their protruding mouths, which were ready to bite, Kassie silently observed as they slowly closed in on Henry. Meanwhile, Henry, as strong and as agile as can be, swiftly grabbed a thick stick from off the ground and was ready to fight them off by himself, directly, if need be. But before he had a chance to hop back onto Midnight to escape from this unfortunate scene, the leader of the wolfpack, which was the biggest and scariest of them all— the true alpha male— quickly leaped straight up into the air and landed right above on Henry.

"Henry!" screamed Kassie, directly from behind.

Following her own instincts, she quickly gathered as many stones as she could from off the ground. After filling her pockets with stones, she quickly climbed up the tree and from there, she began throwing her stones down below and towards the wolves' direction. Most impressively, her aim was very efficient; for she managed to strike each wolf, with every single one of her throws. While Midnight tried his best to kick and push the smaller wolves onto the ground, Kassie continued to cast her stones down towards their direction. After throwing about nine stones below, she successfully managed to scare the smaller wolves away. However, as they quickly fled to the outer reaches of the forest, the alpha wolf remained behind and continued to fight Henry, directly head-on.

By now, Henry's clothes were practically all tattered, and his body was covered in dripping red blood, along with swollen black and blue bruises. While Henry tried his best to beat the alpha wolf with his stick, the pesky beast still would not release his grip on him. After throwing her tenth and final shot, Kassie soon realized that she was now all out of stones. Sadly, she knew that if she didn't have any more stones left on her, then she couldn't assist Henry from up in this tree. If she was going to help him, then she needed to climb back down her tree and do whatever she could to save him. And, dear reader, this is precisely what Kassie did, too.

As she bravely descended down the tree, Kassie continued to watch on as Henry wrestled with the wolf with his bare hands. By now, having broken his stick in half, Henry was now forced to fight with the wolf directly, man vs. beast. Determined to save her beloved, Kassie ran towards his direction. Wanting to serve as a distraction in order to revert the wolf's attention away from Henry and onto her, Kassie quickly whistled as loud and as long as she possibly could.

Her persistent efforts did not go unnoticed, for her loud whistle certainly caught the attention of the aggressive wolf. Upon hearing it, the alpha wolf immediately released his tight grip on Henry and soon abandoned his side. For a brief moment, Kassie felt relieved that her attempts to deter the wolf's attention away from Henry had actually worked. But then, a second later, to her own horror, the wolf swiftly changed directions and was now running towards her, ready to attack!

Determined to face the running beast head-on, Kassie quickly gathered as many stones as she possibly could from off the ground. One by one, she threw her stones directly at the wolf, as he made his way towards her. Unfortunately, for Kassie, unlike her previous aims directed at the other wolves, this time around, her throws targeting the alpha wolf were failing miserably. Whether or not it was her fear or a simple case of bad luck that prevented her success; either way, Kassie's situation was starting to look dire. Sadly, if she failed to scare the wolf away, then sooner or later, she was going to meet a doomful end. As the wolf continued to approach her, Kassie, who was now completely out of stones and had no other loose sticks or weapons to use around her, was currently left vulnerable and defenseless. If Kassie failed to act quickly now, then within mere seconds, she was going to become this hungry wolf's next supper.

Tragically, this was how it was all going to end, she thought to herself. After meeting Henry and spending these past wonderful and blissful weeks within his company, this was how it was all going to end for her. One moment ago, she was making love to the ultimate love of her life, and the next moment, she was facing a wild beast, who was going to devour her, here in the very heart of the enchanted forest. This was it. This was the end. Unfortunately, not only was she going to die young, but she was going to die, before she had the opportunity to finish her research and discover a cure to Henry's curse. And now, it was all over. Her quest had ended, before it had even begun. Not only was Henry's curse going to continue to endure, but that sadly, she was going to be separated from her own soulmate, for the rest of all eternity.

Suddenly, just as Kassie was right about to close her eyes and surrender herself over to the alpha wolf, something miraculous came to be. In that very moment, Henry caught up behind the wolf and to her sheer amazement, a magnificent transformation occurred right there, before her very own eyes. Magically, there, standing right before her, was Henry, whose eyes were now as red and as enraged as the alpha wolf, himself. Staring straight across at Henry's face, it was no longer the kind and helpful gentleman, who had previously helped the elderly traveler from earlier tonight. No, it most certainly wasn't. Instead, this time around, it was the face of another angry beast, ready to kill! Strangely enough, it was as if Henry had transformed into the very devil, himself!

Sneaking right behind the wolf, Henry grabbed a hold of his two back hindlegs and just like a ragged doll, he threw the wolf high up into the air. As the scared animal fell back down onto the ground, it managed to smash its head against a large stone upon landing and as a result, its skull cracked into several tiny fragmented pieces. Along with a bleeding head, the wolf now desperately tried to escape; but sadly, for its own sake, it was far too late. After previously threatening Kassie's very life, Henry wasn't going to allow risking this animal to ever return back for a second time. Determined to finish his execution once and for all, Henry lifted up a log from off the ground— a log, that must have weighed at least a thousand pounds, if not more. To Kassie's continued amazement, not only could Henry easily lift and carry that heavy weight, but upon carrying it, it appeared as if it was no lighter than a feather held within the palm of his hand. Not wanting to lose not a single moment more, Henry released the log from his grip and within seconds, the heavy weapon fell right above the wolf's head; thereby, killing it and smashing the rest of its bones into a thousand pieces. Alas, the deed was finally done. The wolf was dead and everyone else left standing was now officially safe and sound.

"Henry!" cried Kassie, as she immediately ran over to Henry and threw her arms around him.

However, while Kassie was relieved and joyful to see Henry again, safe and unharmed; the same could not be said on his part, in return. Angered by her reckless behavior, along with her general disregard to his prior warnings, Henry confronted Kassie for her inexcusable actions. Pulling her away from him, he held her tightly within his arms, as he shook her violently with rage.

"Why did you follow me into the forest!" he violently roared, with as much force as he possibly could exert.

Confused by his unwelcomed reaction, Kassie just stared at him in disbelief.

"Again," he repeated loudly, "Why did you follow me, after I specifically asked you not to come!"

"But…" Kassie began; however, she was truly lost for words. For deep down inside, she knew that she was at fault.

"You could have been hurt!" he screamed.

In fact, his voice was so loud and angry that even the other small creatures nearby quickly fled the scene, due to his violent outburst and ongoing rage.

"But I just wanted to help you," she quietly whispered, feeling almost embarrassed and ashamed by her actions.

"Kassie, I don't need your help! I'm an immortal. Even if he tore me into pieces, I'd still survive… but *you… you...* on the other hand... *wouldn't*," he revealed, as his eyes suddenly grew filled with tears.

"Henry… I… I'm sorry," she spoke softly, while looking away from his gaze.

"Sorry? Sorry?" he repeated, in disgust. "Sorry isn't enough! Sorry doesn't bring back the dead! Do you understand me?"

"Henry… I… I..." Kassie stuttered, but really, she didn't know what else to say; for truly, he was right. Although her intentions might have been in good faith; in the end, she inadvertently put both of them in harm's way.

"Don't you ever do that again! Do you hear me!" Henry viciously screamed, as he tightened his grip around her shoulders and began to shake her back and forth.

"Henry… you're... you're *hurting me*," Kassie pleaded, as she attempted to pull herself away from his tight hold on her.

Realizing his own failing actions, Henry released her immediately and thereupon, she fell straight ahead and slammed down onto the dirty ground. Regretting his harsh words and disagreeable conduct, he tried to offer his hand to help her back up. But sadly, she refused it. It seemed that Henry's unwelcoming reaction with her had gone too far and as a consequence of his actions, Kassie wasn't so eager to forgive him so easily, either.

"Kassie…" he began to say, feeling regretful for his unbecoming attitude towards her. Sensing her own anger, Henry tried to readjust his overall mood and behavior; but alas, it was too late. Kassie was just as equally angry with him and for good cause, too.

"I came here tonight to try and help you!" Kassie screamed aloud, in defiance. "I came here tonight to see for myself as to what you do, when I'm not around! If we're to break this curse, then I need to know everything!"

"But I've told you everything already," he added, now speaking as calmly as he possibly could. "If breaking my curse means putting your life at risk, then I don't care about it…"

"Henry, that's not the point! You have no right to be so harsh to me!" she exclaimed.

Suddenly, with tears streaming down her eyes, Kassie cried and said, "Henry… when… when… when… did you become such… such… such… a… *monster!*"

Feeling like a dagger had just been pierced straight through his heart, Henry collapsed down onto the ground, while Kassie ran as far as she possibly could away from him. Looking straight ahead, Henry watched as she ran back up towards the direction of the manor. If he was lucky, she would remain inside of her bedchamber. But what if he was wrong? What if he had pushed her to her limits and now, she wanted nothing more to do with him? What if she finally decided to leave him, instead? This time, for good? Go back to her old life and home in the village? Never to return… never to see her, ever again.

Henry might have prevented losing Kassie to the wolf here tonight; but ironically, he might have very well have lost her still, due to his own behavior. Devastated by this heartbreaking possibility, Henry buried his head above his lap. Out of frustration, he pulled at his hair, as he screamed and cursed aloud. Kassie was right. Henry had gone too far. He had been so incredibly cruel to her and now, she was rightfully upset with him. Although it was never his intention to react so harshly with her, he couldn't help it. Seeing her in danger and so close to the brink of death, sent an unrecognizable rage within his very soul. After discovering the love of his life, Henry was going to be damned, if he'd ever allow that alpha wolf to harm not even a single strand of her hair from her precious head. Yes, Kassie was extremely precious and valuable to him. She meant everything to him and more. Truly, she was his world. His universe. The very reason to his own existence.

Staring down at the ground, Henry saw the deceased alpha wolf that he had recently slaughtered and killed. As a result of their battle, the deceased wolf's pool of blood was splashed everywhere: from the nearby trees to the dirt, to the stones and even his own clothing and boots. While observing its corpse that was now smashed into a thousand tiny pieces, Henry noted that the once powerful and mighty alpha wolf was now nothing more than practically dust. However, as unrecognizable as that dead creature now was in contrast to before its demise; so too, was Henry, ironically. Unfortunately, as much as he tried his best to be a true gentleman in front of Kassie at all times; somehow, he let his guard down and displayed his dark side to her tonight– a side, that he never once wanted to reveal to her. Not ever. Sadly, Kassie was right about him. He was a monster. Having behaved so badly towards her, Henry was fearful that he had simply gone too far and that now, it was quite tragically, almost impossible to undo the damages that he, himself alone, was responsible for.

CHAPTER 17

One Hundred Years Ago…

"Knock, knock. Can I come in?" asked Henry, as he tapped away at the wooden door leading into the kitchen.

"Henry? Is that you?" asked the old woman, who was previously preoccupied by stirring a boiling hot cauldron with her trusted wooden spoon.

"Yes, Maureen. It's me," he replied, with a smile.

"Oh, Henry! It is you!" Maureen happily cried, as she dropped her spoon and ran over to his side to greet him with a warm and joyful embrace.

"It's good to see you, too," replied Henry, as he tried his best to pull himself away from Maureen's tight grip over him. But unfortunately, Henry's efforts failed miserably, for Maureen was most determined to keep him close to her.

"Henry," Maureen began, as she finally released him, "Why didn't you write to me earlier to tell me that you were coming back home tonight?"

"I did write," he replied. "But…"

"But what?" asked Maureen, most curiously.

"Well… I started the letter… but afterwards, I decided that since I'm coming home for business anyways, then I might as well just surprise you in-person, myself," he happily announced.

"Aww, Henry, you, devious boy!" cried Maureen, enthusiastically. "Still that kind and generous spirit from when I first met you all those years ago, as a mere baby in the crib… but now… look at you… you're all grown up! Now, you're a man and a lord, at that!"

"Lord or no lord, I'm still Henry. I'm still the same person, who craves your delicious meals in the comfort of your kitchen. A title doesn't change who I am inside," Henry boldly corrected her.

"Perhaps, but after your father's untimely passing, you're still the new Earl of Galloway," Maureen reminded him.

"Sadly, yes. Although I would have much better preferred to have inherited my new title under very different circumstances. However, unfortunately, that's how our laws operate in this country. One cannot inherit a title, without the untimely passing of another… and so on and so forth," Henry somberly reflected.

"Very true. But most importantly, thank goodness your father kept true to his word and left everything to you, and not to that wicked stepmother and half-brother of yours!" exclaimed Maureen.

"Maureen, she's not wicked…Vera is just misunderstood, that's all," Henry kindly pointed out. Even though Maureen was correct, Vera was an odd one at best; however, Henry still found it inappropriate to disrespect and shame her, without her prior knowledge. After all, she was still his stepmother, in the end.

"Well, if that's what you want to believe, then have at it. However, I, on the other hand, believe otherwise," huffed Maureen, in annoyance.

"Anyways," she continued, "I could care less about Vera and Phillip. Besides, I promised your mother on her death bed that I'd look after you always, as if you were my own son. God bless your dear late mother, too.

Sarah was always good to me, just like you. If it wasn't for her, then I'd never find employment here at Galloway Manor. Oh, Henry, I just wish that you could have known your mother. She was the most beautiful and wonderful woman, both inside and out. Even as a distant cousin of hers, she still treated me like close family. And I know that if she were still alive here today, that she'd be so incredibly proud of you… why you're the child of her dreams! Plus, a university graduate from Oxford… honestly, your mother would have been so proud! So very much so, my dear Henry!"

Suddenly, Maureen burst into tears of joy. Wanting to help console her, Henry reached over and gave her another hug. Although Henry had never had the opportunity to meet his own mother, Maureen was the only real mother that he had ever known. Being a widow with only a grown daughter of her own, who had previously married another gentleman several years ago, Maureen served as his own personal surrogate and adoptive mother, ever since he was a child. While his father, stepmother and half-brother preferred to eat their nightly dinners in the formal dining room, Henry often snuck away to eat his meals in the servants' quarters in the company of Maureen and the other servants. As a result, with all of the time Henry spent hidden away in the kitchen, Maureen taught him how to personally cook several delicious and wholesome dishes with his own two bare hands. Furthermore, as an aristocratic boy at the turn of the nineteenth century, Henry grew up to become a modest and humble man, who treated all of the household servants extremely well with the utmost respect and was much beloved by all who knew him. Having developed an acute sense of smell, due to his acquired culinary skills, Henry could already detect that Maureen was cooking his most favorite dish of all.

"Is that my favorite dish that I smell?" asked Henry, hoping to cheer up Maureen's spirits.

"Ah, yes, my boy, it is," replied Maureen, as she wiped away her tears. "Roasted quail, with eggs. You're favorite."

"Maureen," began Henry, with a devious smile, "Why would you be cooking quail, if you didn't know that I wasn't coming? You never cook quail, only but for special occasions."

"Well…" began Maureen, looking a bit guilty. "Perhaps, I suspected your arrival, after all."

"Then, I suppose you already know as to why I'm here, don't you?" asked Henry, trying his best to gather as much information, as he possibly could from her.

"I suppose, I do," admitted Maureen. "But may I ask, why did you agree to marry that young girl?"

"Her name is Julia," Henry clarified and further added, "Plus, it was father's dying wish that I marry her, as she's the daughter of his best friend. It's only right that I honor my late father's wishes by marrying her. Furthermore, her family's wealth will also help to ensure that we maintain the upkeep to our grand estate. Besides, now that I've inherited Galloway Manor, I might as well take a wife."

"Henry," Maureen spoke softly, as she tried her best to delicately address her own concerns about his new engagement.

"Yes?" he asked, in return.

"Henry, marriage is a very important matter. It's not something that can easily be undone. Once you're married, then you're married for life," said Maureen.

"Yes, Maureen, I know. That's why I intend to go through with my marriage vows to Julia, come tomorrow," replied Henry, as a matter of fact.

"But do you love her?" asked Maureen, as she stared deep into his eyes.

"Love her?" repeated Henry, in confusion. For the first time in his life, the thought of loving one's wife had never crossed his mind before.

"Yes, love? Do you love her? Julia, that is?" asked Maureen, once more.

"Well, I never really thought about that, to be perfectly honest," replied Henry, most earnestly.

"Hmm... I was afraid of that," Maureen remarked.

"What do you mean?" asked Henry.

"Henry, I know that as an aristocrat, such as yourself, not everyone in your society marries for love. Often times, marriage is merely a business arrangement, pertaining to estate planning and procreation. But Henry, you're different. You're special. You're not like the rest of them. You might be the new Earl of Galloway, but you deserve so much more. You deserve to marry someone, whom you love. While you might not understand what love is right now, but I promise you that one day, you will fall madly in love with the right girl, when the time is right," Maureen advised.

"Fall in love with another girl, one day?" asked Henry, with a smile. "Pray tell, who would that lucky girl be? Perhaps, another fiery redhead, like you?"

"Very funny, Henry," replied Maureen. "Besides, I'm probably the only redhead in this part of the whole country. Apart from my daughter, we're the only redheads that's lived in this village for years."

"Well, who's not to say that I can't grow to love Julia, in good time? She might have brown hair, but I'm sure that she can be just as feisty and fun, just like you," Henry suggested.

"Henry, I don't mean to alarm you, but I feel that if you still intend to go through with your upcoming marriage to Julia, then I owe it to you, for your late mother's sake, to tell you something," Maureen finally said.

"To tell me something? Maureen, is it something concerning?" asked Henry, now in a more serious manner.

"There's no delicate way to address this, so I'm just going to have to come clean and say it," Maureen announced. "Henry, as of lately, there's been whispers around the manor by the other servants that your fiancé, Julia, and your half-brother, Phillip, are in love with each other. If you still insist on going through with this marriage, then you will condemn yourself to a miserable union!"

"Julia and Phillip? But… but… how's that even possible?" asked Henry, shocked by this new startling revelation.

"I can't confirm it, nor elaborate any further; but either way, I have no reason to doubt any of my sources. Henry, please don't go through with this marriage, come tomorrow! I'm telling you my dear Henry, that your brother is in love with this girl! Furthermore, as the woman, who personally raised you, I beg of you to please think twice about this impending matter, concerning your proposed marriage to Julia," Maureen pleaded.

"Okay, let's pretend that you're correct," Henry began, "But even, if that's the case, then how can I be so sure? It's not like I can personally ask him or Vera for the truth. Heck, Vera is probably already plotting to kill me to reinstate Phillip in my place, as we speak."

"Just observe them tonight over dinner," Maureen advised. "As for Vera, you keep a safe distance away from her. There's also been rumors circulating that she's the one responsible for your father's untimely death."

As much as Henry wanted to avoid further discussing about his stepmother with Maureen, he also knew that he needed to address the white elephant in the room. Although his father's death was technically classified as an 'accident,' due to his severe injuries sustained from an unfortunate horseback riding accident; Henry did, in fact, also hear whispers abroad that foul play might have inadvertently been secretly played at hand. Based upon the circulating gossip that he personally overheard himself, it was rumored that while his father lay in a coma, he had been poisoned by the hands of his own wife, Vera, in an effort to help accelerate his own impending death. Although his father's death ultimately meant that Galloway Manor would go directly to him, as his heir, and not to Vera or Phillip; Henry also knew, at the back of his mind that he also needed to be more careful, too. Had he not been the first-born son, then Galloway Manor would automatically have gone to his younger half-brother— the preferred son to Vera. While Henry had no ill will towards his stepmother, they never really had any sort of a relationship… well… ever. After marrying his father, Vera kept her distance away from Henry. Apart from seeing her during their occasional dinners together, along with various social gatherings, he rarely saw her afterwards. Furthermore, having spent a good portion of his childhood away attending boarding school and then, later on, at university, Henry seldom ever saw nor interacted with either his stepmother or his half-brother. As far as Henry was concerned, they were complete strangers to him. In fact, Maureen probably knew more about Henry than Vera or Phillip combined. And so, if Maureen didn't trust either one of them, then she probably had a good reason for it.

"Do I take it that's probably the real reason as to why neither Phillip nor Vera, picked me up from the train station this afternoon, isn't it?" asked Henry.

"You came by train?" asked Maureen, most surprised that the train was his mode of transportation. "Why didn't you take a private carriage?"

"What can I say, I wanted to experience traveling by train to see the English countryside, while in the company of others," he replied, with a smile.

"Ah, Henry, you're an adventurous spirit! I'm telling you that you've got to absolutely wait, until you find the right girl, who's your equal match! Julia is too dull and unworthy of you!" exclaimed Maureen.

"We shall see," replied Henry, with a raised brow.

While Henry wasn't going to forfeit his engagement to Julia just yet, he still kept an open mind to observe her around his brother this evening, just as Maureen had suggested. If Maureen's suspicions proved to be correct, then Henry, as a man of honor, was willing to let Julia go and allow his younger brother to claim her as his wife. But for now, Henry was going to sit and observe, then make a final decision later on tonight.

"How long are you planning to stay?" asked Maureen finally, as she was secretly pleased that perhaps her attempts of persuasion had actually worked out in her favor rather successfully.

"Well, as the new Earl of Galloway, I suppose that I'll stay here, indefinitely," he revealed.

"Wonderful!" exclaimed Maureen, happily. "Galloway Manor is in desperate need of new management, after the abuse everyone's been forced to endure under Vera. We are all so incredibly lucky to have you here with us, now."

"Thank you, Maureen," replied Henry, with a smile.

"As I still have more work to do in this kitchen, may I ask what your plans are for the rest of the afternoon?" asked Maureen.

"Plans… well… I suppose that I should probably revisit my old bedchamber, as it's been years since I've last seen it… and then, I believe I have an appointment to have my portrait painted," Henry recalled.

"A painting? Oh, how interesting! An official portrait as the new earl?" asked Maureen, delighted by this new information.

"Yes, an official portrait, as the new Earl of Galloway. Really, I had originally planned on having it done next week. However, the painter was most adamant that he paints me today during this sunny weather; therefore, to humor him, I reluctantly agreed," said Henry.

"Finally, after all these years, your official portrait will hang in the gallery, along with the rest of your ancestors. Your mother, Sarah, would have been so proud," said Maureen, beamingly.

"I suppose," said Henry. "Now, I really must be off."

"Oh wait!" cried Maureen.

"Yes?" asked Henry, as he turned around to look at her, while standing in front of the door.

"Just remember what I said earlier. Keep a close watch on those two," Maureen forewarned.

Keeping true to his word, Henry agreed as he exited the kitchen and walked over into the garden to meet with his new painter. After years of living in what had felt like exile abroad, Henry was finally back home at Galloway Manor. While the future still seemed uncertain; but at least for now, one thing remained certain: come tonight, Henry's portrait as the new Earl of Galloway would join the rest of his ancestors to remain forever memorialized, along the walls of his ancestral estate.

CHAPTER 18

Just as Maureen had previously advised him earlier in the day, Henry sat and silently observed his relatives over dinner. As the new head of the family, Henry quietly ate his meal at the front, as he studied each one of his distinctive family members seated at his table. As expected, Vera, his stepmother, remained silent and emotionless, just as she had always been, ever since Henry had known her. Why, she hadn't even uttered not a single word, since his return to Galloway Manor, let alone a kind greeting nor a welcoming embrace. However, Henry anticipated as much… or better yet, that little of her. But sadly, while he predicted almost nothing from Vera; in contrast, he expected so much more from his younger half-brother, Phillip.

While they might not have been full brothers in blood, Henry still regarded Phillip as his darling younger brother, regardless of who their mothers were. Given the fact that both he and Phillip were primarily brought up in separate boarding schools, Henry still hoped that they could grow to become closer in their adulthoods. Possibly, even friends. Even though Henry wrote several letters to Phillip over the years, he never once received a reply back from him. Although most men in his position would have long given up on Phillip, Henry still held out hope that eventually in due time, his younger brother would change his ways and come to accept him as his older brother not only in name, but in his brotherly affection, as well.

Although Henry and Phillip were only four years apart, they were still so very much different from one another. While Henry was charismatic, outgoing and social; Phillip was quiet, reserved and an outcast— much like his own mother, Vera. Furthermore, while Phillip had resembled their father so little; Henry, in contrast, was the spitting image of their father, from head to toe. Ah, yes, Henry resembled their father, only too well. Not only did Henry have their father's dashing good looks, wealth, title and estate; but apart from their shared family's name, Phillip had nothing else to show for it. Was Phillip jealous of his elder brother? That was very much possible. For Henry had everything, while he had nothing… all except for his brother's fiancé, Julia.

Was Phillip in love with Julia? Was she in love with him? Was it an innocent and playful romantic relationship, based only upon flirtatious glances shared amongst one another? Or was it a steamy and physical relationship, that transformed them from mere household acquaintances into secret and passionate lovers? After all, they had both lived together under the same roof for quite some time. While Henry was busy away traveling abroad, Julia previously moved into Galloway Manor some months ago. Upon writing his letter agreeing to marry her to her father, Julia was immediately sent away from her childhood home and relocated into Galloway Manor, as a new resident of the estate. Although they had only met each once before as teenagers, Henry vaguely recalled that she had chestnut brown hair, along with a plain yet sweet and innocent face. However, Henry was not a vain man and beauty had little to do with his ultimate decision to marry her; for his decision to wed her was solely due to his late father's dying wishes and nothing more. However, if Henry felt that his brother did in fact, care for Julia and that she cared for him, in return; then out of the love and affection that he held for Phillip, Henry was willing to sacrifice his happiness, for the happiness of his younger brother. Perhaps, this way, he'd finally earn the lifelong respect and admiration from the brother; whom, after all, was the only immediate blood relation that he still had left in this entire world.

After attending university for a few years, serving in the military, fighting wars on foreign lands and then, traveling some more and spending extra time abroad, Henry had already spent most of his adult life living outside of Galloway Manor. Already a man of thirty years in age, Henry spent more years wandering the European and Asian continents than his own backyard. But now, alas, he was finally home and the time had come for him to get back into his family's business. As the new head of the Galloway clan, Henry needed to care and supervise after the affairs of his stepmother and younger half-brother. Furthermore, although Henry had previously announced his intentions to marry Julia come tomorrow morning; tonight, Henry would ultimately make his final decision about their impending futures.

Watching her from across the table, Henry noted that Julia seemed rather tense and nervous. While sipping her soup with a silver spoon, her hands appeared jittery. Furthermore, her face and eyes remained tilted downwards, never once seizing the opportunity to look up and acknowledge him, nor to strike a friendly conversation with the man, whom she was supposedly promised to marry. Overall, Julia seemed flushed in color and Henry could even swear that a small teardrop appeared to have fallen, straight from her very own eye. My God, was she actually crying?

Suddenly, Henry heard a cough. Ironically, this was the first sounds that he had actually heard all evening. Unfortunately, their dinner was so quiet and uneventful, that even the mere drop of a spoon falling down onto the floor, sounded much more exciting and interesting than anything else happening over dinner. Quickly reverting his attention over to his brother, Henry observed Phillip coughing profusely, as he desperately gasped for air. Dear God, was he actually choking?

Promptly rising up from his chair, Henry was about to make his way over to Phillip, when lo and behold, Julia beat him right to the punch. Without saying another word, Julia rushed over to Phillip's side and in one swift move, she reached over from behind his back and carefully wrapped her arms around him. Pushing against his stomach from behind, Julia beat down across his belly, as Phillip eagerly fought for his very dear breath of life. Thrusting back and forth, Julia moved Phillip up and down like a ragged doll, until finally Phillip spit out an object, right from out of his own mouth. Staring at the disregarded item, Henry saw a tiny piece of a quail bone laying above the table. Covered in saliva, Henry realized that Phillip had mistakenly swallowed on one of the quail bones. Had Julia not acted so quickly and as effectively as she did, then Phillip would have most certainly died right there on the spot, before their desserts were served.

"Phillip, are you alright?" cried Julia, as she desperately clung onto him for dear life.

"Yes… I'm alright…" replied Phillip, as he tried his best to recollect himself.

Feeling a bit embarrassed about the entire ordeal, Phillip promptly excused himself from the table and exited the room. Following in his footsteps, Julia also soon excused herself from dinner, with the excuse of feeling a bit flushed over her part in his rescue efforts. With his fiancé and brother now gone, Henry found himself alone at the table with Vera. Surprisingly, even with her own son so close to the brick of death, Vera, remarkably, appeared unaffected by the entire situation. Whether her son lived or died, it didn't really seem to matter to her.

But apart from Vera, Henry still remained in the dark about the true relationship between Julia and Phillip. While Julia did seem a bit distressed tonight, was it possible that it was simply due to her own nervousness about being a new bride? Was it even remotely possible that perhaps, she was distressed, because come tomorrow, she was going to marry him? Once and for all? But weren't most brides supposed to be happy? Blissfully joyful? Was this sort of bridal behavior even normal to begin with? Or was her cold reaction the very proof that he needed, in order to prove that she loved his brother, instead?

After all, it was Julia who came running to Phillip's rescue and no one else. But did she do that purely from the kindness of her own heart? Did she eagerly rush over to save Phillip, solely due to her humanly compassion for another being? Or, did she rush over to help Phillip, because she secretly loved him? After all, Henry did catch her crying at one point over dinner, did he not? But were those tears meant for Phillip to signify her undying love and devotion to him? Or were her tears directed towards Henry, at the groom, whom she secretly wished not to marry, come tomorrow? Sadly, unlike before, Henry now faced more questions than answers!

Determined to clear his mind, Henry excused himself from the table and at last minute, he decided to visit his favorite horse, Midnight, at his private horse stable. As one of his most favorite pastimes, Henry found horseback riding to be his primary outlet to alleviate his stress and to put his mind at ease. Only through horseback, could Henry plunge himself straight into nature, while abandoning all of his other worldly woes behind. Furthermore, night riding was by far, his most ideal and favorite time to ride, best of all. While riding at day was still a wonderous event, the night was far more thrilling. It was there, during the dark night, where Henry found himself in complete solitude with just him, his horse, the forest and nothing else more. And after traveling most of the world during his adolescence years, riding one with nature as an adult felt like had he indeed, returned back home.

And so, Henry quickly hurried over to his horse stable to ride Midnight, before he eventually, retired off to bed. With most of the servants gone for the rest of the evening, Henry was looking forward to being all alone. Perhaps, in solitude, he would be able to clear his mind and then, make a sound decision about his future. However, as soon as Henry approached the front door leading into the horse stable, he overheard distant sounds and chatter spoken from afar. Pushing the door, ever so slightly, Henry peeked through the crack and to his sheer surprise, he saw his brother and fiancé engaged in what seemed to be a private conversation.

"But you don't love him!" exclaimed Phillip, angrily. "You never have! Now, you need to tell him the truth, before it's too late!"

"It's not that easy Phillip!" Julia yelled, in return. "I promised my father that I'd marry him and now, if I break my word, my father will never accept me back home. I have no other choice…"

"But we must do something! It isn't fair! Henry has everything… the title… the money… the estate… everything. He has everything, but he can't have *you*, too! No, I won't allow it! You're mine… *all mine*!" Phillip passionately yelled!

"We must do something Phillip," Julia pleaded. "I don't want to marry him… I want to be with… *you*."

"Well, if you can't tell him, then we'll have to run away, tonight. Yes, that's it! We'll run away up north to Scotland and get married! There are no formal rules about matrimony up there, so we can freely marry, without our relatives' consents. If we leave now, then we can actually do it!" exclaimed Phillip, happily.

"Do you really mean it, Phillip? Can we really run away together?" asked a hopeful Julia.

"Julia," began Phillip, as he reached over and held her hands within his.

"Tonight, if it hadn't been for you, then I was surely going to meet face-to-face with death. Julia, you're my angel. We belong together. I can't simply stand around, do nothing and allow you to marry him. Julia, we've got one life to live, and I intend to spend the rest of my life with you, even if that means that I must work every day of hard labor for the rest of our lives, in order to support you."

Suddenly, Phillip and Julia embraced and locked lips together in a passionate kiss. Afterwards, she pulled herself away and said, "Alright, Phillip, I agree. I will marry you!"

Upon agreeing to his proposal, Phillip scooped Julia up within his arms and escorted her over to one of the smaller horses in the stable. Once comfortably seated above on their horse, Phillip tapped his whip and instantly, the two lovers rode out of the back exit and just like that, they were gone.

A few moments later, Henry finally walked into the horse stable and made his way over to his horse, Midnight. After hours of contemplation, Henry finally had his answer. While most men in his circumstance would have been heartbroken, Henry surprisingly wasn't. In fact, he was quite relieved actually. In truth, he had only agreed to marry Julia in the first place, due to his father's last dying wish and nothing more. Furthermore, had he known ahead of time that Phillip loved Julia and that she also loved him too, in return; then it was ultimately, going to be an awkward conversation between them as to how to formally and most appropriately, end their engagement. After all, refusing marriage to Julia would be the ultimate slap in the face to her father. At least this way, Phillip and Julia saved Henry that heartache. Perhaps, Maureen was right, after all. Maybe, Henry hadn't yet met his match. The love of his life. Maybe, just maybe, he was meant to wait to meet the right woman, one day, later on in the future. Perhaps, his future bride was going to be a fiery redhead, just as he had always secretly wished for her to be.

158

CHAPTER 19

After exiting the horse stable with Midnight, Henry decided to visit the final resting place of his late mother, Sarah. Although Sarah died in childbirth shortly after his birth, Henry still felt an everlasting connection and attachment to her, even from beyond the grave. Ever since he was a young boy, Maureen frequently brought him to visit his late mother's grave. Over the years, he, along with Maureen, planted several seeds of violets over her plot of land, which was located right in the heart of the forest. Since violets were Sarah's favorite flower above all else, Henry and Maureen made it their own personal mission to ensure that Sarah's grave would one day flourish and blossom into an endless field of purple violets.

Unfortunately, upon his father's marriage to Vera, his stepmother's ongoing resentment over his late mother, even in her death, was unfathomable and unforgiveable. Consumed by her envious jealousy over her husband's first wife, Vera used her powers of persuasion to convince Henry's father to commit the most barbaric and brutish of acts: removing Sarah's tombstone and thus, leaving her grave nameless. Wanting to appease to his new wife's desires, Henry's father reluctantly agreed to Vera's wicked request. Furthermore, as cruel as this unmentionable and unholy act truly was towards the legacy of his late mother, Henry understood very clearly at an early age that his stepmother was ultimately, desperately trying to erase the memory, as well as the history of his dear late mother, Sarah. But as terrible and as horrific as this deed was, even under a nameless grave,

Sarah's violets, ironically, still found a way to grow and flourished, even in the most unfortunate of circumstances. Surprisingly, that spring, the violets came to blossom into the most stunningly beautiful and breathtaking flower bed, that neither Henry nor Maureen had ever imagined or hoped them to be. Amazingly enough, it was as if, even from the very pits of her own grave, Sarah still found a way to claim her revenge in the form of her blooming violets. Eventually, in due time, her own nameless grave and plot of land, transformed into an enchanting field of wild purple violets that consumed the very heart of the forest, which rested along the paths leading up into Galloway Manor.

Although his mother's grave remained nameless over the years, Henry could still locate her final resting place even from afar, purely by following her trail of violets. Strangely enough, his mother's violets never grew any further beyond her plot of land to spread into any other reaches of the forest. Furthermore, due to this strange occurrence, Henry could always find his mother's grave, even in the darkest of nights, simply by following the majestic trail.

Throughout the years, Henry, as her only son, continued to pay respect to his late mother by frequently visiting her grave, whenever he was at home. Even in his most desperate of hours, Henry still took the time to visit his mother, in order to seek her guidance spiritually, from beyond this earthly domain. From discussing about his innocent childhood woes to venting about his teenage-self's internal struggles as he grew into adulthood, Henry spoke to his mother about anything and everything his heart clung onto, as if she were still alive with him and only merely sleeping in her grave. Although, naturally, Henry never got a spoken reply back from the dead; but still, somehow, he silently knew internally as to which actions he needed to take. Whenever he confessed about his problems aloud to his mother in her grave, Henry could always sense from within his own heart, as to the solutions to any one of his pending problems. Somehow, by visiting Sarah's final resting place, whenever Henry closed his eyes to concentrate and meditate about his issue, he always magically encountered a sign and soon afterwards, discovered an answer to his struggles. Whether it was the wind blowing across his face, or the sounds of a fallen tree log from afar, Henry could just sense as to which direction he needed to take, towards solving his woes. While being alone and so in tuned to nature,

Henry quietly listened on, as the forest and his mother's spirit guided him down his journey onto the righteous path and ultimately, leading him towards his own destiny.

Having lost his father and now, his fiancé and brother, Henry thought that tonight, out of all nights, was the night, in which he so desperately needed to gain any sort of helpful guidance from his dear late mother. Therefore, Henry rode Midnight out of the stable and traveled deep into the forest to visit his mother's final resting place, late into the night. Passing by all of the ancient oak trees along the way, which were thousands of years old, Henry entered into the forest from the far reaches of Galloway Manor's back garden. Once he arrived towards the foot of his mother's field of violets, Henry got down from off his horse and then, he securely tied Midnight to a sturdy tree, located nearby. Afterwards, Henry slowly approached his mother's grave, until he finally came to the end of the field, in which the violets ceased to grow any further. Here, at this very spot, was where his mother's tombstone once stood, prior to Vera's interference.

"Hello Mother," Henry announced, as he greeted his dear late mother, Sarah.

Kneeling down above the dirty ground, he touched one of her violets and whispered aloud, "Mother, I feel so incredibly lost, right now. I've returned back to Galloway Manor, our ancestral home; but this time, without Father. Sadly, now, with both you and Father gone; I'm not entirely certain, as to what I should or shouldn't be doing. As the new Earl of Galloway, I want to make you and Father proud of me. I want to make Galloway Manor as prestigious and as glorious as possible, for the sake of our family's and village's honors. I want to treat all of our household servants with the same dignity and respect, that you and Father had previously bestowed upon them all. Had you still been alive, Mother, then I would hope that I'd be the sort of son who makes you proud. Even after being so far away from home all these years, I still agreed to marry Julia, just so that I'd make Father proud; but sadly, this will never come to be. Given that Julia and Phillip are probably halfway up to the Scottish border by now, I will never fulfill that wish to Father. But regardless, I still want to make both of you proud of me; even in death. Oh, if only you were both still alive today! Maybe, then, you could actually tell me on what I shall do with the rest of my life! Mother, please, I beg of you, please send me a sign… any sign, at all. I just need a sign to know that you can still hear me, and that I'm still on the righteous path for my life…"

Suddenly, a darkness emerged and quickly consumed the entire forest. Blinded by this newfound darkness, Henry lost his balance and fell straight down onto the dirt. Struggling to regain his posture, he tried his best to touch and feel his nearby surroundings, in order to find an object to help pull himself back up. However, while still on the ground, Henry started to feel some strange and foreign objects suddenly catch hold of his legs and arms, pulling him back further down onto the ground. After fighting and resisting this unknown and malignant force, Henry screamed, as he desperately struggled to wiggle himself off from this strange gravitational pull. Meanwhile, Henry could also hear Midnight neighing and wrestling with something concerning, as well. Whatever it was, Henry and Midnight were being overpowered by an ominous force, clearly determined to destroy them. While Henry was still blinded by the darkness, he silently listened on as he heard the sounds of various trees and branches fall straight down onto the ground, one by one. As mysterious and unexplainable as all of this really was, Henry felt almost trapped; as if the entire forest, itself, was closing in around him and Midnight. It was suffocating. While Henry no longer had free access to anyone of his limbs, a long strand of ivy emerged and slowly made its move around his neck. Gradually, the vine of ivy targeted and moved to encircle his neck and for every rotation around him, the ivy was pressing ever so harshly against his skin. Within mere seconds, Henry was practically choking and was so-close to the brink of death. And then, suddenly, out from nowhere, a bright and shiny image finally appeared.

"At last, you've finally got, what's been coming to you!" laughed the ominous and evil looking figure.

After staring at the darkness for so long, Henry's eyes struggled to adjust to this new blinding light, as he tried his best to decipher the strange creature standing right before him. After a brief minute, Henry's eyes readjusted and as he looked straight ahead, he saw what appeared to be an ugly witch, standing and laughing ahead.

Dressed in a black robe, the witch's ugly face was filled with several warts and fungus, growing along her nose and cheeks. Furthermore, her skin was as green as the trees grown within this very forest; while her eyes were as yellow as the moon. Meanwhile, her deformed teeth were more fang liked than teeth normally found in humans; and those fangs had overpowered her own mouth and thereby, dangled straight from out of her very lips. Additionally, her hair was long, grey and knotted; and she smelled the most horrific and foul odor, which was comparable to a bad case of molded cheese or spoiled milk. By far, the witch was the ugliest creature that Henry had ever encountered or looked upon before. However, apart from her hideous appearance, her manners and personality appeared to be far worse.

"After all these years, I've finally got you!" the witch laughed on.

"After all these years?" repeated Henry, in confusion. "What do you mean? What are you talking about? Who are you?"

"Who am I? Who am I? Why, don't you know?" asked the witch mockingly, in return; as she continued to laugh hysterically aloud.

"Of course, I don't know, who you are! Now, as the earl of these lands, I demand that you tell me at once, as to who you are!" screamed Henry, as he continued to fight off the ivy that surrounded his whole neck and body.

"Why, Henry, don't you recognize your own stepmother? Why, it's me, Vera," she proudly announced, with a smile.

"Vera? But, how? Why?" asked Henry, stunned by this new startling revelation.

"After all these years parading as a human, this is my true form! Behold, I, Vera, am a witch! And, as I might add, one of the most powerful witches of all time!" she revealed.

"I… I… I don't understand…" uttered Henry, feeling stunned and confused.

"There's nothing to understand. I'm a witch and now, I've come to finish you, so that I can claim your inheritance, all for myself!" exclaimed Vera, as she laughed away.

"But why…. why kill me?" asked Henry, as he desperately tried to gasp for air.

"I'm just doing what needs to be done. After all, it was *I*, who *killed* your father. A horseback riding accident… ha! No, it certainly wasn't. Not on my watch. No, your father died the same exact way, in which you shall die here, tonight!" exclaimed Vera.

"What… you killed my father? But how? Why?" asked Henry, as he continued to fight and defend his body against the evil forces that were trying to consume him.

"The world might have thought it was a horseback riding accident, but it wasn't. Your father also suffocated in a similar fashion, by the very same vines that consumes you here right now, as we speak. Unfortunately, he survived… and so, I made sure that he drank the correct poison, as he lay in his coma. But this time, I intend not to make the same mistake! Tonight, you will die at the hands of this forest, as part of my curse against you!" exclaimed Vera, as she laughed on.

"But if I'm gone, then Phillip inherits my estate. Galloway Manor will go to him, not you!" Henry screamed, in anger.

"No, Henry, I'm afraid not. With Phillip and Julia eloping, I highly doubt that either one of them, will ever show themselves back in polite society, ever again! No, Henry, you might as well count them as good as gone! It's just me, who's left. And now, with both my stepson and son completely out of the entire picture, it is I, and I alone, who will inherit Galloway Manor and no one else!" Vera yelled.

"But why… why do you even care about Galloway Manor, so much? If you let me go, then I promise, I can give you whatever money that you want, in order to purchase new land in exchange for my life," Henry pleaded.

"You don't get it, do you Henry? I don't want other lands! I specifically want Galloway Manor and this forest! You fool, don't you know that there are special elements and properties, which grows spontaneous in these lands? Why, even my own dark powers have never been more powerful, than ever before! No, Henry, there is magic in this land and I intend to harbor them, all for myself!" vowed Vera.

"But how can you be sure that Phillip won't return back to avenge my death? After all, I am his brother!" Henry pointed out.

"Half-brother," Vera made it a point to publicly highlight. "Either way, he's *my* son, before being a half-brother to you. Besides, he hates you. Always has and always will. I've made certain of that; just as I made certain that he fell in love with your little fiancé, too."

"Fell in love with my fiancé? Whatever, do you mean? How can you make someone fall in love with another?" asked Henry.

"Sadly, Henry, you do have a valid point. Even I alone, being a powerful and maleficent witch, cannot force two people... two separate souls to fall in love with each other. No one can. After all, love is free will. It's mightier than even the most powerful of curses. That, along with enduring belief. However, the influence of persuasion can be just as equally a powerful and sinister force, that can also be used to combat true love," Vera revealed. She continued, "In your case, during your absence, I just needed to make sure that Phillip constantly found himself alone in Julia's company. As his mother, I simply made it my business to secretly set them up on various accidental romantic settings; thereby, giving them their privacy and most importantly, the opportunity for them to ultimately, give into their temptations and mutual desires, out of their own free wills. The rest is history. Now, at long last, with both he and you out of the way, I can finally take claim over these lands, all to myself!"

"I will defeat you!" vowed Henry, as he continued to struggle and fight against the elements of the dominating and violent forest.

"Henry, it's too late! My curse has already been enacted! The deed is done. Come tonight, you will die, just like your father before you. Now, Henry, surrender your ambitious desires and come to accept your fate!" Vera laughed, as she suddenly disappeared into the darkness, leaving Henry and Midnight behind alone to fend for themselves.

Meanwhile, as Henry struggled to fight back as hard as he could, his strength was starting to grow weak. In a matter of minutes, the forest was going to completely consume him. Eventually, Henry was going to die here tonight, along with Midnight. Sadly, if he was amongst the lucky, then someone would soon discover their rotting bodies, come tomorrow morning. Realizing that he was indeed dying and right above his own mother's grave, too, at that; a tear suddenly streamed down across his face. As his tear fell and dropped below onto the ground, it managed to land on top of one of his mother's violets, nearby.

"Oh, Mother, please help me! Give me strength to survive this!" he cried aloud.

Feeling helpless and useless, Henry was all but ready to finally accept defeat and to surrender himself over to the custody of the forest, that was currently seeking to consume him, both body and soul. However, all hope was not lost; for a miracle was about to happen. Just like all of the other signs from his past, Henry's mother remained an avid and keen listener to his looming problem, even while resting in her grave. Suddenly, the darkness that had previously dominated the entire forest, was now, miraculously covered in a bright, shiny and white colored light.

Lifting up his head to look at this new figure standing before him, Henry gasped, "Mother?"

CHAPTER 20

Mother? Is that really you?" asked Henry, in amazement.

"Yes, it's me. But my darling, I don't have much time," she said, as she waved her hands up into the air.

Immediately, upon his mother's command, the numerous plants and vines that surrounded Henry, all ceased their hold over him. With the light illuminating from Sarah's aura, everything that previously held Henry hostage, were all forced to release their tight grip on the young man. After much persistence, Henry and Midnight were finally released from their captors.

Falling straight down onto the dirt ground, Henry lifted his head back up to face his mother. Although he had never actually previously met her before, Henry recognized her face from one of her portraits that hung above the walls at Galloway Manor. With her rosy colored cheeks, long blonde hair and emerald green colored eyes— the very same unique shade of green that matched his own— Henry recognized that the angel standing before him, dressed in all white and illuminated by a bright heavenly light, was none other than his own late mother, Sarah.

"Mother," he cried, once more.

"Henry," Sarah replied, with a bright smile that warmed his heart. "My darling son, don't worry. I promise, I will help you."

"Am I already... *dead?*" asked Henry.

After his struggle and fight with the forest, Henry wasn't entirely certain as to whether or not he survived this entire ordeal.... or if he had... well... died. Furthermore, if he did in fact die, then perhaps, this was heaven; for if he was in heaven, then naturally, it would only make sense that the first person to greet him in the afterlife was his own mother.

"Henry," she began softly, "No, you're not dead."

"But Mother, if I'm not dead, then... how... how... are you here? How are you able to save me?" he asked in confusion.

"I heard your pleas all the way up from heaven, my sweet child," she revealed. "But I don't have much time. Now, I fear that I must forewarn you, as to what will happen next."

"Mother... I..." Henry began; but alas, he was already lost for words.

"Henry, it's better that I speak, first. Please just listen to me, very carefully," said Sarah.

"Now," she continued, "Henry, I might have saved you from the clutches of death, but I'm afraid that I, myself, cannot undue what's already been done. Unfortunately, Vera is a very powerful witch, and I'm afraid that her curse is far too powerful to easily undue. Given that Vera is a practitioner of dark magic, she's already made a deal with the elemental forces of nature to claim ownership over your very life. Although I tried my best to reason and negotiate with the forest; I, alone, cannot terminate the deal that they made with her. While the forest has agreed not to claim your life, a debt is still owed to them."

"When you say 'them,' whom are you referring to? Who owns the forest?" asked Henry.

"No one," Sarah revealed. "Not one single being owns the forest, it's owned by all. From the trees to the river, to the sky and the leaves, to the plants and the flowers, nature owns nature. It's all part of the circle of life. This forest operates on universal elements, such as earth, fire, water and air. These are all critical elements, which dictates your world. Given that Vera is a witch, she must bargain with these elemental forces of nature, in order to use them in her magic… just like the curse that she's recently enacted on you here, tonight."

"Mother, what does it all mean?" asked Henry.

"It means, that while your life has been spared; you, unfortunately, are now a creature of the very forest that saved you. From here on out, you will never die, nor age another day. You will forever remain as you are; never to grow old, nor to perish. Furthermore, your humanly attributes will no longer dwell upon you; for you will never again, crave the taste of food, thirst for water or desire sleep. You will forever be trapped in time, never to leave these lands and existing forever more as an immortal," said Sarah, as she tragically revealed this life altering message over to her son, with a heavy heart.

"Never to venture outside of these lands? Do you mean that I'm cursed to live here, for all of eternity?" asked Henry, as he tried his best to hide his growing tears from his mother.

"Yes," whispered Sarah, softly.

"Then, you should have left me to die! At least in death, I had an opportunity to escape! A chance to reunite with you and Father, back in heaven! If I can't live my life with complete freedom, then what's the point of eternity? Death would have been a far better end! Had I but known this sad and bitter truth, then I would have greeted death most welcomely!" he boldly exclaimed.

"Henry, please don't despair. All hope is not yet lost," said Sarah, in an effort to comfort her son.

"What do you mean, that all hope isn't lost?" asked Henry, with a new sense of longing within his voice.

"While you might be cursed to remain as you are, all curses do have a cure… including yours," said Sarah.

"A cure? What is it, then?" asked Henry, most eagerly.

"Sadly, that's as far, as I know. While I might not be enlightened as to the intricate details surrounding your cure; I do, for one, know, without a shadow of a doubt, that all curses have a cure. However, the only person in this world who knows for certain as to how to undue your curse, is, unfortunately, the very person who placed the curse upon you, in the first place," explained Sarah.

"You mean…Vera? Mother, if that's the case, then it's hopeless! She killed my father, pushed Phillip and Julia to run away together and now, recently attempted to kill me out here, tonight! No, Mother, I cannot reason with her. Vera is a wicked witch who's determined to steal my inheritance. Why, she's done everything in her power to even erase you, by removing your very own tombstone! No, Mother, if my fate lies in the hands of Vera, then I'm as good as gone! I might as well accept my fate by living the rest of my existence here on earth, due to this an unbreakable curse!" exclaimed Henry, angrily.

"My son, please don't give into your desire for hate and revenge, so easily. While it might be difficult to believe me at first, but in time, you must try to convince Vera to reveal her cure to you; for she's the only person who can. Please don't act too hastily; otherwise, you might live to regret your actions. Remember Henry, don't act on impulse. Your curse cannot be broken, unless you find your answers to a cure through Vera," Sarah forewarned.

Suddenly, in a flash of light, Sarah disappeared into thin air, leaving Henry behind, alone in the forest with nothing more than endless time and his own thoughts. For one whole month, Henry remained secretly hidden away in the forest, with only Midnight by his side. Trying his best to follow his mother's advice, Henry desperately pondered about the correct course of action to take, regarding his hopeless situation. After all, Henry was justified in his quest for revenge. Not only did Vera murder his father, but she also alienated him from his brother, Phillip. Furthermore, she convinced Phillip to seduce his fiancé and then, helped them to disgrace not only themselves but of their families' honors as well by running away to Scotland. Furthermore, Vera was already a tyrant, who terrified and abused the servants at Galloway Manor, during Henry's absence abroad. Not only had Vera stolen his entire family away, but she also made it her business to steal his life, too. No, Vera had gone way too far! This time, it wasn't just about removing his late mother's tombstone, it was an attempt to terminate his very own existence!

But was killing Vera the right approach? After all, his mother forewarned him not to seek revenge, for a cure was still possible. However, if he gave into his quest for vengeance and pursued his desire to kill Vera— the one woman who knew the truth about undoing her own spell— then he'd be lost in this form forever. While Henry remained hopeful for a cure, he also wasn't a fool. Hell would have to turn over, before Vera was ever going to reveal the cure to him; for that would require her to develop a heart and as it currently stood, Vera was incapable of love nor compassion. No, unlike his own mother, Vera was absolutely heartless. Oh, what a fool his father had been to have married her in the first place, all those many years ago!

While Henry could spend the rest of eternity hiding inside of this forest and away from his ancestral home; in the end, was it really worth it? Was it worth sparing Vera's life, in the hopes of her having a miraculous change of heart? After much reflection, Henry realized that no, it wasn't worth it at all. Ultimately, he was convinced that no matter how much he tried, he could never convince Vera to help him. As it stood, his hopes for a cure were as good as gone. Alas, he finally accepted his doomful fate! The curse had been cast and the damage was already done. From now to all eternity, Henry was going to wander through this enchanted forest, as a phantom or better yet, as a ghost. If Henry failed to take action now, then Galloway Manor would be lost to him forever. Determined to prevent Vera from proclaiming her rights over his ancestral home, Henry was now more than ever, convinced that he had to do everything in his power to stop her. If he was damned already, then he might as well be damned inside the comfort of his own home! And so, Henry grabbed his dagger, hopped aboard Midnight and rode off into the night, heading straight for home!

CHAPTER 21

After one long month, Henry finally arrived at the front doors of Galloway Manor. Although his mother had warned against it, Henry knew what he needed to do next. There was no turning back, at this point. He needed to stop Vera and reinsert himself, as the legitimate head of his ancestral home. Come tonight, he was going to return to the comfort of his own bed, rather than spending another forsaken night wandering aimlessly outside in the chilly forest! And so, Henry reached over and with his bare fist, he violently pounded against the wooden doors with all his might.

Almost immediately, the front doors were opened by a servant, who was surprised to see him standing out there. Had they already presumed that he was long gone and dead? After all, Henry had been missing for over a month. Determined not to waste not a single moment longer, he demanded to know as to where Vera was at this very precise second.

"She's in the dining room eating supper," revealed the terrified doorman, who appeared so frightened that it was almost as if he had just seen a real-life ghost.

Delighted by this revelation, Henry stomped his way over into the dining room. Upon entering the room, he saw her there, now seated at the head of the table in his old chair, eating away at her supper. Disgusted by her resumed humanly appearance and lack of remorse, he quickly rushed over to her side of the table and before she even had a chance to react, he plunged his dagger straight through her heart. Shocked by his swift actions, Vera stared at him in horror… but then, she unexpectedly laughed at him, in a rather sinister way.

"I… I… I… always knew… that you were a… *monster*," she whispered aloud with a smile; and then, she further added, with the last ounce of her breath, "And now… it's too late to undue it… take pleasure in being a *monster*… for the rest of *eternity*…"

Seconds later, Vera was dead. While Henry might have been successful on achieving his revenge; but for some odd reason, now that the deed was finally done, he didn't feel so entirely satisfied. In fact, he felt rather… well… *nothing*. It was as if, his own heart had grown sour overnight, and he was no longer affected by anything, anymore. By killing Vera, he had practically sold his soul over to the dark forces, empowering his own curse. However, before Henry could reflect any further, Maureen soon entered the room and saw the bloody scene. Although Vera had been a much hated and despised woman, Maureen still never expected her to die at the hands of Henry, of all people. However, at the same time, Maureen was also relieved to see the young man, whom she had personally raised since childhood, return back to Galloway Manor, alive and well. Therefore, without any questions nor judgment, Maureen rushed over to Henry's side and threw her arms around him. Afterwards, Henry sat Maureen down at the table and he calmly confessed everything that had transpired over this past month to her.

"A curse that cannot be unbroken?" asked Maureen, with grave concern.

"Yes, and now, with Vera gone, I'm afraid it's too late for me," Henry somberly reflected.

"It's never too late, Henry. As God as my witness, we're going to find a cure for you, even if I must dedicate the remainder of my life to help you," Maureen vowed.

"Maureen, I appreciate your concern, but what can we honestly do? You're not a witch, or a wizard… we're both just average beings," said Henry.

"That might be so, but I still refuse to accept this. One way or another, I'm going to save you from this curse. I didn't promise your mother all those years ago to look after you, only to abandon you right now, in your greatest time of need. No, we will find a way! Even if I need to help you from beyond my own grave," spoke Maureen, passionately.

"Maureen, I saw her there… I saw my mother," Henry revealed.

"You saw Sarah?" asked Maureen, amazed by Henry's admission to her.

"Yes, and she looked just like her portrait, too. That's how I was able to recognize her out there, in the woods," he said.

"My God, Henry, if your mother was able to visit you, as an angel to save you from the brinks of death, then there has to be a cure to undue this spell! But pray tell me, previously you mentioned that Vera said something about the power of love, while she cursed you. What was that all about?" asked Maureen, as she listened on with keen ears.

"Actually, it was about Phillip and Julia, and nothing about my curse, for say. From what I can vaguely recollect, she mentioned that she couldn't force two people to fall in love with each other, and that somehow, love is based on free will. I suppose even her wicked powers cannot carry over to everything, including love. Furthermore, she also uttered that love can withstand, even the most powerful of curses; that, along with the power of enduring belief," Henry reflected.

"That's it! Love must be the cure! Henry, we still have a fighting chance to save you!" exclaimed Maureen, as a new glimmer of hope shined across her cheerful face.

"Maureen, please don't get your hopes up, just yet. Love is the least of my concerns, right now. Besides, who's ever going to fall in love with me? Even in my pre-cursed self, Julia didn't love me and I was her fiancé. Honestly, who's going to love the latest monster, now lurking inside the dark corners of this forest?" asked Henry, now feeling rather hopeless.

"You're not a monster, Henry," said Maureen, in an effort to comfort him. "Besides, Vera was the *real* monster, *not you*."

"But it doesn't matter, I might as well be. After all, I'm cursed," Henry pointed out.

Staring at Henry's latest portrait that now hung above the walls at Galloway Manor, Maureen admired the handsome young horseman in the picture that she helped to bring up. While the portrait was ironically painted the same morning as his accident, Maureen still saw the same Henry that she had always loved, looking back at her from the painting. Determined not to give up on her hopes of rescuing this same young man from the portrait, Maureen vowed to never forfeit her attempts to save him from a hopeless fate.

"I will help you, that much I promise you, Henry," said Maureen, with all her heart.

"I appreciate your concerns Maureen," replied Henry wryly.

Noticing that Maureen was also staring at his recent portrait, Henry further added, "But Maureen, the young man that you once knew in that painting is no longer here. You might as well consider me dead and gone; for I'll never be that same Henry, ever again."

"No, Henry, you're still you," Maureen reminded him.

Not wanting to argue with her, Henry rose up from his chair and walked over to the front door. As he opened it and was about to exit the manor, Maureen cried out to him.

"Where are you going, Henry?" asked Maureen, worried as to where he was about to go, so late into the midnight hour.

"To ride my horse right now, of course. In fact, I can feel the forest already calling out for me," he revealed.

"But Henry…" began Maureen, but alas, it was too late. The damage was already done.

"Like I said before, Maureen, Henry's gone. It's the Dark Horseman, now," he said with a smirk painted across his face, as he walked out through the front door and slammed it shut behind him.

176

CHAPTER 22

One Hundred Years Later…

Henry might have been a monster in the past, but he no longer wanted to be one in the present, especially around Kassie. No matter her faults, Henry still regretted his actions towards her tonight. After spending all these years in constant solitude, he finally discovered the true love of his life and now, he was determined to keep her. But first, he needed to find her and apologize to her, directly. Hopefully, she'd accept his apology and forgive him; for if she didn't, then Henry was truly as good as gone.

Upon entering into Galloway Manor, Henry made his way back into his bedchamber. Hoping that she was still there inside, he slowly approached the door and to his excitement, he saw a faint candlelight burning from within. Indeed, she was still there. In his room. She didn't leave. Had she waited for his return? Henry could only hope. Wishing for the best, he slowly pushed open the door and to his own sadness, he saw Kassie lying there on his bed and hysterically weeping.

Seeing her suffering and in dire pain, brough so much agony to Henry's own fragile heart. A heart, which by all admission, should have been stone cold as of right now, due to his own unfortunate curse. But alas, his undying love for Kassie, somehow managed to melt right through his stone walls and found its way straight into the center of his heart. Watching her in distress, felt like a dagger had been plunged right through into his very own chest. Oh, how Henry wished he could take back everything that had transpired between them tonight!

"Kassie," he spoke softly. "Can I come in?"

"Please, go away!" she yelled, without even bothering to lift her head up to acknowledge his presence.

"Kassie, please, give me a chance to explain," he begged.

"No! Please, just leave me, alone!" she yelled again.

"But Kassie, I've got nowhere to go… after all, you're in my bed," he playfully reminded her, hoping that she'd change her mind.

"Oh!" she cried, as if she was truly unaware and ignorant to the fact that she'd been lying on his bed this entire time.

Upon realizing her own fault, Kassie quickly got up and tried to walk herself out of his room. However, Henry caught her midway and pulled her straight into his arms. Desperately trying to escape from his hold on her, Kassie attempted to remove herself from him; however, Henry continued to fight back. Finally, she gave into his pleas and stood there motionless, as she leaned her head across his warm chest.

"Kassie, I'm sorry," he finally admitted. "You don't need to say anything to me, in return. Please just know that I'm truly sorry for my behavior and actions towards you tonight. It's just that when I saw you there in danger, for the first time in my entire life, I was finally afraid of something. Never before, have I ever feared about anything. Even my damn curse never scared me! Kassie, I've lived most of my life, both as a mortal and as an immortal, being absolutely fearless. Nothing… not the darkness, or the witches, or the wizards, or the goblins, or the monsters, or the criminals, or the beasts alike… nothing in this world has ever deterred me from my comfort zone… at least not until… tonight. Tonight, for the first time ever, in all of my existence, I was truly afraid of losing you. I was absolutely terrified that I was going to lose you to that hungry wolf and that I'd never see you again. Please believe me, when I say that I don't ever want to act like a monster… and especially to you. From the bottom of my heart, Kassie, I want to be a better man for you. No matter what happens in the future, please know that I love you, unconditionally."

Without saying another word, she instantly locked lips with him.

"Oh, Henry!" she cried. "I'm sorry, too! Please believe me, I, too, was worried about you, as well. When I saw those wolves surround you, I almost lost my mind! Sometimes, I forget that you're an immortal and that no harm can befall upon you. And even though my mind screams this fact, my heart refuses to accept it. Henry, I love you, too. But most importantly, I also want to be a better woman for you, as well."

Upon her heart felt admission, Henry leaned in and began to passionately kiss Kassie, as if tomorrow did not exist. Moving his hands along to her waist, he pulled her as close as possible to him, as he held onto her as tight as he could, while his mouth kissed and devoured her. She, in return, continued to stroke his hair with her hands, as her lips intertwined with his.

After the drastic events that took place tonight, Henry was grateful to have Kassie finally back in his arms, where she belonged. However, his patience to consume her was growing thin. Alas, Henry couldn't anticipate any longer. He needed to have her, right there and then.

"I don't think I can wait Kassie…" he whispered into her ear.

"Me either," she whispered right back to him.

Currently, Henry was standing with Kassie in front of his piano. After previously blocking her from exiting his bedchamber tonight, he managed to kiss her, right there, near his entryway. However, given how large and spacious his bedchamber was, his bed was at least, what felt like another mile away. At this rate, he was going to lose himself to complete madness, before he'd successfully make it back across and over to his bed, while carrying her within his arms. No, Henry thought to himself. He couldn't wait that long. He needed her, right here, right now. And so, without a further thought or hesitation, Henry swiftly lifted Kassie up from the floor and placed her right above his piano.

"What are you doing?" she asked, surprised by his unexpected move.

"I'm going to take you, right here, right now," he revealed, as he promptly ripped his clothes off from his body.

Luckily, for Henry, the wolf had already torn most of his clothes to shreds, so it didn't take much for him to remove the rest. Excited by his surprise actions, Kassie squealed with delight, as she closed her eyes and surrendered herself over to her beloved. Determined to have his way with her, Henry tugged at her buttons, and then, he tore off the front of her dress collar; whereby, her breasts were immediately exposed to him. Pleased by the glorious sight before him, Henry bent down and leaned his head against the center of her bare breasts, as he began to lick and suck on her nipples. Thrilled by his hunger for her, Kassie moaned from pleasure, as Henry continued to suck and nibble at her large and voluminous breasts with his mouth.

Meanwhile, as he devoured her nipples, Henry's hands crawled underneath her gown, moving upwards towards her legs. As his hands finally came into direct contact with her inner thighs, he slowly began to push her legs as far apart as possible. Once his hands climbed its way up towards her undergarments, he slowly pushed his hand inside and tightly grabbed at her private areas; which caused Kassie to immediately scream from joy, as she rolled her head and fell into a blissful state. Sensing her approval, Henry continued to touch her and the more he touched her, the more wet she became. Alas, Kassie was ready for him.

Without bothering to rip the remainder of her clothes, Henry instead, pulled her undergarments down, lifted her skirt up, parted her legs as wide apart as he could, and then he positioned himself, right in front of her. Once both he and she were comfortable in their new position, Kassie leaned her hands back onto the piano, as Henry pushed and entered right into her.

With one large thrust, Kassie jumped up into the air, as Henry made his way into her body. Back and forth, he penetrated right into her, as she gasped for air. After spending most of their evening fighting in the forest, they were now making up for their lost time, together inside of his bedchamber. Wanting to bring him even deeper into her, Kassie moved her hands away from the piano and instead, she wrapped them around his back, as she pulled him even closer to her. Holding onto Henry for dear life, Kassie closed her eyes and held on tightly, as he had his way with her. Tonight, Henry was a hungry man and he, apparently, had no intention to stop.

Up and down, back and forth, Kassie bounced, as Henry inserted himself into her body. Meanwhile, their vibrations were so strong, that even the piano keys began to play music, along the way. Faster and faster, he pushed himself into her; and the more he thrusted, the more she screamed from delight. After several rounds, both Henry and Kassie finally climaxed and collapsed onto one another.

Afterwards, Henry pulled Kassie down onto the floor, where they rested together, side by side. While tonight might have started out disastrous, it certainly ended in splendor. Eventually, Kassie, exhausted by their wild adventure, soon fell fast asleep within Henry's arms. Looking down upon her as she peaceful slept, he smiled to himself. After everything that had happened between them, in the end, he still had Kassie and from this day forward, Henry was determined that nothing, and I mean absolutely nothing, was going to come between them, ever again.

CHAPTER 23

"**D**amn it to hell! Where is she?" demanded Walter angrily, as he stared out of the window, overlooking the gardens of Wiltshire Hall.

"It's been well over a month," he continued, "Surely, she would have returned back home by now."

"Don't worry Walter, give her some time," replied Maureen, as she peacefully sat on the sofa located inside of the salon, while enjoying a cup of afternoon tea.

"Besides," she added, "No harm will befall upon her, while she's busy frolicking out and about within our sleepy village."

"But how can you be so sure? What makes you so certain that she hasn't been kidnapped and held for ransom? After all, she's a lady. She's a part of nobility," Walter remarked.

"If there was a ransom, then we would have received a note by now; and as far as I'm aware, we haven't yet received such a thing. Besides, no one in this village would ever dare to kidnap Kassie. Especially, while I'm still alive," replied Maureen, confidently.

"How can you be so confident about that? Aren't you worried that she might be injured out there, somewhere? Or that, she's possibly run away and never will return?" asked Walter, most concerningly.

"Walter, my granddaughter is much tougher, than you give her credit for. Kassie is a classically trained equestrian, and she's knowledgeable about many, many things. Plus, she's trained in first-aid. If she was hurt, then I'm perfectly confident that she'll be able to take care of herself," said Maureen, boldly.

"I can't believe that I'm hearing this! I haven't slept nor have gotten a full night's worth of rest, since the day she disappeared. Meanwhile, you seem to be perfectly fine!" shouted Walter, out of frustration.

"Kassie is an independent, strong and feisty young woman. I suspect that she needed more time, in order to 'adjust' to her new circumstances. When she's ready, she'll come back home to us. In the meantime, Walter, please remain patient and give her some extra time," suggested Maureen, as she took another sip of her tea.

"I'll be more relaxed, once I see her again," Walter replied, in defiance.

"Come now, Walter, take it easy. Why don't you enjoy a nice cup of tea with me, instead?" asked Maureen, ever so politely.

"Tea? Tea? Honestly, Maureen, it's like I'm talking to the wall! I'll take tea, once Kassie returns back to Wiltshire Hall, safe and sound!" exclaimed Walter, angrily.

"Very well, suit yourself," Maureen sighed, as she poured herself another cup of tea.

Staring out at the window, Walter wondered as to where Kassie was at this precise moment. Ever since she failed to appear at the church on the day of their wedding, Walter hadn't had a moment of rest. After searching the estate, park, woods and the entire village all put together, from acre to acre, stone to stone, house to house; he, along with his dedicated search team, still couldn't find her. Oh, where had she gone? Their sleepy remote English village was so small already, that it was virtually impossible to remain hidden for this long! Plus, the next nearest town was several miles away. Had Kassie actually traveled further away, then someone from their mutual acquaintances would have spotted her and informed him of her whereabouts by now. So, with that being said, where the hell was she?

Kassie, the woman, whom Walter had secretly loved and adored, practically all of his entire life. From the time they first played together in the sandbox, Walter always loved her. In fact, even as a child, he already knew that one day, he was going to grow up and marry her. Although Kassie's romantic interest in him never actually seemed to be reciprocated on her part; but in truth, her deficiency in harboring any romantic feelings towards him really didn't matter. Not, in the least. Either way, Walter was still determined to marry her. Eventually, in due time, he was convinced that she would fall in love with him, one way or another. After all, she'd have no other choice, as he was going to be her legal husband, in the end.

Even though Walter knew that Kassie did not love him in return, he honestly didn't care. As long as he had her, then that was good enough for him. He'd take her as his wife, in any shape or form— regardless of the circumstances. Over the years, Walter stood by her constant side, while keeping up the appearances as her dear and sweet childhood friend, who was loyal, supportive and ever so patient. Strangely enough, it was rather ironic too, that Maureen would dare advise him today to remain patient, while they waited for his fiancé's return; for Walter had patiently waited for Kassie for practically all of his entire life. Why, he previously and patiently waited for almost twenty years and counting to marry her… and just when he thought that he was finally done with waiting, she up and vanished, leaving him standing all alone at the altar!

As devastated as Walter was when she failed to appear at the church, he still did not give up any hope. At first, he presumed that she had cold feet; but after a day or two, when she never returned back home, Walter grew more worrisome. Strangely enough, Kassie's own grandmother, Maureen, never once batted an eyelash; for even then, she was somehow convinced that Kassie had run away, all on her own free will. However, Walter couldn't be so sure.

Even though their marriage had been a forced arrangement, Walter believed that Kassie was content with their upcoming union. After all, she was going to marry him; he, her best friend. Plus, Walter was a wealthy man in his own right. Furthermore, their combined wealth and status would finally put Wiltshire Hall back on the map. But was it possible that he was wrong? Was it possible that Kassie secretly despised and hated him? And instead, want nothing more than to escape an unwanted union?

Sadly, the truth was that Walter hadn't been entirely honest with either Kassie nor her grandmother, in the first place. After waiting several years for her, Walter eventually, came to the unfortunate realization that not only did Kassie possess no inclination towards marrying him; but that, she had no interest in marriage at all. Unfortunately, this lack of interest associated with the subject surrounding marriage, proved to be a great obstacle that hindered upon Walter's future plans.

Upon returning back home from university, Walter was once again, delighted to reunite with his darling childhood friend. While Kassie was busy studying at university, he stayed behind to learn more about farming and agriculture locally. Since the Thornton family owned several acres of land in their local village, it was only natural that he would decide to remain within their humble village to study his family's business. As the only child and son of his father, he decided that it was his overall duty to skip over university and to instead, learn his family's trade, firsthand. From planting and cultivating carrots, lettuce, potatoes, strawberries, cabbages and all of the alike, Walter took his time to learn the fine art of farming, directly. By the time Kassie graduated from university and finally returned back home to Wiltshire Hall, he was already a trained and professional farmer, having harvested at least two seasons of his own crops. Furthermore, as a landowner and entrepreneur, Walter was now a sensible and successful businessman. Having managed a twelve-acre farm with a staff of ten, plus selling his own produce at the local markets in the nearby towns, Walter became a successful entrepreneur in his own right. Additionally, with Kassie's recent arrival, plus her being the appropriate age for wedlock, he was convinced, now more than ever, that this was the most proper and ideal time to propose marriage to her, so that they could finally start their lives together as husband and wife, while building a family of their very own for the future. However, those dreams were soon tragically destroyed, the very same day that Kassie arrived back in town.

Excited about her return after a long period of absence, Walter paid Kassie a welcoming visit, while also bringing her a large bouquet of roses to her home. If Kassie could only see him now— he, a successful businessman, who owned his own land, with money saved in the bank, and coming from a respectful family— then surely, she'd want to marry him, after all these years. Even though in the past, she never once glanced at him in that special way before, she'd have to take a second look at him now— especially, with him personally paying her a visit at her home, along with a fresh bouquet of flowers. After all, didn't all women universally love flowers?

Sadly, Kassie wasn't like most women, at all; for the very moment that Walter entered into Wiltshire Hall with his fresh bouquet of roses, she simply laughed at his face, upon his entrance. Remaining completely innocent and ignorant regarding his romantic affections and intentions for her, Kassie mistook his gesture as another regular welcoming gift. Devastated by her unexpected reaction, Kassie inadvertently plunged a rejection dagger straight through his heart, when she later announced that evening that not only did she not have any intentions of ever marrying, but that she actually wanted to move to London to work as a governess, while at the same time, pursuing her dreams of writing her first novel. After several long and agonizing years of patiently waiting for her to finally come around and acknowledge him as a possible potential suitor, Walter was left utterly heartbroken and completely devastated beyond words. Instantly, overnight, his lifelong pursuits and dreams about their shared future together, were violently shot down to the ground. Oh, how tragic this really was too!

While most men would have simply accepted defeat and moved on to the next debutante, Walter simply couldn't. Although there were plenty of other lovely, available and respectable young ladies in their village, who were also eligible to marry; sadly, none of them were her. Kassie, his sweetest and dearest Kassie; the mere sound of her name, brought an endless amount of joy to his heart— even though she, in return, failed to reciprocate his same romantic feelings for her. But either way, it didn't matter; for Walter still loved her, regardless. From her fiery red hair, to her soft and delicate skin, to her adventurous and courageous spirit, to her fearless attitude about life and the world, Walter both admired and loved her. Although Kassie was the polar opposite of his own shy, reserved and conservative self; she was everything that he could have ever hoped or aspired to be.

And so, after that dreadful night, rather than crying himself to sleep, Walter concocted a decisive plan: if Kassie wasn't going to marry him freely based upon her own free will, then he was just going to have to force her hand to do it, one way or another. Although Walter knew that it was wrong to force an unwanted marriage onto her; in the end, he didn't care, for Walter was willing to have her by any means possible, regardless of the circumstances. Ah, yes, morality and honesty meant absolutely nothing to Walter, for they were merely just useless and inanimate words to him! And so, because of these reasons, he secretly plotted away and devised a most devious plan in private, never to reveal the real truth about his deception to anyone. Not a single soul.

Given that Kassie was an heiress and the sole person, who stood to inherit Wiltshire Hall, with no other male relatives in line to interfere with her inheritance, everything seemed well on her part. As a wealthy heiress, who came from a noble and respected family, Kassie had the true freedom to choose her own path in life— a rarity to most women of her time. However, wanting to prevent such freedom, Walter knew that if another male relative existed, then they could challenge Kassie's legal claims over Wiltshire Hall. Plus, given the high costs and expenses on maintaining the estate, eventually one day in the near future, Kassie was going to run out of money, as well. And so, Walter researched her family's tree at the local library to locate a possible male relative. Sadly, after much research, Walter could not locate not a single living male family member. However, this lack of findings did not stop him, for he was still most determined to succeed. If Kassie did not have a living male relative, then he was simply going to have to find one… even if he had to create one. And so, by picking a random name from off her family's tree, Walter chose a 'Douglas Marley' from one of the distant branches from her male line. By selecting a distant cousin, whom, no one had ever heard of before, Walter knew that his plan was more likely to succeed, for who would dare to question them? After all, Kassie did technically have a Douglas Marley relation; except, he died several years ago from a shipping accident at sea. Alas, his plan was too good to fail! If Walter could find and hire someone to pose as Douglas Marley on his behalf, then Kassie would have no other choice but to marry him. She'd have to; otherwise, she stood to lose her childhood and ancestral home over to a total stranger. Plus, Walter was a decent man, a family friend and had the means to pay off this so-called distant cousin. Therefore, without further delay, Walter hired one of his farmers to pose as Douglas and brought forth his plans into action.

With his pen in hand, Walter forged a letter addressed to Maureen directly, signed by a 'Douglas Marley,' regarding his valid 'claims' over their estate. Naturally, both Maureen and Kassie were innocently fooled by his deception. Furthermore, to Walter's great joy, both the Stanton ladies leaned upon his longtime friendship for his support during this troubling time. Delighted by their reactions, Walter suspected that Maureen, who had already spent the greater half of her life living at Wiltshire Hall, wouldn't be so easily keen on seeing her late husband's and late son's estate transfer over to an unknown and distant cousin. Furthermore, given that Kassie was Maureen's only grandchild, Walter calculated that Maureen would be more inclined to be persuaded towards giving Kassie's hand in marriage over to him. Feeling highly confident about his treacherous plans, Walter quickly acted in haste and soon afterwards, he made his formal proposal directly to Maureen. To his great relief, she accepted on Kassie's behalf. Although Kassie was previously fooled into believing that it was her grandmother's original grand idea for the marriage proposal; it was actually the opposite, for it was Walter's direct hand in the matter that started the entire course of action. And so, this is how Walter became engaged to Kassie. Even though he had to lie, trick, blackmail, and deceive in order to make it happen; but in the end, it still happened and that's all that mattered… at least, not until now.

Previously, Walter had planned everything, from the date and time of their wedding ceremony, to the transfer of his property over to hers, to the wedding décor and invitations, and even down to Kassie's own choice of bridal gown, which was personally preselected by him— everything had been meticulously and carefully sorted out, without any interference from the bride's part. All that Kassie needed to do was to simply arrive to the church in time for their ceremony. That was all. Nothing more. But sadly, that didn't happen. Unfortunately, the one thing that Walter failed to ever consider was the remote possibility of Kassie disappearing on him, on the day of their wedding. After years of waiting, Walter was supposed to turn his lifelong dreams into a reality. Literally, he was mere inches away from calling Kassie as 'his wife;' but alas, it still failed to happen. What was meant to be a day of celebration, turned out to be the worst day of his entire life.

Rather than celebrating their first night together as man and wife inside the comfort of their own home; Walter was instead, desperately searching for his missing bride out in the cold and darkness, while growing madder by each passing minute.

Did she have another lover? Was it possible that perhaps, Kassie had eloped to marry another? Or did she actually secretly love someone else? Walter couldn't help but wonder. But whether or not she did, it didn't matter; for as far as Walter was concerned, Kassie was already as good as his. Had there been another man, then it was purely irrelevant; for Walter still intended to have Kassie all for himself, regardless. Ah yes, Walter was completely obsessed with Kassie and one way or another, he was going to have her… even if he had to wrestle with the very devil, himself!

In the meantime, he needed to remain patient… at least, just for a little while longer. After waiting these past twenty years for her, he was willing to wait a few more extra days or even weeks, if he had to. But either way, in the meantime, Walter just needed a sign, while he patiently waited. A sign that she was still alive and well, and that she would soon return back home. And then, suddenly, a servant arrived into the room, with the most startling announcement.

"Sir," said the servant, as he stood in front of Maureen and himself.

"Well, what is it?" asked Walter, with high hopes.

"It's regarding Lady Kassandra," announced the servant.

"Kassie?" Walter repeated, with a glimmer in his eye. At last, had she finally returned?

"Her horse, Faith, was recently discovered down by the riverbanks today," replied the servant.

"Was Kassie with her?" asked Walter, eagerly.

"No," he replied. "Faith was discovered alone, with no trace of Lady Kassandra."

Suddenly, a brilliant idea came to Walter's mind. If Kassie had indeed run off, then she would have left on horseback, riding Faith. Furthermore, if Kassie was still hiding somewhere outside there, then Faith was sure to know! All that Walter needed to do right now was to ride Faith outside and have the horse lead him the way.

"Take me to the horse, right now," Walter demanded.

"Really, Walter, do you know what you're doing? Is this even necessary?" asked Maureen, concerned by his sudden and impulsive behavior.

"Maureen, I know precisely as to what I'm doing. And yes, it is absolutely necessary," he bitterly replied.

Reverting his attention back over to the servant, he commanded, "Prepare the horse. I intend to ride it, immediately."

Without a further delay, Walter had the servant escort him directly over to Faith, where he intended to track and relocate his lost bride, once and for all.

CHAPTER 24

"What about these violets?" asked Kassie, as she showed Henry her dried wedding bouquet, which included a few magical violets that she previously gathered out in the forest on the first day he rescued her.

"What about them?" Henry asked, as he bent down to sniff them.

"I gathered them in the forest. They're magical. In fact, I even witnessed it miraculously cure a wound to an injured bunny. Maybe, if we try, it can also serve as a cure to your curse?" asked Kassie, with high hopes.

"Kassie, these violets are meant to cure mortal wounds and diseases, not to reverse one's immortality. Besides, how can it cure me, when I suffer no ailments?" he asked, with a raised brow.

"But we can always still try," Kassie suggested.

"Actually, Kassie, I already have," he revealed.

"You have? But how?" she asked, most surprised.

"Believe it or not, but these violets are a part of my late mother's final resting place. They grow right above her nameless grave. It's how I've been able to locate her grave too, through her blooming violets. I cannot tell you as to just how many times I've touched, rolled and sniffed them... at least a million times over, this past century. More than I can even count. Trust me when I say, I'm completely immune to them," he confessed.

"Your mother's grave? That's where your mother is buried? Wait… is this the same place, where your curse was originally enacted?" asked Kassie, most intrigued by this surprising revelation.

"Yes, the very same place," he admitted.

"Is that why they're so magical, then? Because of the location? Where your curse was cast?"

"Perhaps… or perhaps, not. I honestly, don't know. But according to legend, these lands have been magical for centuries," Henry revealed.

"You know Henry, it's funny that you mentioned that, because my grandmother used to say much of the same, too. But in all honesty, I've never really understood as to why exactly that was. Do you happen to know?" asked Kassie.

"I've never been entirely certain myself; but from what I do know, these lands were once occupied by wandering druids. In ancient times, they regarded this territory as the ideal location for the seasonal solstices. Apparently, this forest rests on the perfect celestial alignment, where the sun and moon eclipses at the precise angle that's adjacent to Venus and Mars, every so often. Perhaps, these violets happen to rest upon the very same place, where the druids previously worshiped. But it's so long ago, that we really can't prove anything for certain. Apart from the oral history foretold by the former elders that I, as a young boy, used to listen to over the years, I don't think there's much information or documentation written about it in a book. Besides, all of the past elders perished a long time ago," he said.

"It all makes sense now! If the ancient druids worshipped these lands, then maybe that's why Vera was so obsessed with acquiring Galloway Manor and this forest, all those many years ago. Perhaps, to cure your curse, we just need to wait for the next eclipse!" exclaimed Kassie happily, as if, after all this time, they finally had their lead.

"Kassie, in the past one hundred years, there's been hundreds of eclipses, both solar and lunar, and not once, has it cured me. Had there been a connection or even, a remote possibility of an eclipse curing me, then trust me, it would have happened long ago," he sadly revealed.

"Well, we've got to try something!" she exclaimed. "We can't just sit around here and do nothing!"

"Okay, okay, please don't despair Kassie. We're making progress… heck, this is more progress than anything else that I've ever attempted to do before, especially in these past one hundred years or so," he said with a smile, while hoping to cheer her back up.

"Henry, please do be serious! We really must find a solution to your curse, for both of our sakes," Kassie proclaimed.

"Alright, but are you sure that we haven't done enough already? At least, for today?" he playfully suggested. "After all, I'd much rather prefer that we pick right back up in our bedchamber, for my lips already miss yours…"

"Henry, behave yourself!" Kassie shouted, in an attempt to redirect their focuses back to their mission. After spending most of today performing various experiments, Kassie wasn't about to allow them to get too distracted by another round of their lovemaking… at least, not until tonight…

"Alright, I promise to act more serious," said Henry, as he took a seat across from her in the library.

"Now," he continued, "Please remind me on what we've tested and experimented with, thus far."

"Okay, okay, let's see," began Kassie, as she reviewed her notes from her notepad.

Noting as to just how many pages she was silently reviewing, Henry remarked, "It seems like we did put in much of a good effort today, didn't we?"

"Yes, alright, I've got it," Kassie continued, "Thus far, we've tried true love's kiss… and that sadly, did not seem to work…"

"It might not have worked, but it still doesn't change the fact that we love each other," Henry made it a point to remind her.

"Yes, you're probably right," she agreed.

"Probably?" he asked, with a raised brow. "Does that mean there still remains the remote possibility that you don't love me, in return?" he inquired, in a playful manner. However, deep down inside, Henry already knew in his heart that they were both equally and madly in love with each other.

"Haha, very funny Henry," Kassie teased him, in return. "You already well know that we're soulmates."

"Soulmates… hmm… I like the sound of that," Henry said, as he reached over and grabbed a hold of her hand.

Not wanting to give into his distractive affections, Kassie gently pulled her hand away and continued on with reading her notes.

"Moving on," she continued, "We've also tested confessing our love for one another… and that didn't work either…"

"But Kassie, pray tell, why do you presume that true love's first kiss or even confessing our undying love for each other, should break my curse?" asked Henry, most amused.

"Well… for starters… it worked for Sleeping Beauty and Snow White… so naturally, I also presumed that it would work for you, too," Kassie innocently confessed.

Amused by her honest and sweet answer, Henry laughed, in return.

"Kassie, my love, do I look like Sleeping Beauty? Or even, Snow White, at that?"

"Well… not exactly…" she shyly admitted.

"Given the obvious *no*, then why do you assume that their same remedies will work on me? Besides, I'm a man… not a damsel in distress," he remarked.

"Man or woman, it doesn't matter," Kassie huffed, in retort. "True love is meant to be the cure for all."

"Perhaps, but maybe there's still another way. What else have we done so far?" he asked, again.

Refocusing back to her notes, Kassie stated, "We've also tested wearing silver, smelling garlic and walking outside in the sunshine."

"Interesting. Pray tell, what were the points to those particular solutions? Isn't silver used to destroy werewolves? And garlic and sunshine to rid away vampires?" he asked, with humorous suspicion. Somehow, Henry suspected that Kassie might have confused her remedies with other legendary creatures that didn't apply to him.

"Yes, that is true. But I thought that it was still worth a try," Kassie reflected.

"Come now, Kassie. Do not worry, nor take offense. Please do go on," said Henry, as he leaned against his seat, lifted up his feet and placed them above another chair to get more comfortable.

"Okay, okay," Kassie said, as she reviewed the remainder of her notes. "Let's see… we've already tried bathing in tomato juice during a full moon, as well as drinking a warm bowl of chicken noodle soup…"

"Hmm… and what was the point to all those experiments?"

"Umm… well… some legends believe that tomato juice cures repulsive smells and bad spirits, while chicken noodle soup is supposed to cure various ailments," replied Kassie, still as serious as ever.

"I see," replied Henry, as he privately smiled to himself. Somehow, he couldn't find the heart to tell her that chicken noodle soup was primarily served as a remedy meant to cure a common cold or the flu, and that bathing in tomato juice was also meant to cure… well… a foul odor caused by… well… a skunk.

"What else?" asked Henry, once more.

"Well… you also tried drinking green tea with honey, as well as trying all of the various potions that I've concocted, along the way. But sadly, you still seem to be… well… you," Kassie sighed, at long last.

"My love, don't feel bad or defeated. You've tried your best and your best is good enough for me," Henry remarked, in an attempt to console his disappointed lover.

"No, Henry, I refuse to give up! We will find a way! This much I promise you!" Kassie vowed.

"Kassie, really, it's honestly alright," he said, now, in a more serious manner. "I've already accepted my fate long ago."

"But I haven't," replied Kassie, boldly. "Henry, we've only just recently found each other. I refuse to allow anything to come between us, again!"

"Kassie," began Henry, as he stood up and slowly walked over to her side. Kneeling down in front of her, he said, "Nothing and I mean, absolutely nothing will ever come between us again. Curse, or no curse. You have my word."

"I know," replied Kassie, with a smile.

"You, see? Then, you've got nothing to worry about," Henry added.

"But Henry, all hope isn't lost," she reminded him. "According to my notes, you've already been changing, as we speak."

"Changing? In which ways?" asked Henry, now, most intrigued. This was certainly news to him!

"Well, according to my notes, when I first arrived at Galloway Manor, you claimed that you never slept and that you never ate; for you lost your desire to sleep, as well as your tastebuds at the time of your curse. However, ever since I've been here with you, this doesn't seem to be entirely true. In fact, just last week, I caught you sleeping in bed and… well… how do I say this delicately…"

"Delicately? Kassie, please don't linger! Come out and say it!" he begged.

"Well… snoring," Kassie bashfully admitted.

"I, snore? Nonsense!" replied Henry, who ironically, appeared to be offended by the mere fact that he snored, rather than anything else.

"That's not the point," Kassie quickly retorted. "The main fact remains that you *slept*. Henry, you actually *slept*."

"My God, if that's true, then that's certainly something new, indeed," Henry acknowledged.

"Yes, it really is," Kassie agreed. "Plus, the week before, you even complemented me on my cooking. Don't you remember? You said, and I quote, 'Kassie that was your best attempt on baked quail, as of yet.' Afterwards, you actually ate two whole birds, not just one!"

"That's right!" exclaimed Henry, in astonishment. "I did say and did that, didn't I?"

"Yes, you did," Kassie confirmed.

"Kassie, so what does this all mean? Am I turning back into a mortal, again? Because this has never once happened to me before. Certainly, not in this past century, at least," Henry reflected.

"Either you're relearning how to be a mortal again simply by being around me, or that, our love means something. Maybe, in time, our love will ultimately save you," said Kassie, remaining hopeful.

"Perhaps, you're right," agreed Henry.

"Henry, let's try something different," said Kassie. "You've stated that you can't leave the boundaries of this forest; so maybe, if we try leaving together with me by your side, then maybe, this time around, we can actually do it."

"Are you sure that you really want to try this?" he asked, very seriously.

"Why not? Why shouldn't we try? We've done everything else, thus far," Kassie reminded him.

"I know. It's just that I don't want you to get your hopes up, only to be disappointed later on, if the outcome doesn't go in our favor, that's all," he admitted.

"Don't worry, Henry. Even if it doesn't work out the first time, then we will find another way. Trust me. Please, let's do it now," she pleaded.

After a century of living within the ruins of Galloway Manor and the enchanted forest, Henry was ready to give it a try. At this point, he had nothing else to lose but everything to gain. For the first time in a hundred years, Henry finally had hope. Hope that maybe, just maybe, there was a cure to his curse. A solution to his eternal damnation. Perhaps, Kassie was always meant to serve as his savior. Maybe, this was the sole reason, as to why he needed to wait all these years, just for her. Because as it currently stood, Kassie had already changed his life for the better. She alone was the sole reason for this new smile that currently rested upon his face. After everything, Kassie was his soulmate; the love of his life and his better half. Surely, if she thought there was a remote chance and possibility of them living a life together, outside the forbidden boundaries of this enchanted forest, then at the very least, Henry needed to meet her halfway and give it a try. Thus, with a hopeful heart, Henry agreed to Kassie's proposal.

An hour later, Henry and Kassie rode off together aboard Midnight to the far reaches of the enchanted forest. Once Midnight was safely parked to a nearby tree, Henry escorted Kassie over to the edge of the forest, which served as the official boundary between his ancestral lands and the village. After witnessing numerous travelers cross these boundaries for over a century, Henry finally held out hope that maybe this time around, he would be able to successfully cross over onto the other side and thus, break his century long spell. With Kassie by his side, Henry closed his eyes, followed her lead and stretched his right foot forward, as he attempted to walk a path that had long been forbidden to him these past one hundred years and counting.

CHAPTER 25

With Kassie standing over the boundary, Henry closed his eyes as he put his right foot forward to cross over into the forbidden path. Cheering him on the other side, Henry listened on as Kassie encouraged him to walk forward to her. After waiting all these years, at long last, Henry was going to finally leave his world behind and enter into a new territory!

Had the world changed so much, when he last ventured out? Were the people still much of the same; apart from their general clothes and overall appearances? Did people still ride in trains and in horse carriages, or did folks nowadays prefer to use other modes of transportation? Who was the current King of England and did high society still recall his family's name? Would anyone in the village still remember him as Lord Henry Galloway, Earl of Galloway, or would he only be recognized as the legendary Dark Horseman, instead? After pondering about these thoughts for over the past century, at long last, Henry was finally going to discover the answers to these looming questions for himself. What a joy this was! A world filled with new opportunities and endless possibilities!

Putting his first right foot forward, Henry was mere inches away from crossing over, when suddenly, a mysterious force immediately jolted him backwards, about ten feet away. Surprised by this unexpected outcome, Kassie quickly ran over to his side. Meanwhile, Henry was currently lying down motionless, with his back pressed against the grass. Staring at him below, much to Kassie's relief, Henry wasn't physically injured. However, although Henry might have lacked any external injuries, the same could not be equally said with regards to his internal self. For at this precise moment, Henry's facial expression said it all: he looked gravely disappointed. More disappointed than what Kassie had originally anticipated.

"I was afraid that this was going to happen," Henry confessed, as Kassie helped to pull him back up.

"What happened? One moment, I saw you there crossing and then, the next moment, you were pulled backwards. It was almost as if…"

"Almost as if an invisible force, pushed me back," he responded, with great frustration.

"Yes, that was it," Kassie agreed.

"It's part of this damn curse!" he sourly admitted. "This isn't the first time, too! And now, sadly my dear, I dare say that it won't be the last, either."

"Does this happen every time, whenever you attempt to cross over?" she asked, out of great concern.

"Precisely," he bitterly replied. "Which is why I can't ever leave this godforsaken forest! I'm forever bounded to these lands, like a prisoner held captive by an invisible force. It's what kept me in for over a century, in the first place."

"Okay, so we failed on our first attempt. We can always try again," Kassie encouraged him.

"Kassie, what's the point? Even with you by my side, apparently, nothing's changed. As you can see, I'm still trapped in here," he sadly acknowledged.

"Henry, you mustn't think this way. We just need to retrace your steps and think of another solution," she said.

"Another solution? Pray tell, what else do you have in mind?"

"Well… if you can't walk in, then perhaps, you can fly over," Kassie thought aloud.

"Fly over?!" exclaimed Henry, in sheer surprise. "And how do you suggest that we do that?"

"For starters, do you happen to have a hot air balloon? I've only ridden in one once before, but that was several years ago."

"A hot air balloon? Kassie, have you gone mad! Of course, I don't own such a thing!" exclaimed Henry, in disbelief.

"Okay, if you don't, then we can try to build one, together. I know that it probably isn't the most conventional solution that you might have wanted, but it's still worth a try," Kassie insisted.

"If that's the case, then I might as well use Midnight to try and jump over that invisible force, while we're at it," Henry remarked sarcastically.

"Good idea! Let's try that, too!" exclaimed Kassie, excitingly.

"Kassie," Henry spoke softly, this time. "I think we need to have a serious discussion, right now."

Unfortunately, Kassie knew that now wasn't the ideal time to suggest any more escape routes. After their first failed attempt to cross over, she was well aware that Henry was gravely disappointed by their results. With just one look at his face, his facial expression sadly, said it all.

"Kassie, I love you with all my heart," he began.

"And I love you too, Henry; with all my heart," she interrupted.

"Yes, I know," he said. "But I need you to understand that right now, this is going to have to be it. This is going to be the life that we're going to have, if we're to stay together. While I don't want us to ever give up hope; however, at the same time, I also ask that you find it within your heart to accept this ultimate truth, too. As long as we're together, this is going to have to be it. The forest, Galloway Manor… *me*… that's all that I have to offer you. If that's enough for you, then I promise to do everything in my power to make you happy… but if this isn't enough, then it's better that you come to accept this reality now, so that you can make other arrangements, while you're still young…"

"Henry, what are you saying?" asked Kassie, as she began to tear up.

"Kassie, you have your entire life ahead of you. You're young, beautiful, smart, thoughtful and kind. You still have a chance to live your life to the fullest, the way you want to. As much as I love you, it would also be selfish of me to hold you back, if this isn't the sort of life that you desire. You deserve so much more. Kassie, I love you so incredibly much that I'm willing to sacrifice my own happiness for yours. To give you the freedom to live your life the way you envision it to be," Henry confessed, with a heavy heart.

"Henry, my life is with you. By your side. There's nowhere else that I'd rather be, than with you. Period. End of story. I only suggested that we break this curse, because I want us to grow old together," she admitted, with tearful eyes.

"But that's it, too. You deserve to be with someone who's a mortal, like you. At first, I'll admit, I only thought about this inequality of me being an immortal and you being a mortal, from my perspective only. I never previously thought about it from your side before... at least, not until now. Kassie, are you going to be okay growing old, while I stay forever young? Will you miss the outside world, while you age here, with me? Kassie, I love you for you. Unconditionally. Youthful or elderly. It's all irrelevant to me. I love you, as you are, in any shape or form. You are the very essence to my being. The love of my life. My better half. My soulmate. But apart from my own personal opinions, are you going to be okay with this inevitable reality? Will you be able to bear the unbearable?" he asked, as his own eyes grew teary.

"Henry, I don't want you to speak anymore of this! I love you so much, and I'm going to stay with you, for however long God permits us to be! Curse or no curse!" she shouted, as she threw her arms around him and hugged him for dear life.

"Shush, Kassie, it's going to all be okay," he said reassuringly, as he held her tightly within his arms. "I just needed to say this, because I love you so damn much."

"Henry, no matter what happens, we will be together. This much I promise you," Kassie vowed, as she leaned against his chest.

Pleased by her spoken words, Henry smiled on, as they rested together on the grass and stared out across at the forest's forbidden boundaries. While Henry might not ever have the chance to cross over it within the span of Kassie's own lifetime; he was now content, that no matter what happened from this point forward, Kassie had finally accepted their fates. But more than that, she was also jointly content with their modest, but humble life together. As relieved as he was, Henry was also grateful that she did in fact, agreed to stay with him; for had she not, then Henry was afraid that very decision would have really been the end of him, curse or no curse.

CHAPTER 26

After wandering through the village for the past several hours, Kassie's horse, Faith, finally brought Walter to the foot of a mysterious dirt road leading into an undiscovered forest; a place, which he had never once seen nor heard or traveled to before. Within this past month, Walter had previously searched and inspected each and every square inch of their small country village; however, this new road was on unchartered territory. Clearly, this unknown path leading into an undiscovered forest was extremely significant and deserved to be thoroughly searched, as well. But why hadn't he ever thought to look in here before? How did Faith manage to stumble upon this strange and foreign territory? Or better yet, why didn't he know about this forest's very existence, until today?

Curious about this new potential lead with regards to his ongoing search for his missing bride, Walter continued traveling further down this unknown path. Somehow, Faith led him on this strange and mysterious journey, and into a gothic style forest. Furthermore, as far as Walter was concerned, he knew that this couldn't be limited to a simple coincidence. No, this all meant something. This all served a purpose. In fact, he could feel that something was off; it was penetrating right down into his bones and entering into his very own soul. A premonition. An intuition. An overall, supernatural sense that this forest was the very key to this current crisis. Something dear and precious to him was nearby, in this darkened place. And as unexplainable as this feeling was too, Walter could simply still just feel it, nonetheless.

If Faith had brought him to this location, then Kassie must be hiding somewhere, inside of here. In fact, the more he thought about it, the more convinced he became. For the past month, Walter previously lacked any leads. Even though he searched in every house, room, business, barn, field, lake and river, Walter still couldn't find her. It was as if, come overnight, Kassie had simply vanished into thin air; however, logic and reason dictated that this was absolutely impossible. One way or another, Kassie was somewhere hiding and now that Walter had just crossed over into this strange and mysterious forest, he was now convinced without a shadow of a doubt, that she had been hiding in here all this time, right under his very nose.

Allowing Faith to take the lead, Walter sat back as Kassie's horse rode him through the dark forest. Passing by several ancient oak trees, Walter could already tell that this forest was very old, indeed. Silently, he observed the surrounding small forest creatures, plants and mushrooms. The further he wandered into the forest, the more perplex he became. If Kassie was indeed alive and living inside of this place, then how on earth, did she manage to survive this long, out in this wilderness? Although Maureen had previously told him that Kassie was skilled in the art of first-aid, Walter still had his own personal doubts. Even with a young woman, who was as smart, determined, feisty and skillful as Kassie, everyone had their limits. Especially, when left alone to care for themselves, out in the wild. Walter, himself, was also doubtful about his own abilities as well; for had the roles been in reverse, then he wasn't entirely certain as to whether or not, he, a grown man, could have even fended for himself in such a bleak and isolated area.

Suddenly, Faith came to an abrupt halt. Curious as to why Faith decided to stop right in the middle of the forest, Walter climbed down. Quietly, he listened to his surroundings and to his amazement, he heard chatter from afar. As Walter listened in, his ears detected that the sounds appeared to be human speech; a conversation. Ah, yes, it was a conversation spoken by two individuals, a man and a woman, in English. But who were they? Who could possibly be conversing in a private conversation, out in the middle of nowhere? In this godforsaken forest?

Slowly, Walter tiptoed behind until he reached a rose bush, which managed to conceal his entire body. Carefully, Walter bent down and kneeled behind the bush, as he gazed ahead to spy on the couple in front of him. Watching them from behind, Walter initially saw the couple lying down together on the green grass. With the man seated half up and leaning his back against a tree, the woman's head was resting alongside his chest. At first glance, Walter could only see the man's face. From what he could tell, the man was tall, muscular, with broad shoulders, along with a handsome face. Near him, was the female. Although Walter couldn't catch a glimpse of her face; however, from her behind, he could see that she had long flowing red hair. Additionally, her hair was so remarkably bright in color, that from afar, it looked as if a fire was burning against the surrounding forest. Furthermore, as vivid and as lively as her hair was, Walter was completely enchanted by it; for he had never seen such a vibrant hair color before… well… apart from Kassie's.

Other than his own sweet and dear fiancé, Walter had never seen such a woman with similar hair… and then, the most unexpected of occurrences happened: the woman finally turned around and alas, Walter was able to finally see her face! As he squinted and stared across at the woman, he was surprised to see that not only was she so incredibly and breathtakingly beautiful, but that she was also young and cheerful. Gazing closer upon her face, Walter finally came to the realization that this very same young woman, was none other than Kassie! His Kassie, to be precise! His sweet and dear Kassie! Alas, Walter finally found his lost fiancé, but in the arms of another man who wasn't him!

Almost immediately, Walter's shattered heart sunk deeper into his chest. After desperately searching for his lost bride, he finally stumbled upon her, out in this secluded and mysterious forest, hidden away from the rest of humanity. Unfortunately, after many sleepless nights, Walter now, at long last, finally had his answers. Not only was Kassie still alive and well; but at the same time, she also seemed to be actually enjoying herself in the arms of her lover. Furthermore, by the looks of it, she looked far more beautiful and lovelier than ever before. In fact, her facial expression, body language and overall mood, seemed much more relax, joyful and happier than when he had last saw her on the eve of their wedding.

Did Kassie voluntarily leave him at the altar for this other man?

Her lover? Did she know him from before, when she previously agreed to marry him, instead? And who was this man? Walter had never once seen him before at their village, and he knew practically everyone in England. Did he come from another respectful family, like his? Was he also equally wealthy as he? Would this mystery man provide the same economic means of comfort and status that Walter could offer her, as well? Suddenly, Walter's mind was plagued with a million unanswered questions; questions that he had never thought to contemplate before. After patiently waiting and plotting to take Kassie as his bride, he finally lost her against his own will to another man; whom, at this very moment, had his arms wrapped around her waist!

Damn it to hell, Walter thought to himself! Never did he imagine that he would lose Kassie to another, especially when he came so incredibly close to marrying her! Not only did she have another man, but from the looks of how familiar they were with one another, Walter doubted that Kassie was still an innocent virgin anymore! Oh, how that crushed his very heart into pieces! How he waited and longed to be the one, and only one, to have rightfully claimed her virginity on their wedding night! Curse be to God on how much effort he recently placed into meticulously planning their wedding ceremony and for arranging their future lives together! In fact, Kassie didn't even have to lift a single finger, for Walter had taken care of everything. But in the end, it almost didn't matter, for he still lost her. Sadly, as much as Walter tried, he could never really have her; for he never truly had her in the first place. Although he remained by her constant side as one of her oldest and dearest of friends, Kassie never once looked at him in that special way... the way in which she currently looks at this stranger, right now, at this very second.

Oh, what Walter would have given to have Kassie just look at him with those same yearnful eyes! Even for a split second! Oh, how much he had waited, prayed and hoped for her to see him, just as exactly as she stares into the eyes of this other man! In fact, Walter would have gladly traded his own soul with the very devil, himself, if it meant he could have Kassie see him in that same light! Tragically, Walter's love for her was one sided. Although he hoped and half expected that in due time, she would eventually grow to love him, just as much as he loved her, in return; but sadly, now, from the looks of it, that no longer seemed to be a feasible option anymore.

Now, her arms were around another and this reality was absolutely maddening to Walter! Here he was, standing so close to Kassie and yet, so far. If he really wanted to, then he could practically stretch his arms and reach out to her… but what was the point? Obviously, she didn't want him… and truth be told, Kassie never really wanted him… well… ever. Sadly, the only reason as to why she agreed to marry him at all, was because she was forced to. Had it not been for his devious plans, then she'd never have gone through with their engagement; let alone, their wedding. But alas, this was the sad truth and bitter reality that Walter currently faced. Now, with a crushed heart, he was at a crossroads with his very own life.

What was he to do, now? Was he to just turn around, leave and move on with his life, as a single man? To forget about Kassie and marry another? To pretend that he no longer loved her; when, in truth, it was far from it? To erase the past twenty years, he spent pining away over her? Wishing and praying, with all his heart that they were soulmates, who were always meant to be? To forget all about the lies that he told to her and her grandmother, in order to secure an engagement with her? Was this truly the end?

Staring at the happy couple, Walter was disgusted beyond measure. Not only had Kassie become such a loose woman, who freely gave herself to this despicable man, but this same stranger also had the audacity to fondle with a young, innocent and once respectable woman like a common whore, whom, he most likely wasn't even married to. At least with Walter, he had the decency to honor and respect her reputation by offering marriage to her. And the more he pondered about this, the more Walter grew convinced that out of Kassie's two suitors, he, and only he, had been the true gentleman, out of the two. Somehow, one way or another, Kassie had been bewitched and seduced by a spiteful man. If Walter were to leave her now, then surely, this man would eventually come to abandon her and thus, Kassie would then, be regarded as a fallen woman. A disgraced lady of nobility, who would never again be welcomed back into high society. Sadly, she would be shunned and turned away from all of the respectful members of their inner circle, and her family's name, as well as her own reputation, would forever be ruined. Furthermore, what if she was already with child?

Carrying the bastard offspring to this forsaken beast? What would become of her and her unborn child?

As much as Kassie had destroyed his heart, Walter was still determined to save her from this unfortunate fate. While Kassie certainly wasn't the first runaway bride to flee from her chosen groom into the arms of a secret lover; Walter believed that she would not be the last, either. Why, hundreds of other women in society had done much of the same; but in the end, they always returned back to their betrothed. And had Kassie already been impregnated by this man, then the urgency for her to marry would be far great. Perhaps, if Kassie could return back home, even just for a single night, then he could convince her to marry him again; and if not for her sake, then for the sake of her potential unborn child. At least by marrying Walter, then he could offer her an honorable and respectable name to her child… who, would otherwise, surely be abandoned by this beast of a man and be born as a bastard!

Watching straight ahead, Walter knew that bringing Kassie back home was going to prove to be a real challenge. After all, her arms were practically glued to this wicked man. But Walter, being the determined young man that he was, refused to easily surrender and let go. No, he needed to be creative, in order to snatch her away. While her lover was very well built, Walter already knew that it was absolutely pointless to fight him off, for he would surely lose the battle. However, on the other hand, if he could use his wits to convince the both of them otherwise; then maybe, just maybe, he still had a chance. And so, Walter devised a new plan within his mind and after a few minutes of pondering on the precise execution style, he was ready to finally take action and set his new devious plan into motion— all in an effort to reclaim his bride, once and for all.

"Ah, the things we do for love," he whispered to himself aloud, with a sinister smile, as he took a step forward.

For as happy and as content as Kassie was beside Henry, little did they know that apart from Henry's looming curse, another form of evil had just arrived and was now lurking right behind them out in the woods.

CHAPTER 27

While Kassie rested her head against Henry's chest, she peacefully shut her eyes and was about to fall asleep. However, upon closing her eyes, she suddenly heard footsteps creeping away from afar. Curious as to what this noise was, Kassie reopened her eyes wide. With Henry currently preoccupied with his deep relaxation, he failed to hear these sounds. Not wanting to disturb him, she briefly excused herself to inspect this lingering noise.

Slowly pacing forward ahead, she followed the sounds, where it eventually, led her to a prickly rose bush. Carefully, she stood a good distance away from the rose bush, as she proceeded to grab a large wooden stick nearby from off the ground. From the looks of it, the sounds didn't appear to be that of a wolf… therefore, whatever it was, Kassie presumed that she was completely safe from any physical danger, for what could be more dangerous than a wolf? Using her wooden stick to push through the rose bush, to her sheer surprise, upon peeking through one of its branches, she saw a familiar face! To her astonishment, the face to the man staring right back at her was none other than Walter!

"Walter?!" Kassie gasped in surprise.

"Kassie!" Walter happily cheered, as he pushed his way through the thorny branches.

Remarkably, Walter was not pricked at all by the rose's prickly thorns. Instantly, he quickly arose from straight out of the bushes and within the blink of an eye, he was there, standing right in front of her. Not wanting to wait for a single moment longer, Walter immediately threw his arms around her and released a big sigh of relief.

"Thank goodness, you're alright Kassie! We've all been worried sick about you!" Walter ecstatically exclaimed, as he held onto her tightly. Finally, after much physical contact, he finally released her.

"Walter, I'm perfectly alright. There's no need to be alarmed," she swiftly said, in an effort to put him at ease.

"Yes, I can see that. You seem rather well, but—" he began; however, Kassie stopped him midway.

"Walter, I'm sorry to have kept you all worried, but I'm perfectly fine. In fact, I'm better than I've ever been before. Needless to say, I have no intentions of ever returning back home," she boldly declared.

"Not returning home?" he asked, in astonishment.

It was as if, Walter had never once considered the possibility that she wouldn't voluntarily want to return back to civilization with him. That she would actually choose the wilderness over a life of luxury. Was this even the same Kassie? The girl, whom he grew up alongside with? Had her jungle lover bewitched her this much? Had she fallen victim this easily and so deeply into his spell?

"Yes, that's right. I'm not returning back. The forest is my home now," she declared.

"But what about Wiltshire Hall? Your ancestral home? If you don't return back with me, then you're guaranteed to lose your inheritance and family's estate over to your cousin," he reminded her.

"I'm well aware of the consequences of my decision, but my mind is made up. I've decided to stay here permanently for good," said Kassie, sternly.

"I see," replied Walter, in disappointment.

For whichever reasons, Kassie was certainly starstruck with this man of hers. Had she not, then she would have never in a million years, ever think to relinquish her rights so easily away to a distant male cousin and thereby, leaving her own grandmother homeless and penniless. This was so unlike her!

"But what about Maureen? What shall become of her?" he asked.

"My grandmother has plenty of her own money, that was previously set aside for her long ago. My grandfather took care of all of that. If we're to lose Wiltshire Hall, then I'm more than certain that my grandmother can take up residence elsewhere, while I live my own life," replied Kassie.

"Let me get this straight," Walter began, "You would much rather prefer to stay behind in this godforsaken forest, then to return back to the village to marry me and live comfortably for the rest of your life at Wiltshire Hall? Am I understanding you, correctly?"

"That's precisely what I'm saying," replied Kassie. "Listen Walter, you and I both know that our engagement was not born out of love. Our relationship has never been a romantic sort of pairing. Besides, Walter, you've got a kind, gentle and decent disposition; you deserve to find another nice and fine young lady, who can better adapt to your agricultural world. Someone who's far more compatible to be the perfect farmer's wife... more than I could ever be."

"I see," remarked Walter, as he did his best to force his facial muscles to display the fakest of smiles across his devastated face. In the meantime, he felt as if his own heart had been stolen from right out of his chest, thrown into the muddy ground and then, aggressively stomped over by the sole of her shoes against it; and thus, turning it into a thousand fragmented pieces. Lastly, with each passing new word, the remains to his heart were being further crushed into dust, even as she continued to speak.

"Now, let's call a truce," she began, "Walter, I wish you well on your new life and journey, as I do the same. Shall we let our past stay in the past and promise to remain as we always were, before all of this? As dear and sweet friends?"

Seeing her hand extended across from him, Walter finally recognized that no matter what he said or did, Kassie wasn't ever going to change her mind. After patiently waiting years for her, his ever-enduring patience ultimately proved to be useless. For every lie he told and for every scheme he plotted in order to win her over, he lost practically every single battle. No matter how much he tried, one way or another, he could never win over her heart. While he never previously had any competition before, at long last, he finally did. Furthermore, this mystery man had not only seduced her; but in the process, he also won her heart, fair and square, as well. Unlike him, her new lover didn't force her to love him; no, Kassie actually chose to love him, out of her own free will. As devastating as this truly was, this stranger was able to accomplish the one thing that Walter could never achieve. No matter how much wealth, honor or prestige that he possessed, the one thing that Walter could never own was Kassie's heart. Therefore, after much defeat, he reluctantly accepted Kassie's olive branch and shook her hand in solidary with their continued friendship.

"Yes, we shall always remain friends Kassie, no matter what," he said.

Smiling back at him, Kassie was delighted by this new and unexpected turn of events. After leaving Walter back at the altar, she now had a clear conscience to move forward with her own life. With her past finally put behind her, she was ready to enjoy her future with Henry, the true love of her life.

Suddenly, Henry appeared and promptly came over to join Kassie's side. Curious as to who this stranger was, he quickly interjected and inquired about his whereabouts. However, Kassie decided to take the lead and explain the entire situation to Henry in her own words.

"This is Walter Thornton," began Kassie, "He's a childhood friend of mine, who came to see how I was getting along, here in the forest. He just wanted to see if I was alright, that's all."

"A childhood friend? Is that all?" asked Henry, with a raised brow. Recalling how he had first encountered Kassie wandering through the forest, while wearing a white bridal gown; somehow, Henry couldn't help but think that perhaps, this new gentleman might have been her lost groom from before.

"It's true, we are childhood friends," interrupted Walter, as he helped to confirm her story. Noticing that Kassie had very distinctly left out the key fact that he was also, most importantly, her former groom, Walter decided to go along with her story. At least, for now, that is.

"I see," remarked Henry. Reverting his attention back to Kassie, he asked her, "And is everything alright, now?"

"Yes, everything is perfectly alright. I've already told Walter that all is well and that I plan on staying permanently in the forest with you. Given that I'm doing well, he plans to leave and return back to the village right now, aren't you Walter?" asked Kassie, eager to send him as far away as possible. The sooner, the better.

"Ah, Kassie, actually, there's something that I must tell you," said Walter.

Given that this was probably going to be his one and only chance to persuade her otherwise, Walter decided to enact his plan. Although he might have previously accepted Kassie's friendship proposal just a moment ago; however, he still wasn't going to give up on her so easily. One way or another, Walter was determined to return Kassie back to Wiltshire Hall, come hell or high water.

"Yes, what is it?" Henry answered, in Kassie's place.

Already sensing Henry's overbearing protectiveness over Kassie, Walter knew that he needed to outsmart the both of them. Observing Henry's muscular built and alpha demeanor, Walter treated his words very carefully and wisely in front of them. Whatever he decided to say next, he needed to be very strategic and succinct with his choice of words.

"It's about your grandmother," Walter finally announced.

"My grandmother? What about my grandmother? Is she not well?" asked Kassie, who was now concerned about this new and troubling revelation.

"Ever since you left, your grandmother has slowly fallen ill. Sadly, her condition has gotten worse within these past few days. At this point, her last dying wish is to see you, one last time. In fact, it's why I came here in the first place. I promised her that I would find you, so that I could personally deliver her final message to you," said Walter, as he bent down his head and secretly smiled to himself.

"Oh my, I see," replied Kassie, with a heavy heart.

Although Kassie refused to leave Henry's side, she still felt incredibly heartbroken about the prospect of losing her grandmother to death. Never had Kassie ever imagined that her grandmother would have fallen ill, so shortly after her disappearance. After all, her own grandmother was another feisty woman, just like herself. But lo and behold, Kassie now faced a difficult dilemma. While she didn't want to leave Henry, she also didn't want to neglect saying her final farewell to her own sweet and dear grandmother. After all, Maureen had helped to raise her, after her own parents' unfortunate demise. But given these dire circumstances, Kassie quickly made up her mind.

"Walter," she began, "Please tell my grandmother that I love her very much, with all my heart. Also, please let her know that I'm safe, happy and that she never needs to worry about me, ever again. That's all."

"Wait, are you honestly saying that you have no intention of coming back with me to Wiltshire Hall? Not even to bid your dying grandmother a final farewell?" asked a confused Walter, who did not ever consider the remote possibility that Kassie would still refuse to leave the forest, even after hearing about Maureen's ailing condition.

"That's precisely what I'm saying," said Kassie, boldly.

However, Henry wasn't so equally convinced. Given these unique circumstances, Henry knew that the only right and honorable action for Kassie to take was sadly, to return back to Wiltshire Hall with her friend; at least, for one last time. While he was going to terribly miss Kassie in her absence, Henry also knew that eventually, she would return back to him in due time. Either way, in the end, they would soon reunite with each other, once again.

"Kassie, can I speak to you, privately?" Henry requested, as he made his move to lead her away from Walter and back over to the tree, in which they were previously resting together, just a few short minutes ago.

"Yes," Kassie replied.

"Kassie, you've got to go. It's the right thing to do, and you and I both know it," he finally said.

"But Henry, I can't go without you! I won't go! Not until your curse is broken, first!" she protested.

"The curse might not be broken anytime soon; but in the meantime, your grandmother still needs you. Plus, she might not have that much time left either, and you owe it to both her and yourself, to say your final goodbyes. Kassie, do you realize what I would give to see any one of my relatives again, even if it was for one last time? Why I never had the chance to say goodbye to either one of my parents, let alone to anyone else in my life. To have a second chance, that's something beyond words. A true and rare blessing. Remember, you and I love each other and we still have a future together. No matter what happens next, we will find each other again and then, we can spend the rest of our entire lives together, in blissful happiness. But for now, you've got to go back home. At least for one last time, to say your final farewell, the proper way," said Henry.

"But what if I can't find this forest again, for a second time around? What if… if… I never see you… again?" she asked, with tearful eyes.

"You will find me again, because you still have unfinished business in this forest. Remember, only those who have unfinished business are allowed to step a foot in this place. It's why your friend was able to discover here. He was probably meant to find it, in order to deliver your grandmother's last wishes," he said, as he pulled out a violet from out of his pocket and gently placed it behind her ear.

"Plus, this magical violet will lead you back to me," he said, with a smile. And then, he reached back into his pocket again and in an unexpected move, he handed over a dagger and placed it right into the palm of her hand.

"Just in case anything happens along the way, I want you to remain safe, even while I'm not around," he said. "Now, will you promise to go? The sooner you leave, the sooner you'll return back home to me."

Looking straight into his eyes, Kassie nodded in agreement. As much as she wanted to remain by his side forever, she also knew that he was right. After everything that her grandmother sacrificed and did for her, she owed it to her to see her one last time to say farewell. And so, with Henry's blessing, Kassie walked over to Walter's side and together, they hopped onto Faith, as they rode off into the direction leading back to the village. As Kassie waved farewell to Henry, he forced himself to smile and to wave back at her, in return. As much as he tried to put on a brave front, he secretly hoped that his prior speech to her about having unfinished business wasn't just about his own hopeful wishes. With all his heart, Henry silently prayed that this wasn't going to be the last time that he'd ever see her again. That eventually, soon enough, she would return back to him again, safe and sound.

CHAPTER 28

Upon their arrival to Wiltshire Hall, Kassie hurriedly ran over to the entrance, eagerly pushed through the front doors, and then, she loudly shouted her grandmother's name aloud. As her voice echoed across the entire premise, Kassie forcefully entered into each room, as she desperately sought to find Maureen. After opening practically every door on the first floor alone, she finally approached the salon; which ironically, was the very same place where Henry's portrait was also displayed in.

Since the room was currently empty, Kassie decided to take a brief moment to rest and collect herself. Sooner or later, she was going to be reunited with her grandmother. Therefore, in the meantime, Kassie decided to cease this rare opportunity to admire her beloved portrait of Henry, one last and final time. Placing the dagger that Henry had previously lent to her down onto the table near the front entrance, Kassie proceeded to walk over to far corner of the room.

From there, she gazed at his fine portrait hanging up upon the wall. My, how much had evolved and transformed within her own life, since she last gazed upon this very portrait. After admiring his portrait and face for so long, Kassie finally met him in real-life. Furthermore, not only was he real, but he turned out to be the true love of her life. Her partner. Her equal. Having spent this past month in constant and blissful happiness within his loving arms, she finally came to learn as to just how wonderous it really was to truly be in love and to be loved in return, by the right person. Luckily, Kassie had narrowly escaped her own ill-fated marriage to Walter and instead, she found herself crossing paths with Henry and moving into his grand estate at Galloway Manor. Now, staring back at the painting once more, everything had finally come in full circle. While the Dark Horseman had previously been a mysterious figure, who had dominated most of her childhood fantasies; at long last, her admiration for him was no longer limited to only a mere fantasy... no it was in fact, a true reality; for the Dark Horseman was no longer the Dark Horseman to Kassie, he was Lord Henry Galloway, her friend... her lover... her protector... her soulmate.

But as handsome and dashing as he was in the portrait, Kassie noted that he was far more attractive in-person. In fact, his portrait truly did him no justice, at all. Gazing across at the background of the portrait, something strange and peculiar caught her eyes. There, located within a miniature estate that appeared to be Galloway Manor off in the far background, appeared to be a woman standing at the window. Since the image was so small and obscure, Kassie had to actually squint her eyes, in order to see it more clearly. Staring closer at the image, she could see traces of long red hair, along with a fair and smiling face... that ironically, just so happened to look just like... herself?

Shocked by this unexplainable sight before her, her jaw dropped from this unexpected image. Never before had she ever seen this image painted there on this portrait. No, not ever... not even once... and Kassie had stared at this portrait for at least a million times over, since her childhood. How was this even possible? Clearly, based on appearances, that woman in the window was Kassie; for apart from her own family, she was the only other redhead in their entire village. In fact, her trademark red hair had been a family trait that she had directly inherited from her Grandmother Maureen, herself. Did someone recently paint her onto this portrait, while she was away? Or had magic played a part in this strange mystery?

However, before Kassie could ponder about this subject any further, she heard footsteps from behind. Someone had just entered into the room. Turning around to see who it was, to her surprise, Kassie saw her grandmother walk straight into the salon, looking as healthy as ever.

"Grandmother?" cried Kassie, aloud.

"Kassie! My dear, you're back!" exclaimed Maureen, joyfully. "Have you gotten everything settled now? Oh, I'm so glad that you've made it, right in time for tea."

As Maureen walked herself over to the sofa, she rang the bell for the servants to deliver her daily afternoon tea. Once she was comfortably seated down, Kassie stared at her in utter amazement. Unlike the fragile disposition and deathly description that Walter had previously told her about, Maureen appeared to be in the complete opposite state. Not only was her grandmother not on her deathbed, but she also appeared to be in good spirits, too. In fact, it seemed like everything was back to normal again, and that Maureen hadn't even been worried nor concerned about her prior disappearance, not in the least bit. Suddenly, Kassie realized that Walter had not only deliberately lied to her, but that he had actually tricked her into returning back home with him, too!

Grabbing the portrait from off the wall, Kassie walked over to her grandmother's side and took a seat beside her, along with the painting in her hand. Determined to get solid answers to this mystery, Kassie looked straight into her grandmother's eyes and decided to take this rare opportunity to press her for the truth.

"Grandmother," she began, "I take it that you're in perfectly good health, am I correct?"

"Why, yes, my dear, why wouldn't I be?" replied Maureen, with a raised brow.

However, just then, the servants opened the doors and entered into the room. With the tray of afternoon tea and desserts in hand, they gently placed them above the coffee table. While Maureen was busy preparing her afternoon tea, Kassie continued on with her questions.

"Grandmother, I'm glad to hear that you are well. I am doing equally well, myself," she said.

"Yes, I know, my dear," Maureen interjected, as she took a sip of her tea. "In fact, I've always known that you were perfectly alright, too."

"You did? But how?" asked Kassie, surprised by her statement.

"Why the portrait of course," replied Maureen, as a matter of fact.

"As you can see," she continued, as she reached over and using her index finger, Maureen pointed towards the image of the woman in the manor. "That's you."

"How… how… how… can you be sure that it's even… me?" asked Kassie, in amazement.

"My darling girl, of course, I can spot my own granddaughter, especially in a painting," Maureen remarked, as she took another sip of her tea.

"Although I must confess," continued Maureen, "Initially, I was worried about you, after you failed to arrive to your own wedding. But then, once I saw you in the painting, then I knew that you were alright and most importantly, that you were with him."

"Wait, you've known, this whole time? You mean to tell me that somehow, I was in this painting the entire duration, while I've been gone? But how? Is this somehow, a part of the curse?" asked Kassie, while desperately searching for more concrete answers.

"Yes, the entire time. But Kassie, you can't be entirely so surprised. After all, this is a magical portrait and you've always known that, too. Ever since you were a little girl," Maureen reminded her.

"I just don't understand… how is this all possible?" asked Kassie, in disbelief.

"My dear, belief is a powerful thing. If you don't believe me, then look at the back of the portrait. Go ahead, go ahead and take a look," advised Maureen.

Following her grandmother's instructions, for the first time in her life, Kassie looked at the back of the portrait. To her amazement, the following message was written right behind the portrait:

"Nothing is more powerful than a curse,

apart from everlasting love and the enduring belief in it."

Upon reading this wise, but true statement aloud, Kassie looked straight at her grandmother. Slowly, but surely, these magical words started to take a hold upon her heart and in her soul.

"Kassie, his curse is not permanent. It's not unbreakable. With the right person, it can be broken," said her grandmother, smilingly.

"But I don't understand…" uttered Kassie.

"No, Kassie, you do. Think hard. Think really hard. Why is it that you could always see him in your dreams, even as a young child? Why you even found him out there in the forest, in the first place? It's because you always *believed* in him. And now, if you're to help him to break this curse, then you *both* need to start believing in each other and in your love for one another," said Maureen, with much conviction.

"But we've already shared true love's first kiss. Plus, we both tried to cross over the forest's boundaries together and still, he couldn't cross over it," added Kassie.

"That's because he didn't believe that he could. Kassie, belief is a mighty and powerful thing, just like love. Both are very powerful forces in nature. They go hand and hand, with each other. Just like true love cannot be forced, neither can belief. You both have to trust and believe in your love, in order to defeat Vera's curse. Only then, can you two be united in your love for one another," said Maureen.

"Grandmother, I think that perhaps you're right. Looking back at it all, Henry has already been slowly changing. He's been eating and tasting food. And as of lately, he even fell fast asleep, alongside with me. Honestly, neither of these things were even possible before I…"

"Before you arrived," interrupted Maureen, as she finished Kassie's sentence. "It's because you were always meant to break his curse. You're his cure. His savior. You and only you."

Suddenly, the doors abruptly slammed shut behind them. Startled by this unexpected commotion in the middle of their heartfelt conversation, Kassie and Maureen looked over and saw that Walter had now arrived into the salon. However, rather than joining them at the sofa, he kept a safe distance, that wasn't too far away from the front doors. Picking up the dagger in his hands that Kassie had left behind at the front table, Walter looked at them with such a strange and ominous stare, that Kassie, herself, could barely recognize him, anymore. The once kindhearted, sweet and dear friend from her childhood was no longer there. He was long gone. Instead, standing before her was a man, who not only lied to her about her grandmother's health, but also appeared to have the most evil and sinister look upon his face. Sadly, after all of this time, he now looked like the very devil, himself.

"Walter, what is the meaning of this? Why did you shut the door so loudly?" inquired Maureen, as she tried to pat her ringing ears, caused by such a loud and unnecessary commotion.

"Oh, shut up you old hag!" Walter yelled, most angrily.

"Hey, watch your tongue! That's my grandmother that you're speaking to!" shouted Kassie, as she stood up and was right about ready to leap across the room and strangle him for deliberately disrespecting her grandmother. However, fearing for the worst, Maureen, tightly grabbed a hold of Kassie and sat her back down beside her.

"Kassie, please remain calm, my dear," Maureen forewarned.

"Well Kassie, you better start getting used to it, because as the new man of this house, I will refer to whomever or whatever, by whichever title that I prefer or feel like addressing. Is that understood?" asked Walter, as he released the most sinister laugh.

"Walter, what are you talking about? You're not... and I repeat, not the new man of this house!" exclaimed Kassie. "Besides, in due time, my cousin Douglas Marley will soon be taking over."

"Ah, yes, Douglas… about that. Well, since you decided to mention him, then I might as well come clean to you, dear Kassie. Especially, given that we'll be man and wife soon enough, you should probably know that there is no Douglas Marley. No, Kassie, that was a lie. Your ancestor Douglas Marley died long ago. No, the person, whom you previously met was one of my farmers. Unfortunately, since you refused to ever take notice of me, I sadly had to orchestrate this whole inheritance fiasco, in order to gain your attention and get you to finally agree to marry me," Walter revealed.

"What? What are you talking about? Do speak up, Walter," said Maureen, this time, most angrily.

"It's true. I lied. But what can I say, I did it for us," said Walter, with a smirk.

"Walter, you're well aware that I have absolutely no intention with going through with our previous engagement. We will never marry. Not now, not ever. And the very fact that you lied; well, I especially, have no other reason to ever marry you, let alone, remain as your friend!" Kassie hissed, in rebellion.

"Really? What about the fact that you've been whoring yourself, over at that forest of yours? Don't think for a single moment that I, or anyone else in respectable society, will ever believe that you're still a virgin. Especially, after being alone with that… that… disgusting beast of a man!" shouted Walter, angrily.

"He's not a beast! He's a man! He's Henry! And I love him!" shouted Kassie, in return.

"Walter, don't you ever call my granddaughter by such a hateful term. Unlike you, she's a born lady," Maureen scolded him harshly.

"A lady or a whore, it makes no difference to me. And love, ha! Please, beast… or Henry… it doesn't matter; unlike me, he'll never make you a respectable woman. Besides, if you're pregnant, then you'll have to marry me, either way… especially for the sake of your unborn child. Honestly, Kassie, you don't want your first-born child to be born a bastard, now do you? I think not; which is why I've already made prearrangements with the priest to have us married today by sunset," Walter revealed.

"Married today by sunset? Walter, have you gone absolutely mad!" Kassie yelled, in defiance.

"Kassie, one day you'll come to love me, just as much as I've always loved you. But in the meantime, if this is the dire extremes that I must take, in order to secure you as my wife, then so be it," he announced.

Looking directly at Maureen, he further added, "If you're wise Maureen, then don't plan on doing anything stupid, while I'm away. Furthermore, to make sure that this time around, Kassie doesn't get away, I'm going to lock you and dear grandmama inside this salon, until it's time for the wedding. Until then, I bid you both, adieu," he said, with a bow.

Walking back to the front door, he was about to exit, when he unexpectedly turned around one last and final time and said, "Also, I'm taking this dagger with me, too, as you won't be needed it any longer. But as a word of advice to Maureen: if you want to continue living underneath the same roof as Wiltshire Hall, then I highly suggest that you start listening to and taking orders from me directly… otherwise, I'll have no other choice, but to commit you to a mental hospital for the elderly, after we're married."

Finally, at long last, Walter slammed the doors forcefully shut behind him, as he exited the room for good.

With fearful and worrisome eyes, Kassie looked at her grandmother for guidance. Moments ago, she was joyful in the knowledge that at long last, there was the possibility of a real cure to Henry's curse. But now, sadly, that same hope was slowly fading away.

"Oh, Grandmother, what are we to do?" she asked.

Staring straight across at the window, Kassie saw that it was now approaching midday. In a few more hours, the sun was going to eventually reach the horizon. If they failed to act quickly, then by sunset, Kassie was going to become Walter's wife and this time, it was going to be for good… and the very thought of it, felt like a dagger had already been plunged deep within her own heart.

CHAPTER 29

"**D**on't worry Kassie, you've got plenty of time to escape," said Maureen, calmly and unaffected by Walter's threats.

"But how can you remain so calm? We're locked inside of here. If we're to escape, then we'll need to break through those windows and jump down!" exclaimed Kassie.

"Nonsense," huffed Maureen. "Why should I jump out of a window, when I have the key to the front door?"

"Wait, you have the key?" asked Kassie, in amazement.

"Of course, I do. Don't think that I was ever stupid enough to entrust the only set of our keys to him alone, after the two of you got engaged," replied Maureen.

"Oh Grandmother, you're the absolute best!" exclaimed Kassie, as she threw her arms around her grandmother and gave her a grand hug.

"Careful my dear, I almost spilled my tea and we don't want to get any blemishes on the carpet. Especially, given that this carpet is at least a hundred years old… which ironically, is about the same age as your Henry, I dare say," remarked Maureen, with a smile.

"Listen Kassie," began Maureen, "Extraordinary people are not meant to live ordinary lives. This is why, my dear, you've struggled to accept your fate with Walter. Finally, I, myself, recognize this, too. Seeing how cruel Walter's behavior and actions have been, I'm glad that you refused to marry him. Truly my dear, I only previously agreed for you to marry him, in order to save Wiltshire Hall for you and only you, alone. I wanted a piece of our family's history to remain with you, along with your descendants, always. Not for me. I've already lived my life, and I am grateful to wherever God shall place me, moving forward. Kassie, as your grandmother, I only want the best for you. Please know, that I personally give you and Henry my blessing. Besides, Walter is the beast due to his ghastly behavior, and certainly not Henry."

"Thank you, Grandmother, that means so much to me," said Kassie, with tearful eyes.

"Kassie, did I ever tell you about my own grandmother before? Did you know that I was actually named after her?" asked Maureen.

"No, you didn't. Was her name Maureen, as well?" asked Kassie, in return.

"Yes, her name was Maureen and once upon a time, she was the former chef at Galloway Manor," Maureen revealed.

"A chef at Galloway Manor? Did she know Henry?" inquired Kassie.

"Yes, she did. In fact, she helped to raise him, too. As a distant relative of his late mother, Sarah, she vowed to look after the boy, upon his mother's own death bed. Staying true to her vows, my grandmother raised him from infancy on up, until he was a grown man. And in return, she loved him, as if he were her own son," Maureen revealed.

"My God, I had no idea," Kassie admitted.

"Kassie, you see, when I last told you that we were distant relatives to Sarah, I didn't lie to you. We were… are… through my grandmother, who's the mother to my own mother," explained Maureen.

"I see," said Kassie.

"But most importantly, Maureen was there with him on that memorable night, in which he murdered Vera and thereby, sealed his own unfortunate fate. My grandmother loved Henry so incredibly much, that she was also determined to help find a cure to end his ungodly curse, such as yourself. In fact, she spent the remainder of the latter half of her own life, trying to desperately find a solution to break his spell. But sadly, she was never able to do so successfully, even into her old age. Eventually, she retired from Galloway Manor and afterwards, she moved into Wiltshire Hall. By then, her daughter, who was also my mother, had married my father and together, they resided in Wiltshire Hall— which was the ancestral home of my grandfather's family, before passing to my late husband. Upon her arrival to Wiltshire Hall, Maureen brought only herself, along with Henry's portrait, as a last and final reminder of the beloved boy, whom she once loved and cherished, as if he were one of her very own. It was through her enduring love and undying devotion to Henry, that his portrait took on a magical shape, so that our family would always remember him and Galloway Manor throughout the century, spanning from generation to generation. While history might have forgotten about Henry and Galloway Manor, our family continues to remember; for we are specifically tasked to do so. Afterwards, upon Maureen's death, this painting was passed down to my mother, and then eventually, my mother passed it down to me. And now, my dear Kassie, it's finally my turn to pass this portrait down to you, at long last. Like the rest of us before, we've each been fascinated by his portrait throughout the years. However, you've been the one and only one, who's been fascinated by him the most, by far. And now, I finally understand why; it's because you were always destined for him, as he was always destined for you. You're both destined for each other. Regardless of Walter, he doesn't stand a chance between the likes of the two of you, no matter how hard he tries; for love can never be forced. It's like chemistry, it must come naturally. Love is another form of nature. It's what keeps the world going. Plus, as it currently stands, you and Henry are soulmates. Time and space knows no boundaries between the two of you. Kassie, like I said before, love is the most powerful force in the entire universe. That, along with belief. Believe in your love for each other, and I promise you my dear child, nothing will stand in your way," said Maureen.

"Thank you, Grandmother, for sharing this incredible story with me. I promise to make you and all of our ancestors proud," Kassie vowed.

Looking straight at the clock, Kassie wondered as to when Walter would return back. Not wanting to lose their one chance to escape, she said to Maureen, "Should we go, now?"

"Yes, the time has finally come for this curse to be broken," announced Maureen, with great pride. "Come now, Kassie, let us go."

Walking to the front door, Maureen used her spare key to open it. With Walter still gone, Maureen escorted her granddaughter over to the horse stable. Once Kassie was safely seated upon Faith, she bid her farewell, as she made her journey back into the enchanted forest. Watching from afar, Maureen could see a faint rainbow peek across up in the sky, right above Kassie. Privately, she smiled. After waiting over a hundred years and counting, her ancestors could finally breathe a sigh of relief up there in heaven, for Kassie was finally making her way with the determination to break Henry's curse, once and for all.

CHAPTER 30

Wandering through the woods for a second time around, proved to be more challenging than her first. In fact, it was rather difficult, given that Kassie hadn't yet been able to locate it. After encircling the park nearby her estate for at least a good mile; unlike before, Kassie didn't find herself transported back into the enchanted forest. Alas, this was proving to be a real challenge. What was she to do? How was she going to get back in? What if she couldn't find it again?

Suddenly, Kassie's heart fell down to her stomach. The very thought of not finding the enchanted forest and thereby, never seeing Henry's face again, truly felt like the end of her entire world. If she failed to reunite with her beloved Henry, then what was the point of it all? What was the purpose of continuing on with her mortal life, without him? What was the reason of even living?

Remembering her grandmother's wise words regarding the power of love and belief, Kassie took hold of herself. If she was ever going to reunite with Henry again, then she needed to remain strong. She needed to trust in their enduring love and to fight for him. She needed to start believing wholeheartedly that their love was stronger than Vera's curse, in order to defeat it, once and for all— for in the end, what else is more powerful in this universe than love, itself? After all, it's through the very act of love that all living things are born.

As tears began to form within her eyes, Kassie reached into her pocket to retrieve her handkerchief. However, to her surprise, she instead pulled out the violet that Henry had previously gifted to her. Recalling its magical properties, she decided to say a little prayer with all her heart, wishing to be once again reunited with her estranged lover. As her tears streamed down across her face, one of her many tear droplets managed to land right above Henry's violet; which at this moment, was currently held within the palm of her hand. Thus, as a direct result of her internal woes, something unexpected and magical was about to take place.

Suddenly, out of nowhere, a bright ray of light burst out onto her path. Following the light and looking straight ahead, Kassie saw that below the hill from her was the forest! At long last, she had finally spotted it! Determined to reunite with Henry, Kassie quickly tapped against Faith's reins and instantly, the pair were swiftly galloping off down the hill and making their way back into the enchanted forest!

As they rode downwards, Kassie's heart continued to beat faster and faster. After narrowly escaping her second wedding from Walter, she prayed that this time, it was finally for good. Never again, did she plan on returning back to Wiltshire Hall... at least, not without Henry. Unlike before, after acquiring the necessary knowledge on how to break his spell directly from her grandmother; this time around, Kassie intended to finally undue Henry's curse, once and for all!

A few minutes later, Kassie arrived back at the enchanted forest. While she continued to travel down the muddy pathway, she eventually arrived at the infamous field of violets, located deep within the heart of the forest. It was there at that very field, where she saw Henry knelling down and saying on what appeared to be a silent prayer. Recalling his own origins tale, Kassie remembered that this magical field of violets was not only the original site of his curse, but it was also the final resting place of his late mother, Sarah.

"Henry!" Kassie joyfully cried, as she hopped down from her horse and came frantically running over to him.

"Kassie? Is that really you?" Henry asked, almost in utter disbelief.

"Yes, my love it's me! I've returned!" she happily exclaimed.

As the two lovers ran over to embrace one another, they welcomed each other in open arms, as they each planted several kisses along the other's lips. Eventually, Henry slowly pulled himself away from her and finally ask, "But Kassie, how did you return? How did you come back to me? All this time, I was secretly worried and afraid that I wasn't going to be able to see you again?"

"See me again? Of course, you were going to see me again! Why, before I left, it was *you*, who said that I still had unfinished business in the forest, did you not?" she asked him in return, with a raised brow.

"I did. However, at the same time, I must confess that I wasn't entirely certain as to whether or not, it really was the truth; or my own heart hoping and wishing for the best," he admitted.

"Henry, that's part of our problem. We lack belief. We cannot break this curse, until we both start believing that we can, together. My love, we cannot defeat this curse, until we trust and believe, with all of our hearts, that our love is stronger than this curse; for truly, that *is* the cure," she revealed with a smile.

"Wait? Is this true? Where did you come to learn of this?" he asked, with his heart rapidly pounding with excitement.

"From my grandmother. She knew your chef, Maureen, who was my own great-great grandmother. She said that 'Nothing is more powerful than a curse, apart from everlasting love and the enduring belief in it,'" Kassie revealed.

"My God, I think you're right. All those years ago, Maureen believed that it was love that would set me free. But my goodness, who would have known or thought that the love of my life was going to be one of Maureen's descendants," he said, in amazement.

"It's true Henry," said Kassie, "And now, we must both start believing that our love alone, can save you. Save us."

As Kassie leaned down to kiss Henry upon his sweet lips, they both closed their eyes to embrace this new startling revelation. For a moment, everything seemed all but perfect. After waiting this past century for a cure, Henry finally found it through Kassie. Whether it was her kiss, or her smiles, or her embrace... in the end, it was her love. Her love was what he had been missing all these years. In fact, it was always missing in his life. That empty void that he once harbored within his stone heart, was no longer there... for it had already been filled by Kassie. Whether it was her love, his love, or their combined loved for one another, Henry realized that Kassie was his cure. She'd been his cure all along. She was the key. His missing link. His better half. His soulmate. And now, after waiting all these years, he finally had her in his arms.

"Kassie, I love you more than anything else in this entire world. More than I can even say. You are my entire world, wrapped up into one being," he confessed aloud.

However, instead of hearing a response back from her, Henry was confronted by complete silence. Kassie might have been many things, but quietness was never one of her distinctive list of qualities. Her silence was so peculiar and unlike her; especially, after confessing his undying love and devotion to her. Curiously, Henry opened his eyes and to his horror, he saw a large blood stain suddenly appear across Kassie's dress!

Immediately, Kassie collapsed right into his arms, as the two of them both lost their entire sense of balance and fell downward onto the ground, landing on top of the violets, along the way. Never leaving sight of her not for a single second, Henry saw that the trail of blood not only covered her entire gown, but that it also originated right from her chest... from her very own heart. But how... how... how was this possible? What could cause such an injury? There was no one else in the forest, but them...

Suddenly, Henry heard the most sinister laughter from right behind him. If he hadn't known better, then he'd say that the laughter sounded almost identical to Vera. In fact, it was the same evil and devious laugh that he last heard on the day of his curse. But alas, this time, it was not the voice of a woman laughing... but of a man.

At long last, Henry soon realized that the 'old sweet and dear friend' that Kassie had recently traveled back to the village with, was the very same person, who was now, currently left standing and laughing away at them. Somehow, this bastard not only followed Kassie back into the enchanted forest, but in a state of pure madness, he managed to sneak up behind them and stab her, right through her heart. Ironically, unbeknownst to Kassie, this was the very same dagger that Henry had previously used to slay Vera and seal his own fate. And now, most tragically, in a sinister twist of fate, this very same dagger that he once gave to Kassie as a form of protection, was the very same weapon used against her.

"Hahaha!" laughed Walter, in the most mocking of tones. "Now, you will *never* have her! She will *never* be yours!"

In a fit of rage, Henry was ready to pounce over and kill him for attacking Kassie, but before he even had the chance to make another move, Walter beat him to the punch.

"Before you come after me, know that the damage is already done. Your beloved Kassie has been stabbed right through the center of her heart, and it is I, who's the guilty party! I take great pride in that! Furthermore, as I speak, know that she's already at the threshold of death... dying right there, beside you. No matter how much you cry or plead to God of your case, there's not a damn thing that either one of you can do to reverse it, right now! The wheels are already in motion! Because in the end, she was never yours to begin with... she's mine... and she's always been mine, not yours! As God as my witness, you will never, ever, have her! And now, I... I... unlike *you*... I plan on joining her in death! Meanwhile, as you remain living forever cursed away in this godforsaken forest of yours until doomsday, take comfort in knowing that it will be I, and *I alone*, who will reunite with her in heaven. If I cannot have her here on earth, then I shall take her as my bride in heaven, for all eternity!" Walter shouted, in pure madness.

And then, using the same dagger that had already been covered in Kassie's wet blood, in one swift move, Walter sliced open his own throat. Falling immediately down onto the ground, Walter stretched his arms wide, pointing in the direction of Kassie. Shortly afterwards, he died there instantly, within a pool of his own blood, while positioned on the ground and adjacent from Kassie. Even in death, he was still determined to never be separated from her.

With Walter now out of the way, Henry concentrated on Kassie. As she continued to lie there still and bleeding profusely on the ground, in a pool of her own blood; Henry desperately sought to stop her bleeding. Pushing down on her wound with his bare hands, he tried everything that he possibly could to save her. But alas, it was too late. Unfortunately, her injuries were far too severe and as much as Henry fought hard to save her with all his might; in the end, there was nothing more that he could do...

After stupidly assuming that she would live until the ripe old age of ninety, Henry never once considered that Kassie would die young. Not once, not ever. But tragically, evil in the form of Walter, found them and now, it was too late. Whether or not his curse would continue on for the next one hundred years, it was now, all irrelevant. For as it currently stood, Kassie was here right now, lying within his arms and... dying. Tragically, as much as Henry was willing to trade his own soul to the very devil himself in order to save her; alas, there was nothing else that he could do. After wishing for her, finding her, and loving her... now, this was the ultimate end. The heartbreaking finale to their epic love story. Although Kassie might have miraculously reunited with him today back in the forest, their happy reunion was short lived; for tragically, his sweetest, dearest and darling Kassie, was now dying within his loving arms.

239

CHAPTER 31

Devastated beyond words, Henry cradled Kassie within his arms, as he carried her lifeless body away from Walter's vicinity. Upon transporting her across his own mother's grave, Henry watched as Kassie's dripping blood fell and splattered down across the growing purple violets and surrounding soil nearby. Laying her down gently above a clean patch of violets, Henry brushed her hair away from her face and laid it softly against the earth. As she rested there peacefully, Henry knelt down and began to cry.

After waiting over a century to find her; sadly, he had lost her in an instant. One moment he was in a blissful state of pure heaven and the next moment, he was in a living nightmare... a true version of his own hell. Oh, why had God forsaken him! Why did fate rob him of his chance to enjoy true love for the very first time! After a century of solitude, at long last, he had finally discovered the true love of his life. Rather than spending the next ninety years in ecstasy; unfortunately, now, he was left with nothing but her memory. Sweet and unforgettable memories of kissing her, of holding her, of watching her, of admiring her and most importantly, of loving her. Just her. His dear, sweet and lovely, Kassie. After patiently waiting for so long on a chance to finally break his curse; alas, his one and only chance was stolen by a ruthless and spiteful man!

Reverting his attention away from his beloved and back over to Walter; he watched as the wolves descended down from the hills and made their way over to his deceased body. One moment, Walter rested there lifeless on the ground; and the next moment, his remains were violently ripped into shreds by the vicious wolves. Life had come in full circle. A life for a life. And nature was right there, to claim his remains. As much as Henry passionately hated and despised this despicable man, who stole his only chance for happiness; he also took great pleasure on witnessing his corpse being eaten by the hungry wolves. Meanwhile, as they bit and ate into his flesh, Henry noted that the origins to the very flesh devoured by them, once stemmed from a man, who was worth nothing more than the very dust that they pranced upon.

But sadly, as Henry came to learn the hard way, revenge itself, was never enough. Even after killing Vera all those many years ago, it never truly brought him much satisfaction afterwards. A second of pleasure, never lasted beyond just that. Furthermore, just like Vera's death before couldn't undue his curse; Walter's death couldn't resurrect Kassie back to life. Now, after witnessing Walter's corpse turn into dust— ironically, by the very same wolves that Henry had often battled with in this forest— his heart remained unaffected by this action. For truthfully, Henry's heart was already shattered. With Kassie gone, what was the point of it all, now? How could he continue on living within this state of madness, without her? To endure this curse alone, without her being by his side? Especially, after knowing and loving her, how could he ever go on?

Tightly holding onto her with his bare arms, Henry rocked and cradled her back and forth, as he yelled at fate in anger! How cruel she was to have brought Kassie into his life, only to snatch her away from him so early! It wasn't fair! None of this was fair! Kassie didn't deserve to die this way! Especially, by the hands of a man, whom she once regarded as an old sweet and dear friend!

"Curse be to all!" Henry yelled aloud into the forest.

Devastated by his own unfortunate fate, Henry began to violently weep. What had started as a single tear, soon grew into two… and then four… and then… eventually… he began to cry buckets of tears. Tears that were so heavy in quantity, that Henry's own tears actually began to water the very violets, in which Kassie peacefully rested upon.

"It isn't fair!" he yelled, once more.

Staring down at Kassie's corpse, Henry finally realized as to just how important her final message to him truly was. True love's first kiss wasn't enough to break his spell. Neither were any of their past experiments, nor persistent attempts to cross over the forest's forbidden boundaries. Kassie was right all along. Their past failures were directly due to Henry's own lack of belief. Sadly, he never truly believed within his heart, that there was ever a cure to his curse, in the first place. Even when Vera first cast her spell long ago, Henry still negatively presumed that this was the end for him. Over this past century, he lacked belief in both discovering love and finding a cure to break his spell. Even when he first met Kassie, he still never truly believed that she'd stay by his side for the remainder of her own life; let alone, finding a cure to his curse. However, after witnessing her undying devotion and relentless determination to reunite with him today, Henry finally began to believe that maybe… just maybe… their love was enduring. Everlasting. Perhaps, even in Kassie's own death, their love would continue to live on…

"Kassie," he began, "I understand now. Truly, with all my heart. Sadly, having lost you, I finally understand. Once upon a time, I thought that my curse was the worst possible outcome in my life… that is… until today. Today, marks the end for me. This day, is by far, the single worst day in my entire existence. Losing you is going to be unbearable, that I know; but I won't allow our love to die in vain! Do you hear me! My love, thank you for finding me. Thank you for loving me. Thank you for helping to change my life for the better. For making me become a better man. It is because of you, and you alone, that Galloway Manor has transformed back into the wonderous treasure that it once was from a century ago. It's because of you that I started to regain some of my mortal traits again. And wherever your soul is right now in this universe, please know that I love you, Kassie. Even from the moment, when I first laid eyes upon you on that memorable night, when your horse stumbled upon these woods. Even then, I admired and loved you, before I even had the pleasure to really know you. It was always love at first sight, when it came to you. I have no regrets about anything we've shared together, my dearest and sweetest Kassie. Kassie, I loved you then… I love you now… I love you still… and I will always love you… forever. And had you lived long enough, then I know, without a shadow of a doubt, that this time around, we would have broken this curse together; for now, I *finally believe* that *our love* is *stronger* than Vera's curse. It's stronger than any mere earthly curse or any other natural calamite sent from nature. Our love is forever enduring. It's everlasting. It's timeless. It holds no boundaries. For if I can still love you, even after your death, then nothing… and I mean absolutely nothing… can ever come between us… not even *death*, herself!"

Leaning down, with tears streaming down his eyes, Henry looked upon her sweet and dear face. As he leaned down to place a final kiss upon her cold and blue lips, he whispered, "Kassie, I will *always* love you… *forever.*"

Closing his eyes, Henry placed one final kiss upon his beloved, Kassie. For a long moment, Henry stood still in his pose, as he desperately tried to gather up all of his inner strength to even release his lips away from hers. However, unbeknownst to Henry, something magical was about to happen next. Suddenly, a bright light burst onto the scene. Ironically, it was the very same bright light that had first emerged on the memorable night of his curse. Out from nowhere, a gravitational force violently pulled him away from her and pinned him back down onto the ground. As Henry fought to open his eyes, he was instead, blinded by it. Whatever magical force was present here in the enchanted forest, Henry simply couldn't see it; for it was far too powerful for his own eyes to see. Instead of resisting and fighting back, Henry finally surrendered to the forces of nature. With his eyes closed, Henry remembered Kassie. He remembered how beautiful and lovely she was. From her silly cooking to her comical hunting abilities, and even their attempted dance lessons together; Henry remembered everything and anything that he could about her. Suddenly, the flash of light disappeared and to his sheer surprise, he heard Kassie call out his name.

"Henry?" Kassie cried, as she stood back up, as if she had just awakened from a deep sleep.

Upon hearing his name, Henry immediately reopened his eyes and ran over to her side to help her back up. Amazed by this unexpected miracle, Henry smiled on and gave thanks to God for granting his silent prayer and restoring Kassie back to life. Whatever had just taken placed, Henry didn't think too much of it; for as long as he had Kassie, nothing else mattered.

"Yes, my love," Henry answered in return, as he held onto her tightly within his arms.

Pushing him briefly away, Kassie was amazed to see that a tiny strand of hair that hung forward above Henry's forehead, had somehow turned grey.

"Henry," she began, "Is that a strand of grey hair, right above your forehead?"

"What?" he asked in surprise.

Pulling the loose strand of hair from out of his head, Henry stared at it. She was right. It was grey. But how was this even possible? He had never had grey hair before.

"And that? Is that a wrinkle that I see on the side of your mouth?" Kassie asked, as she began to inspect the rest of his body.

Touching his face, Henry immediately felt that very same wrinkle near the corner of his mouth. Kassie was right! Not only had Kassie been resurrected, but his curse had been broken as well! At long last, Henry had finally been restored back to his mortal self!

"Oh, Kassie! We've been saved!" Henry yelled at the top of his lungs, as he grabbed her in his arms and spun her up in the air.

Once Kassie landed back down onto the ground, she looked at him straight in his eyes and said, "Henry, then you know what we must do next."

Silently, Henry nodded in agreement. Pulling Kassie to his side, together, they walked over to the far edge of the forest's forbidden boundaries. While Henry might have failed to cross over the barriers the last time; this time, he was ready. Determined to move forward, Henry grabbed Kassie by her hand and together, they both took a step forward. And to their amazement, for the first time in over a hundred years, Henry was finally able to successfully cross over and join Kassie on the other side of the forest. At long last, Henry was now cured. Looking over to Kassie, he gave her another kiss, as they enjoyed this newfound freedom, together.

CHAPTER 32

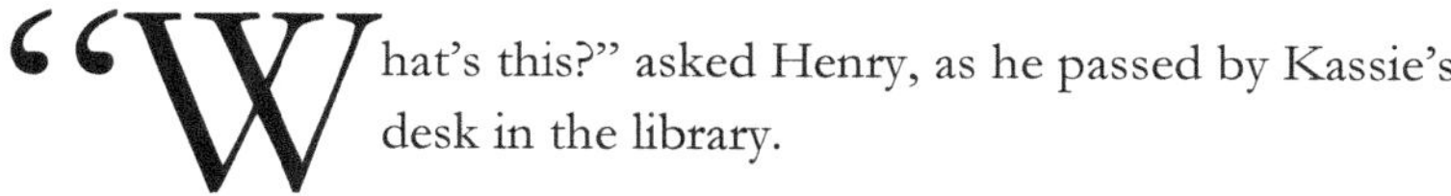

"What's this?" asked Henry, as he passed by Kassie's desk in the library.

Picking up on what appeared to be some sort of a manuscript, he read the following title aloud, "The Curse of the Dark Horseman by Lady Kassandra Galloway. My dear, have you turned our personal life experiences into a new book?"

"Actually, yes, my love. It's going to be my debut novel. I figured that after documenting all of our past experiments pertaining to your former cursed self, I thought that it was only fair for us to share our knowledge with the rest of the world. At least, just in case," she replied with a huge smile.

"In case there's another similar curse, that's reenacted again in the near future?" he asked in return, with a raised brow.

"Why, of course," said Kassie, as she rose up from her chair, wrapped her arms around Henry and gave him a kiss.

"Besides," she continued, "People need to understand that the cure to such a curse is love."

"And the enduring belief in everlasting love such as ours," he added.

"Yes, such as ours. Forever and ever," Kassie said, as she gave him another kiss.

Pulling away from her, he said, "But let's not forget that you chose to use your married name and not your maiden name."

"Well, why wouldn't I? After all, we're married," she said, as a matter of fact.

"Not quite," he replied. "Soon-to-be married. There's a big difference."

"Soon-to-be, or already are; both are the same to me. I mean… technically speaking, we did marry once, back in the forest. But either way, it still doesn't change the fact that I love you," she said, with a warm smile.

"Well, I do care. I want the whole world to recognize you as my lawful wife. Now, and forever. Besides, it's getting late and we don't want to keep the priest waiting. After all, it took quite a bit of convincing to get him to even agree to marry us, in the first place," he reminded her.

"Ah, that's right. After my last wedding, it did take you some effort to convince him to appear at what would be my what… second… or… third wedding ceremony? But Henry, unlike before, this time around, I can assure you that you've got absolutely nothing to worry about. I promise to be there, right on time," Kassie vowed.

"Oh, no you don't. I'm not taking any chances. I won't make the same mistake, as your last groom. This time, we'll ride together to the church," he said, with much conviction.

"Wait, are you actually contemplating the remote possibility that I might actually run away again? Henry, I can assure you that will certainly never, ever happen. My days as a runaway bride are long over," she said.

"Either way, we'll ride Midnight together. Besides, after riding in the forest for over a century, he could use a change of scenery," he said.

Pleased by his request, Kassie accepted Henry's proposal. After exiting the library together, she quickly changed into her new bridal gown. Wearing a silk embroidered dress that had been Henry's own late mother's gown, he beamed with delight upon seeing her. Excited about their new future together, Henry and Kassie exited Galloway Manor and walked over to the horse stable. Once seated together above Midnight, Henry tapped at his reins and in seconds, they were off.

Looking deep into Henry's eyes, Kassie said, "Henry, I love you."

"I love you, too, Countess Galloway," Henry said with a smile, as he addressed her by her new title.

"Ah, that's right, I'm going to be a countess now, aren't I?" asked Kassie, playfully.

"Yes, and now my love, it's time," Henry announced, as he tapped against Midnight's reins once more, as they rode off into the sunset to finally, at long last, get married… and this time… married the proper way, too.

EPILOGUE

Five years later...

Lady Kassandra Galloway stood firm and still, along with her husband, Henry, and their young daughter, Violet, by her side. After marrying into the Galloway family five years ago, Kassie decided that at long last, it was high time that an official family portrait be painted of them in their honors. Just like their ancestors before them, Kassie and her family's pair of portraits would hang above the walls at Galloway Manor and Wiltshire Hall. Since the family split their residences between both houses, in which their spring and summer seasons were reserved at Galloway Manor and their winter and autumn seasons spent mostly at Wiltshire Hall, Kassie requested that two identical portraits be painted of them, one for each of their ancestral houses.

Upon breaking the curse, Henry and Kassie married and a few months later, their daughter was born. In honor of the magical violets that grew within the enchanted forest, as well as after Henry's mother and Kassie's grandmother and great-great grandmother, the child was named Lady Violet Sarah Maureen Galloway. While Violet might have had Kassie's red hair and feisty spirit, she also inherited her father's emerald green eyes and his universal love for horseback riding. Furthermore, just like her father before her, Violet was a most impatient child; whom, currently, as of right now, had much rather preferred riding her horse with Henry, instead of sitting still for yet another hour of posing.

"Mama, can't I go and practice riding on Midnight or Faith?" asked Violet, hoping that her mother would oblige with her request.

"My darling, please be patient. Soon enough, we'll be done and then, we'll have a beautiful family portrait that we can always cherish forever," Kassie reminded her daughter.

"Kassie, don't you think that we've stood still long enough by now? After all, we've been posing for weeks. I'm certain that your skilled painter has already memorized our faces from long ago," remarked Henry, also hoping to persuade his wife otherwise.

"Henry, you're not helping," Kassie whispered aloud, while still trying to hold her pose.

Although Kassie did her best to maintain her composure, the same could not be equally said with regards to her husband and daughter. While Kassie sought to ignore them and to continue on smiling ahead at the painter, Henry let out a little yawn. Meanwhile, young Violet grew distracted by a small butterfly that just so happened to fly right by her. Given that the family were gathered and posing outside in the garden of Galloway Manor, they were also inadvertently left exposed to the elements of nature. And so, as the orange monarch butterfly flew pass Violet, the young and curious child immediately broke loose from her pose and promptly, she started chasing down the flying butterfly across the field. As Violet fled the scene and was busy running around the garden, Henry quickly excused himself to chase after their daughter. And so, much to her dismay, Kassie was left standing alone, feeling greatly frustrated and disappointed in the process.

Sensing her uneasiness, the painter quickly reassured Kassie, by saying, "Don't worry Countess Galloway, the earl is correct. I've already come to memorize your husband's and daughter's faces. I can take it from here."

Relieved by the painter's admission, Kassie immediately took great comfort. While Kassie loved her family dearly, they were also both such a huge handful to take in. Suddenly, Kassie heard the sounds of trotting approaching from behind her. Turning around, Kassie saw that Henry and Violet were already aboard Midnight and together, they were riding off and entering back into the forest. Amazed by their joint efforts and fast attempts to avoid posing with the painter, Kassie silently smiled to herself. Even though Henry's curse had long been broken, his love for the forest still remained… and ironically, it was also a trait that their daughter, Violet, now shared with him, as well.

"Countess Galloway, if you'd like, you can come and take a look at the painting, now," announced the painter.

Curious about their new portrait, Kassie walked over and took a peek. Much to her approval, the portrait was absolutely stunning and perfect. It was everything that Kassie had always envisioned and wished for it to be. Capturing their looks and personalities to the core, the portrait had Kassie and Violet seated down on a chair in the front, with Henry standing up behind them on the back row. Furthermore, the gardens of Galloway Manor were also used as the official landscape backgrounds behind them and right across from Henry, stood both Midnight and Faith, also painted onto the family portrait.

Suddenly, a tear formed within Kassie's eyes. After staring at Henry's Dark Horseman portrait for years, it was touching to finally see a new painting of all of them together, as a loving family. A portrait that would ultimately come to stand the test of time to serve as a new family heirloom for their descendants, for several more generations to come. A moment forever captured in time, through a painted portrait that would foretell the great and epic love story of their family's history and legacy. A story about curses and persistence; love and honor; and belief and faith. Important lessons and morals to be shared across and remembered amongst their children… and their children's children… and their children's children's children… and all others, who gazed upon this portrait, forever more; spanning across time and space, for all eternity and the hereafter. But the most important lesson above all else, is that no curse is immune to the power of love and belief; for that was precisely the case for our beloved Henry and Kassie. At long last, the Dark Horseman had finally been transformed into the loving husband and father, who would now forever be known to history as Lord Henry, the fifth Earl of Galloway, along with his adoring wife, Lady Kassandra, the fifth Countess of Galloway, and their faithful daughter Lady Violet Sarah Maureen Galloway; whom, herself, would one day later grow up to marry a prince and become a princess in her own right… but that's another tale… for perhaps, a later time…

AFTERWORD

To all my readers, thank you for taking this wonderous journey with me through the Enchanted Forest.

And this saga continues on with our next heroine, Lady Violet Galloway, in…

The Sleeping Knight

About the Author

Kristina Stangl is an American author. She was born and raised in San Francisco, California, USA. She holds a Master's degree in Public Administration, MPA; a Bachelor of Arts in International Relations, with a minor in Middle East and Islamic Studies from San Francisco State University; along with Teaching English as a Foreign Language (TEFL) credentials from the University of Toronto, Ontario Institute for Studies in Education. Before writing her first novel, Kristina previously worked in both the public and private sectors, having served in the United States federal government for nine years. In addition to writing, Kristina enjoys traveling across the globe and visiting famous and historical sites, which she documents on her social media accounts. To date, she has traveled to over thirteen countries, three contents, and speaks three languages. When Kristina is not traveling or writing, she's at home experimenting with baking new desserts, pies and other sweet treats.